DARK OF THE MIND

C.S. McMillian

ISBN-13: 978-0-9912989-1-4
ISBN-10: 0991298918

First Edition

Cover art by Angela McMillian

Edited by Charles Gulotta

For Kari.
Forever and ever.

The Five Stages of Grief

Some scream, some cry, and then there are others who calmly take the path. We naturally resist, denying the inevitable that lies in front of us as still as a lifeless tree displayed in our living room. We desire more, crave an immediate comprehension of the chaos in our head. We are burning mad, and we desire justice. We reach out to try and grasp the lingering flake of hope floating off into the distance. We think we know what is happening and why, at first, but our understanding is shaken and pulled apart into unrecognizable pieces that seem impossible to put back together. Then we return to the room with open arms, a sudden clarity that the darkness will take over no matter the struggle, no matter the fight. It's over.

— Tryke Harper

Year One

Chapter 1

I was curious when my partner Dave Higgins asked, "Is your adrenaline flowing yet? Are you pumped?" I stared at my reflection in the side mirror of the ambulance. There were no apparent signs of excitement or nervousness. That was surprising, because it was my first code call as a paramedic. My first dead patient.

Actually, my heart was racing, but not for the same reasons as my partner. Dave felt overjoyed at being able to help a fellow human being. He explained to me, on our first shift working together, how he experienced a saint-like feeling after patients thanked him for saving their life. He went so far as to say it felt exhilarating. Euphoric, even. Maybe if I wasn't so preoccupied with my own infatuations I would have been able to see his perspective, but then again, probably not. I just couldn't afford to think like Dave or become sidetracked by a path to righteousness.

"You want the head or the monitor?" he asked, parking the rig against the curb. I quickly learned how Dave worked.

He liked order and loved giving advice. Given the chaos of the streets, he believed order was the only thing that was reliable. I couldn't argue with his logic, but it seemed like a pretty boring mentality.

"I'll take the head," I said. I figured that would be the best place to spot an unusual occurrence if it were to happen. Although things can get a bit messy at the head at times — vomit, spit, blood.

We entered the house with bags and heart monitor in hand. The victim was an elderly man who had collapsed in his living room after dinner. His wife led us over to him and then hovered in the corner, smearing her makeup with a tissue and trying to conceal her terror. I briefly pondered which stage of grief she was currently in. I guessed the denial phase — most linger there as long as the brain allows because that's where they can still feel warm and hopeful.

Dave slapped the fast pads on the man's bare chest. I stared into the lifeless eyes hoping to catch a glimpse of something extraordinary. I even went so far as to run my hands over his eyes in an attempt to trigger a response.

"Tryke, you going to work or what?" Dave whispered.

"Yeah... sorry," I said, and quickly pulled the laryngoscope from my bag and slid the ET tube down the old man's trachea. My hands moved fluidly, as if I had done it for an entire career. I was calm and repetitious as I unwrapped the valve mask, hooked it to the tube, and began inflating the lungs. But my mind was elsewhere, waiting for something to emerge. Anything.

"Good job," Dave said. I sensed curiosity rather than praise. After a momentary pause, he started rapidly compressing the man's chest, as the droplets of sweat down his own face increased to a steady flow. "Clear!" he yelled, halting his compressions to glance at the heart monitor that still showed a steady flat line. Dave's passion was obvious. His dramatic moves and shouting of every syllable was hard to ignore. I've always envied his passionate nature.

The save rate for cardiac arrest victims is around eight percent. You have far better odds of avoiding a sexually-transmitted disease in a whorehouse than surviving a heart attack. However, even though they are few and far between, I have heard of "comebacks," those patients who temporarily escape the reaper and are able to be successfully resuscitated.

I was searching for not only a "comeback", but also one who could be resuscitated more than once. This particular old man wasn't a candidate. Ten minutes of asystole, or flat-line on the monitor, was a good indicator he wasn't returning. Even epinephrine — pure adrenaline — couldn't budge that perfectly flat line.

I took over compressions while Dave radioed Mercy General Hospital and bagged with his free hand. He quickly explained to the ER physician how long the man had been down without change in status, and described the array of meds that we vigorously circulated through his veins.

Dave gave me the signal to stop and we called it at 1815 hrs. This was my first time informing a family member of a loved one's death and, unlike the hospital, I didn't have the luxury of taking the wife to a nice quiet room to break the news. I had to make do with my immediate surroundings, which in this case included the deceased's living room chair.

I sat his wife down gingerly and began relaying the information. Her last glint of hope faded from her wrinkled eyes as she released a flood of tears into her cupped hands. Despite my inexperience, I wasn't upset. I was focused. In fact, I didn't mind the task at all, because for reasons I cannot explain, I was drawn to her sorrow. The grieving energy emanating from her was palpable and I wanted to reach out and feel its warmth.

• • •

That night, while lying in bed at the station, I found myself thinking about the old man. I could still vividly see his glazed eyes and the perfect stillness of his body. I wondered how long he stared into nothingness before he departed. The literature says the brain is active for ten minutes after the heart stops. It's the last ten minutes of everything one knows, filled, I imagined, with an anxious wait for the next step. That must be the strangest, most exciting ten minutes of a person's entire life, much like the anticipation a child feels on Christmas morning. I fell asleep with a smile on my face.

A few hours later, I was shaken from a deep sleep by the dispatcher's annoying voice. Call after call, we were up and down from our beds all night long. I learned quickly how 911 was merely an abused showgirl caked over with layers of make-up to cover the bruises placed by society. All damn night, not one real emergency. We were glorified taxi drivers with a light bar on the roof.

I felt miserable by the time seven a.m. arrived. I groggily made my way to the kitchen to brew a pot of coffee. I piled in the coffee grounds, not stopping until the filter was full. Dave followed a few minutes later carrying his own cup that he had stored in his locker. *Coffee, give life to save a life* was printed on the front in bold red letters.

His love for EMS was obvious from the beginning, and went way beyond his personal coffee mug. Below the pictures of his wife and daughter in his locker was a collage of stickers with random EMS sayings. My favorite by far was: *If this ambulance is a rockin', someone's giving CPR.* It wasn't clever, but it represented him well.

"Some night, huh?" Dave said, sighing, as he plopped down at the table. Where is your adrenaline now, Mr. Pumped?" I smirked under a tired frown.

"Bunch of crap calls. What the hell are we doing out there anyway, taxiing people around?" I said.

"Nature of the beast, man. It's what we do. You know how it works: 'You call, we haul.'"

I knew he was right. I'd made enough calls during my ride outs to know how the system worked, but it still pissed me off. Dave had made it past the point that some never get to. He'd managed to avoid the burnout stage. I didn't know yet which I was to become, a burnout or an acceptor of the inevitable, but I'm not easily swayed from my principles.

Not every call was going to present a dying patient, I knew that much, but what I hadn't realized when I started this venture was the vast amount of sideshow nonsense I was going to have to deal with. There is a never-ending crowd of perpetual drama addicts, just waiting to pounce on any soul willing to pay attention.

If I was to survive this endeavor I had to be patient and remember that this was only the beginning of my career. There was no need to be hasty. The busy city of Dallas would afford me many opportunities to view death. An abundance of people jammed in a hot city is a perfect breeding ground for mayhem. I needed the freshest form of death available. What better way to accomplish that than let the victims call, and invite you to the show?

Chapter 2

My infatuation with death started when I was twelve, at least consciously. The memory associated with that infatuation is the reason I began my hunt. I wasn't always an only child; I had a younger sister named Katy who was five years old at the time of the incident. She had big beautiful sapphire eyes and long hair the color of autumn that my mom put up in ponytails. Of course, Katy would immediately undo them once my mom left the room. She also had a giggle that I still can't get out of my head, and hope I never do.

It had been raining for two days straight and the above-ground pool in our backyard was overflowing, shuffling water over its edge. Our dad was at work, and our mom had just gone to lie down because of a migraine. I went to the kitchen to make Katy and me grilled cheese sandwiches for lunch while she watched cartoons on television.

After lunch she kept hounding me to go up to the tree house in our backyard. It was covered by a tightly stretched blue tarp, which kept most of the rain out. Katy had an uncanny ability to charm, and I gave in after a few minutes. We put on our rain gear and trudged through the soggy ground and up the slippery nailed boards to the hideout. We sat in the driest area and began our game of storytelling. She had an amazing imagination, and we immediately set out for a land with upside down trees and talking lollipops.

On my turn I needed a prop from inside, a square piece of cardboard to simulate a TV set. I was gone for just a few minutes.

When I returned, the tree house was empty. I searched the yard, assuming this was part of her usual antics of hiding from me and wanting to be sought out. I looked in and around the tool shed and the sides of the house, but she was nowhere to be seen. I decided to check the tree house again because she was clever enough to have snuck around me while I was searching.

I felt a nauseating worry come over me when I peered up through the cracks and didn't see her. I flew up the ladder and called her name, but there was no answer. I stepped out onto the small porch of the tree house and looked down. I froze in fear.

My sister was face down in the pool with her autumn hair sprawled in the water. I stared in horror unable to move. In that brief moment I saw something in the water surrounding and under her small body. It was a transparent blur fluidly moving with the small ripples. I quickly wiped the rain from my eyes and it was gone. I flashed back to reality and yelled her name, then leaped into the pool below.

I turned her small body over and saw that her lips were blue and her eyes were empty. My sister was gone.

I was convinced that what I saw in the water surrounding her body was her soul. After the funeral I waited day after day for her to return, to say goodbye. Every shadow, each blur, kept me hanging on. I was grasping for anything to release me from my guilt, but it never came.

I asked myself endless questions. Was there something I

could have done to prevent her death? Was there a greater force in the universe controlling it all, pulling levers and twisting knobs of fate? Are we all destined to fade away into the organic abyss below our feet? I didn't know, but my infatuation with the subject continued to grow, along with the need to know where my sister had gone.

After the incident, I would often dream of my own death, alone in a casket surrounded by nothing. The worst part of these dreams was the feeling of being alone and drifting away into blackness as if I had never been born — never existed. To me these thoughts and images were more frightening than being chased by an ax-wielding maniac, or falling from a twenty-story building.

I read many books on death, some religious and some scientific. I even went so far as to read about ancient aliens, but I could hardly go searching for an alien to answer all of my probing questions. None resolved the burning curiosity inside me.

• • •

After our three-shift tour ended, Dave invited me to his house for dinner. Normally I'm not one for family gatherings, but since we were going to be partners, I supposed we should get to know each other away from work. Besides, I needed Dave to trust me; I might need a favor in the future, depending on where my endeavors led me. And what better way to earn that trust than over a drink or two and a home cooked meal?

When Dave answered the door, he told me not to mention work in front of his wife. He said it made her nervous, so I filed a mental note to keep to safer topics around her.

His wife met us in the entryway wearing a flowered apron. She was an attractive woman — petite and blonde — not my type, but still quite beautiful. She reminded me of a housewife from the early 1960s.

"Hello Tryke, nice to finally meet you. I'm Claire." She wiped her hands on her apron and offered one for me to shake. "Dave doesn't talk a lot about work, but he has mentioned you a few times around the dinner table."

"I hope it wasn't all lies," I said, shaking her small cold hand.

She laughed but it seemed as if it were forced. "Can I get you something to drink?"

"Sure, I'll have whatever Dave is having. Thank you."

"Good choice," Dave said. "I hope you don't mind if it's light beer. Claire keeps an eye on my waistline."

"I have to look out for my Davy's health," Claire said with a heavy smile. She returned a few seconds later with a cold beer.

Claire was a gracious hostess and an even better cook. Her potato salad was the best I had ever eaten. But despite her obvious positive attributes, she gave me the creeps a few times during the meal. I caught her staring at Dave once or twice and the look on her face wasn't loving or seductive, but seemed to say, "I'm going to eat your soul once I'm done with this juicy medium-rare burger." Her smile reminded me of the Joker from the *Batman* movies, and sent shivers down my spine. I was pretty sure she was hiding something behind that vicious smile, but then I reminded myself that it was none of my business.

After dinner Dave gave me a tour of his home while Claire changed their daughters ketchup saturated shirt. Everything was neat and tidy. The entire kitchen was labeled and the living room couch was still covered in the original plastic. I asked Dave if a seventy-year-old woman lived there. He laughed and blamed it on his wife. Even their two-year-old daughter's room was immaculate, with not a toy in sight. It was little wonder Dave was clean and orderly at the station.

One of his routines is that before every call, he pulls out his trusty black comb and rearranges his thinning, pale brown hair. And he never goes on a call without his belt. He's a neat country boy. However, I certainly couldn't criticize his ways. I had my own self-satisfying obsessions at the moment.

As the afternoon wore on, Dave and I sipped our beers on the patio.

"You have a great family," I said.

"Thanks. So what's your girl status? Any future Mrs. Harper out there?"

I laughed, "Nah, I'm not ready to have your life. Besides I'm too young." In truth, I wasn't really comfortable around the opposite sex when it came to… well, sex. No, I'm not a virgin, but have managed to avoid the relationship aspect. Though I am inexperienced in that department, I still know that eventually vague discussions turn into personal analysis. My feelings are safer kept neatly in my head.

"Nonsense, I'm only five years older than you and I've known Claire for four of those years."

I quickly changed the subject. "So, you think we'll get any good calls next shift?" I glanced over my shoulder to make sure Claire wasn't around.

"Don't worry, she's still inside with the kid," he said.

"Close one."

"You mean dead or mangled people?"

"Huh?"

"The calls next shift?"

"Oh, right."

"That'll pass, your eagerness to see everything. Besides, they're more work. I'd much rather take care of a few sprained ankles or neck pains from minor wrecks, easy reports, and no medications to give," he said.

"Yeah, I guess. I'd still like to use the skills and medications I learned in school, or I'm afraid I might forget it all."

I was lying. The truth was, I knew my drugs well, down to their chemical makeup. I am somewhat of a chemistry geek. And all the rest seemed to come natural to me for reasons I can't explain. I'm not boasting, because other things in my life I have yet to understand, and may never. But I'm optimistic about the future.

"Don't worry about that. There will always be plenty of mayhem in the world for our profession. They need us out there."

Now it was time to boost his ego to see where it would lead. I wanted to know where he stood on one particular issue. "I just hope someday I'll be as good as you," I said, and lowered my head with a sigh.

I was worried for a moment that he wouldn't buy my false modesty, but he patted me on the shoulder and said, "Give it time, my friend." He drained the last drop from his beer, crushed the can, and tossed it into the trashcan beside us.

"You've been doing this for over five years now. What do you think about death? What do you think happens after we die?" I said.

"I knew that question would come. I just didn't think it would come so soon."

"It's been bugging me since the code we had second shift," I said.

"Well, I for one believe our souls are taken by God and brought to heaven. What about you?"

I'd known he was a religious man before I asked the question. He most likely attended church every Sunday. It wasn't surprising, considering his love of order. Not that I thought it was a bad thing to be religious. I would love nothing more than for God to pull me aside and answer all of my questions about death.

"Same here," I said. "I was just curious." The truth was, I didn't know what to believe. The subject never failed to confuse me. Of course I didn't dare tell Dave that, because I learned a few years ago that arguing about religion or politics is futile.

We both stared into the distance and fell silent, sipping our fresh beers until they were empty.

Chapter 3

My second shift was not a disappointment. As I arrived at
0800, we were dispatched to a possible GSW, or gunshot
wound. There is always the potential for death when a gun is
involved. Even a small-caliber bullet can travel along any
contour of the body and enter a major organ or vessel.

The call was a block away from the station and there was
an elementary school close to the address. That worried me. I
had yet to make a call on a dead child and I didn't know how
it would affect me. When I contemplate death, I don't usually
think about kids, nor do I want to. However, I can't see how
their demise would be any different from that of an adult.
Death wasn't prejudiced; it didn't care about age. My sister
was witness to that.

When we arrived at the scene, thankfully the victim wasn't
a child. There was an adult male about my age, lying face
down beside an eighties station wagon parked in the
driveway. The police had already cordoned off the area with
bright yellow crime scene tape. I lifted the tape and entered

the small war zone. Countless bullet holes lined the side of the car leading up to the shattered front window of the house. Bullet casings littered the yard, which was stained with sprays of blood.

I sat my bag down next to the victim. His body was as motionless as the damp grass lying under him. I slowly reached my gloved hand toward his neck to check for a pulse, but a piece of protruding bone impeded my attempt. I went to check the other side, and as I turned his head, I felt crepitus: his skull was in pieces under the skin. The shards crumbled in my hands like dirt. As I suspected, there was no pulse from the other carotid artery. Dave and I flipped him over for a quick sweep of his body. It looked as though all ten pints of his blood were hiding beneath him, turning the morning dew to crimson.

I could've stuck a small child's fist through the torn bullet hole in the man's exposed chest. His soul could have easily snuck out through that open door as he released. The rest of his body was pelted with more bullet holes than I felt like counting, so I stopped after number eight. It didn't matter anyway, because he had already qualified for the nontechnical term DRT, or dead right there.

Criteria for DRTs include decapitation, or any situation where the victim has an injury that is incompatible with life. This guy met a couple: brain matter seeping from his skull and the red fluid that brings oxygen to his tissues had completely leaked out of its container. I covered his body with a yellow blanket and left the rest to the police.

After the call we grabbed a quick breakfast sandwich from a gas station. I hoped this wasn't going to be a trend — filling my body with questionable foods from convenience stores — but once we left for the day, we sometimes didn't make it back to the station until the end of our shift.

• • •

Since the 0800 GSW, the calls kept coming in, and showed

no signs of slowing down.

We didn't get another potential death until that evening, when a call came in from a local nursing home. I had heard many horror stories about the elderly prisons, including my own few visits — a constant smell of piss and helpless old people sitting in their dirty diapers begging for help. This was a chance to find another possible candidate.

According to dispatch, an elderly woman had fallen, but Dave and I knew never to believe the information provided on NH calls, or any call for that matter. I got used to surprises quickly. On the way over, Dave regaled me with a story from his rookie days.

He had been dispatched to an elderly male who had supposedly fallen, according to the call dispatch received from the NH. When they arrived at the room, which happened to be a five minute trot through the building, that it was actually a *difficulty breathing*, which had now turned code. The only equipment the paramedics had brought in was a C-collar and backboard, and those provided little help with respiration. Dave vowed never to be caught again in that situation.

When we arrived on scene, we packed all of our equipment on the stretcher and headed in. The smell of piss assaulted me as soon as we opened the front doors. This was one of the more rundown NH's in the city, but I had yet to visit any that didn't leave a foul odor in my nose for the rest of the shift.

We were searching for room 406A. The damn place was a labyrinth. We went down two long hallways, came to a crossroad and then took a left, and then down two more. I imagined an aerial shot of the place being in some obscure shape I'd never seen before, maybe a trapezoid converged with a star. I saw a few nurses scattered about, along with elderly people who appeared to be either dead or sleeping in a corner. No one seemed to be in a hurry, and we weren't offered any information. I assumed no one was critically ill, but I've been wrong before. Callousness and complacency form a disease that's easily spread among the weak-minded.

Unlike me, Dave didn't seem surprised or irritated by the lack of greetings or offers of assistance. It was as if we were regular patrons of the place, only dressed a bit differently. I was about to take a seat and hold out my hands for my daily meds when we finally reached the door to 406A. The nurses' station was as barren as the hallway.

"Where the hell is everyone?" I asked.

"They're probably eating, as usual," Dave said. "Who knows, maybe they went home for the night and expect us to take over."

We halted at the door before entering when we heard what sounded like a bedspring being punished. "This ought to be good," Dave said, nudging the partially-open door with his foot. "Did someone call an ambulance?"

I was caught completely off guard at the scene unfolding in front of us. I stood in place, stunned, and time seemed to stop as I mentally began counting and circling all the things wrong with the picture.

A three-hundred-pound female nurse was straddling a ninety-pound elderly woman on her bed and rapidly pushing on her chest. The brittle woman was struggling to yell and flailing her arms in the air.

The sweat-drenched nurse stopped mid-compression and looked over at us. Obviously exhausted, she said through pursed lips, "Sh…she wasn't breathing when I came in to check on her." She paused for a deep breath. "We just switched shifts… my relief told me she had fallen and then called y'all before leaving." She turned back to the old lady under her. "Thank you, Jesus! Thank you, Jesus! I saved Ms. Eddy." Then she rolled off, nearly toppling onto the floor. The blood rushed back to the elderly woman's horror-stricken face.

"The only thing you saved her from was suffocating under your fat ass!" Dave said. "We are here for 406A. That is

406*B*." I glanced over at the bed with the letter A above it. "Shit!" Dave yelled.

The woman in the other bed appeared dead: jaw slightly ajar, eyes open and fixed. Dave immediately began rubbing his middle knuckle into her chest — a sternal rub — a move that is also quite efficient to arouse stubborn drunks. She didn't budge. He moved his hands to her neck.

"No pulse!" he yelled. "Tryke, grab the monitor!"

I yanked myself back from my baffled trance. After ripping open her flimsy flowered blouse, I stuck the fast pads to her bare frail chest and then glanced at the monitor. "V-fib Dave," I said. He stepped back. Ventricular fibrillation is one of the most lethal heart arrhythmias. The ventricles of the heart are quivering and not contracting.

"Clear," I said calmly as I pushed the charge button on the monitor. Dave looked at me with that curious expression again. "Clear!" I yelled this time, which seemed to satisfy him. A soft revving sound emerged from the monitor and then I heard a constant beep, telling me it was fully charged and ready to go. I pressed the button and watched as the unseen electricity traveled along the cables to the pads and then *bam*, her body flinched, slinging drool that had been resting softly on her cheek into the air.

I waited a brief moment before shocking her again to see if there was any change in her rhythm. There wasn't. "Still V-fib," I said as I increased the voltage on the monitor. "Clear!" I repeated, amplifying my voice for Dave's benefit. Her limp body flinched again. The line along the monitor was now flat — the ventricles had stopped moving all together.

I began compressions while Dave secured an airway and placed an IV in her right external jugular vein. Stretching my right foot over to the vials of epinephrine and atropine that I had removed from the drug box, I slid them to Dave. I sure as hell couldn't count on the nurse to give them to me, nor did I trust her at that point. After a few rounds of compressions to circulate the meds, I glanced back at the monitor that was now displaying a sinus rhythm.

Dave checked for a pulse and said, "It's weak, but she has one. Let's give her a 150 mg of Amiodarone and get her the hell out of this place."

As we wheeled 406A down the grim labyrinth to our rig, it occurred to me that we had a "comeback" in our presence. I should have been watching her as close as I could for any signs of… well anything.

"Dave, do you mind if I take this one and you drive in?"

"You think you can handle it?"

"Of course," I said. The half grin on his face told me that he could sense something different about me. He probably thought I was breaking out of my shell and becoming like him. Little did he know that my passion came from a very different place.

"She's all yours," Dave said, as he walked around to the driver's seat.

Before I shut the side door of the rig, I heard a woman's voice yelling for us to stop. It was the nurse who had saved 406B from sleeping, and she was wielding a bundle of papers in her right hand. I supposed that the patient's history and personal information would be helpful, but that wasn't what she was holding. Instead, she handed me the damn woman's DNR paperwork. I saw the words "Do Not Resuscitate" in bold red letters staring back at me.

"A little late for that, isn't it?" I said as I took the papers from her hand and slammed the door in her face before she could respond. I was irritated by the sloppiness of the NH and the total disregard for its occupants. My anger was soon replaced by the thought that I was in the back of the rig, all alone with an honest-to-God comeback.

"Guess what I got?" I said to Dave through the small window separating us.

"Her phone number?" Dave said.

"Hell, no!" I said. "This poor old woman's DNR paperwork."

"You got to be shitting me."

"Nope," I said.

He laughed and put the rig in gear, and we began the five-minute drive to the ER. He yelled back to me, "Your first comeback a DNR. That's classic right there."

All right, lady, I thought. It's just you and me back here. Now what the hell happened while you were dead? I looked down at her softly-closed eyes and then at the tube shoving air down her throat every few seconds. This was as fresh as I was going to get. I hadn't seen any ghostly spirits enter or exit her body. I glanced at the paperwork for her name. Martha Greenwell.

"Ms. Greenwell, can you hear me?" Nothing...the monitor still displayed a sinus rhythm and her pulse was steady. Where the hell was she? For the rest of the short trip, I pondered the "ten-minute window" theory. Maybe she was stuck somewhere and unable to make it back. For all I knew, demons or aliens were battling for her soul.

Though this woman was a "comeback", she still didn't meet my requirements. I needed her to die again so I could witness the release. I was saving her only to wish for her immediate death. It sounds morbid, but I did my part. Now I was merely a bystander.

Another failed call.

• • •

Later that evening we made it back to Mercy General to drop off a chest pain. I inquired about Ms. Greenwell and learned that she had coded again. Because the hospital had the DNR paperwork, they didn't attempt to revive her.

I had a restless night due to a new dilemma weighing heavily on my mind. Why hadn't I seen anything? Though I didn't witness her leave after her comeback, I was there when she returned the first time. I should've seen something. Was Ms. Greenwell's passing too calm? Did the soul need trauma, or a violent jolt to reveal itself? Every question that arose in my mind seemed to confuse me further.

Chapter 4

It was 0300 and Dave was snoring loudly from the bunk across the room. We'd only been back for twenty minutes from our last call and he was already fast asleep. With each log he sawed, I envied his ability to doze off so quickly. I'd never been able to fall asleep as soon as my head hit the pillow. I flipped on the soft light over my bed and skimmed through a *Popular Science* magazine. If I were lucky, I'd be able to shut my eyes in the next hour.

Thirty minutes later, just after I was lowering the magazine and drifting off, the bell ringing and the dispatcher's voice calling out our unit number startled me awake. We were being sent to an apartment fire, and because I hadn't been on a fire call yet, I found myself looking forward to it. The frustration I first felt when the bell interrupted my brief nap quickly faded away.

I knew we would probably just be providing first-aid to the firemen, but I have always found fires fascinating. I hadn't treated a burn victim yet and that type of trauma could very well be one thing that could bring a soul to the surface.

Dave mumbled a few curse words and began his rant. "I hope to hell it's not a big damn fire. We could be there all night if it is, depending on the district chief."

"What do you mean?" I asked.

"The district chief at the fire determines when we leave. And if he thinks his firemen might get hurt for any reason, and I mean any reason, he'll keep us there."

"How can he do that? We don't work for the fire department."

"It's all connected down at city hall. And we're at the bottom of the pot. We're the scrapings, and we do what we're told."

"That's bullshit," I said. I really didn't mind if we had to stay at the fire. I doubted I'd be sleeping much anyway. However, I didn't like the thought that some other agency had the power to tell us what to do. We were more than capable of consulting with one another and determining our own actions. "So we can't discuss things with the chief?"

"Discuss, hah. I guess maybe, depending on the chief, but if it's Chief Fuzzy Nuts from district four, then we don't stand a chance."

"Chief Fuzzy Nuts?"

"Yeah, the firemen in his district named him that because one of them saw his nuts in the shower and said they looked like the skin of a peach."

"All right then," I said, "let's hope Ole Fuzzy Nuts isn't working tonight." I didn't inquire about the event that led to the firemen being in such close proximity to the nude chief as to make the accusation of fuzzy nuts. I really didn't want to know.

The apartment complex turned out to be single story and looked more like a half-square motel. The fire was out by the time we arrived, and they were in the process of putting the exhaust fan at the entrance of the apartment to clear out the residual smoke.

"So, do we get out or do we stay in the truck and wait for them to call on us?" I asked.

"Up to you really, but if it's nighttime I usually stay in the truck, so I can get a nap in if we're here for a while. We can go up there if you want. I think I see Fuzzy Nuts. I'll introduce you to him."

We exited the rig and headed toward the chief's Suburban. The exhaust fan had finished clearing the remaining smoke from the apartment. It didn't appear to have been a very large fire. Maybe an overheated pot on the stove or a lit cigarette dropped onto a blanket. I didn't see any damage to the outside of the complex or many bystanders milling about.

Now, what about the potential victims?

The chief was wearing a white helmet and talking on his portable radio as we approached him. From the other end of his radio I heard the words amplified, "We have a victim." My heart instantly began pounding with excitement. I felt guilty for being enthused, but it was short-lived, because I was on a mission.

The firemen were in the process of wheeling something out the front door. "What the hell is that?" Dave asked as we raced toward the apartment. I didn't answer; I was just as baffled.

As we got closer, the object became clearer. It was a partially charred wheelchair, and it appeared to be motorized. The fireman dragged it backward out the apartment's front door. The skidding of the burnt, flattened wheels along the parking lot concrete amplified in the quiet night air. All eyes were on the chair. When he wheeled it around and faced us, it still wasn't clear what was seated in its cockpit. The red and white strobe lights only made the thing harder to identify, until the engine company shined a halogen light directly on it.

There was definitely an obese body sitting in the wheelchair. A burnt quilt still covered the midsection and a pair of worn cheap tennis shoes protruded below. The head was covered with a black trash bag and a black belt cinched around the neck. Whoever was under there was obviously dead, but Dave or I still had to check for a pulse.

Dave was looking the other way, obviously not volunteering. "I guess I'll do it," I said.

The smell of the burnt blanket and charred flesh engulfed my nose as I neared the body. With gloved hands I attempted to loosen the worn belt but it wasn't releasing easily. I turned my head and took a deep breath and tried again but it wasn't budging. It was bound so tightly around the neck that I eventually gave up and cut it away with my trauma shears.

Slowly, I lifted the bag just enough to check for a pulse. I slid my fingers along the indentations in the skin caused by the belt — nothing. And of course there was no chance of a return. The soul most likely slipped out with the billowing black smoke before we'd arrived.

I lowered the bag back down and placed the belt in a red biohazard bag. "We have one more," a fireman said, dragging another body from the apartment. The head was also covered with a black trash bag and a belt around the neck. This one was stiff, with one hand pointing above the head as if perpetually stuck in a 70's dance move.

No one was volunteering to check the pulse on this one either. I felt like everyone was silently looking at me and nodding toward this new monstrosity. This was getting ridiculous. I was apparently immune to some debilitating disease, and that left me as the only one who could touch these burnt husks.

After checking the second male, I looked over at the fireman who had dragged the last guy out and asked, "Anymore in there?"

"No, that's it."

"Good," I said nodding my head in relief. Considering the neighborhood, these guys were most likely involved in a drug deal gone bad, or owed someone money. Or both. They had obviously pissed off the wrong person because they weren't only beaten, but strangled and partially burned as well.

As I headed back to the rig with the biohazard bags, I handed them over to the first police officer I saw. He told me that the victims were in their early forties and well-known drug dealers of the neighborhood. The cops were there at least a few times a week for noise disturbances and occasional fights. The louder of the two men was a quadriplegic, paralyzed since he was seventeen after being shot in the back. He went on to say that it was just a matter of time before something of this magnitude happened. Still, the officer seemed disturbed by the way the paralyzed man had been killed, even if he was a known scumbag.

I looked around for Dave and assumed he was waiting impatiently in the rig for Chief Fuzzy Nuts to release us. I found him hunched over, hiding behind the rear double doors and spitting residual vomit chunks from his mouth. When I approached, he attempted to conceal a small pile of orange puke beside his boots.

"It must have been those damn tacos we had earlier. My stomach has been bothering me ever since we ate them," Dave said.

I tossed the jump bag into the back of the rig.

"Huh. I feel fine," I said with a smile. "I believe we ate the same thing, if I'm not mistaken."

"I don't know, maybe it was something I had before work."

"Yeah, maybe," I said. Dave, like most of the firemen at the scene, seemed to be in shock, even though I'm sure most of them had seen worse. It might have been the wheelchair that did them in. Or maybe the smoldering quilt lying across the victim's lap brought back memories of their grandmothers.

To me, the bodies were nothing but empty capsules, and I was emotionally detached while checking them. I noticed some of the firemen looking at me oddly. They probably thought that because I was a rookie, I was fulfilling some morbid sense of curiosity. I decided to play it that way.

When I walked by them with the biohazard bags I said, "Strangled and partially burnt patient. Oh wait, and in a wheelchair. Now I can cross that one off my list. What's next?"

The chief held us another thirty minutes until the coroner arrived. Dave was furious, but it was short-lived. His instant ability to calm at night kicked in as we headed back to the station. I wondered why the two strangled men had such a powerful impact on him. There's no doubt it was a disturbing sight, but I didn't understand the vomiting. As paramedics we get to view death in all its glorious variety. I thought he would have been used to it by now. I guess not.

During moments such as these, I suppose I am obligated to inquire about my partner's feelings or maybe offer him some philosophical advice. Or I could just listen to him rant, if he weren't so tired, about how life is cruel and unpredictable. However, in this particular case I would have to argue that it wasn't *entirely* unpredictable. Those men were tempting fate and their luck finally ran out. In the end, it all plays out the same.

I suppose if Dave hasn't figured this out after more than five years on the city streets, I really couldn't do much to help. Surely he has some sort of plan to help him deal with all the crap we see. Hell, I'm the rookie. He should be offering *me* advice, asking if I'm okay.

I knew better than to discuss my real views with him. It would most likely piss him off. Besides, I was still searching, and confusion only seems to make people more uncomfortable. Everyone assumes you should have a viewpoint, even if it is opposite of their own. That way they can argue with you, though no one is really listening.

Chapter 5

When I arrived home the next morning, my apartment was dark and inviting. I poured myself a glass of Scotch, plopped down in my recliner, and opened the book I had been reading yesterday. It was an old book about lost souls, spirits of the damned, and I became absorbed in its contents. Some would call it supernatural babble, though I like to think of such books as describing the natural world to people who can see it. I hoped to become one of those people.

I fell asleep four pages in, but was suddenly awakened from another of those dreams that always leaves me feeling alone and isolated from the world. Once awake, my life wasn't much different. It wasn't as if people didn't like me. I've had my share of friends or acquaintances along the way. I just prefer solitude mostly, and friends have a way of disappearing when you lose contact.

I pressed the silver button on the side of my watch and it read 1830 hrs. I had been asleep for a solid six hours — a new record. I felt the need to get out of the apartment, so I took a walk.

It was only September, but darkness was already seeping in. The full moon hung low in the sky, growing brighter and brighter as twilight slowly drifted away. The Texas wind was warm, but pleasant. Normally it doesn't get cold until the end of October and it usually didn't stay cold. I can remember many Christmases when I wore short-sleeve shirts. I don't mind the mild temperatures, although a change of season would be nice on occasion.

I passed the abandoned Peter's Grocery Store where my dad had retired. I couldn't help but think of him every time I passed by the place. He drove to work each morning, though I grew up only a few blocks away. To this day I'm still not completely sure why, because he certainly wasn't a lazy man. He was a manager, so maybe he thought driving to work maintained his stature in some way.

Overall my dad was a good man. I can't recall any abusive punishments or cruelty. He did like to drink, but he wasn't a mean drunk. He laughed a lot, big hearty bellowing laughs that were contagious. He managed the grocery store for as long as I could remember. He wore pressed white long-sleeve shirts every day with dark suit pants, a thin tie, and obsessively shined shoes. He always made it a point to tell me that appearance was the key to most of life's encounters.

His advice is the reason I make sure my shirts and pants are immaculate when I leave for work. Of course, in my job they don't stay that way, and by the second or third call I am usually a mess. It's useless to try keeping every tiny piece of human debris off my clothes, so I learned to let it go.

My father died two years ago from cancer at the age of sixty-two. He also had heart disease, which leaves me with a lot to look forward to. He and my mom were married for thirty-five years, and I would have to say that their marriage was way above the standards of today. Of course they argued on occasion, but most of the time they were smiling and holding hands. They even managed to get through my sister's death, but not without tension and pain. The house was solemn for a year and I spent most of it alone while my parents tried to extract some sense out of the senseless.

I'd sometimes go to my mom's house, the house where I grew up. I'd notice the kitchen light on, and I'd stop on the sidewalk at the end of the driveway. Usually I'd decide not to go in. Her shadow moving along the wall told me all I needed to know. I just couldn't handle seeing her in continual mourning.

I lived close by and tried to be in touch in case she needed me for any reason. She seemed so much more vulnerable without him, and I worried about her. I can imagine her being easy prey for the demons of the night, stalked by sadness. She has yet to recover and continues to walk around like a mindless zombie, repeating stored questions. Everything sounds rehearsed, as if some outside force is guiding her body. Maybe it was those damn aliens.

The night felt good and I didn't have much to do back at my apartment, so I decided to take a longer stroll. I figured I'd be up most of the night anyway and I find nights pleasant, a nice break from the unrelenting Texas sun. I took the long way back through my old neighborhood.

The walk always stirred up a few childhood memories and this time was no different. I thought of Darren, my best friend growing up. His house was one street over from mine and sat directly behind ours. It was convenient when we wanted to have backyard camp outs.

As I neared his house, his dad was in the process of pushing the trashcan to the street for tomorrow's morning pickup. I waved and said, "Hey, Mr. Moore."

He kept his head down and waved a quick hand to me. "Tryke," he said treading back up his driveway and disappearing into the dark house. I wasn't surprised by his short response. Darren had been their only child, and he and his girlfriend died in a car wreck in high school. Death struck once again, leaving a once vibrant family submerged in a grey world of forgotten graveyards.

I heard sirens in the distance, but approaching, as I entered the street to my apartment. A fire truck rounded the corner, horn blaring. A few seconds later one of the ambulances from my department screamed by, followed by two police cars. They all turned into my apartment complex. I couldn't even get away from work when I was off.

The emergency vehicles parked in front of my building. Most of my neighbors were watching; some were poking their heads through their curtains while others were outside forming small cliques around the light show. Who says bright lights only attract flying insects?

A police officer stopped me as I tried to make my way up the stairs to my apartment. I showed him my ID and he began asking me questions. He wanted to know if I had heard or seen anything before I went on my walk.

"No, sir, everything was quiet. Why, what happened?" I said.

"Your neighbor, Mr. Thompson, was robbed and beaten," the officer said.

"What kind of person would beat a brittle old man who is bound to an oxygen bottle?" I asked.

"Probably some addict looking to score some fast cash. So dang high they don't think."

"That's no damn excuse," I said, seeing the paramedics carrying Mr. Thompson out on a backboard.

"Hey, Tryke, what are you doing here?" one of the paramedics said. I didn't recognize the voice until he faced me. It was Mark, another medic from across town whom I'd met at the hospital a few times. He was tall and skinny with short dirty blonde hair and glasses, clean-cut except for a small devil tattoo wielding a pitchfork running from the bottom of his right ear down his neck. When I first saw it, I wondered where the angel was for the devil to contend? Sweet teenage rebellion…it lives on forever.

"I live next door. How's he doing?" I said following them

down the stairs to the rig.

"He took a pretty good hit to the head and I'm fairly certain his right leg is broken."

"Is he conscious?"

"He mumbles a little, nothing discernible."

"You mind if I try and talk to him for a minute?" I asked.

"Give it a shot. I still need to put an IV in him and get another set of vitals."

"Thanks," I said and climbed into the back of the rig. "Mr. Thompson, hey, it's Tryke." I placed my hand on his shaky bloodied left one. He squeezed lightly, letting me know that he was there. He tried to lift his head, but it was bound to the board with tape — our standard C-spine precautions. I gently pushed his head back down and told him not to move.

"Heee... he had a tattoo on his elbow, a bird," Mr. Thompson said and then began a coughing fit, spitting a broken tooth from his mouth. I wiped the blood away from his face with a 4x4 bandage.

"I'll let the police know, don't worry," I said. "I'm glad to hear you speak. Where are the keys to your apartment? I'll lock up when the police leave." He pulled them from his pocket, a single key attached to a beaded chain and a small plastic coin purse, the kind you squeeze and the slit opens. I noticed the faded Peter's Grocery Store logo stamped on it.

"Thank you," he said.

"Ok, Tryke, we gotta go," Mark said.

"I'll come visit you tomorrow if you're not out of the hospital by then," I said, and thanked Mark again. I shut the double doors and pounded twice on the back of the rig. I watched as the ambulance sped out of sight.

When I first moved in to my apartment, Mr. Thompson met me at the bottom of the stairs. He helped me carry box after box up to my place, even though I insisted he shouldn't. He said it was important to him. I could feel the pride seeping from him as he tread up the stairs carrying stacks of boxes in his arms, sweat glistening on his brow, and his oxygen bottle slung over his shoulder in its black pouch and knocking the railing with each step.

After that, we became friends. I enjoyed listening to his stories about the neighborhood and he always had a bottle of Scotch on hand. Mr. Thompson told me he enjoyed any company he could get, and I took that as a compliment, broad as it was. He told me that he and my dad were friends, and that since he had moved back fifteen years ago he had conversed with him at the grocery store quite often. He divulged many stories of how my dad helped families who couldn't afford to buy groceries. Making exceptions for them meant that at the end of the day, the groceries came out of his salary. Mr. Thompson repeatedly made it a point to tell me that my dad was one of the best people he had ever known.

The stories made me swell with pride, but also with sadness, because I realized I didn't know my own dad as well as I had wanted.

Once the police left I entered Mr. Thompson's apartment. An anger like I've never felt before washed over me as I thought about the atrocity that happened to him. Broken drawers were sprawled all over the floor, emptied of their contents. Lamps were tossed around and shards of glass and papers littered the floor. He must have put up a fight.

Mr. Thompson looks twenty years older than he actually is, and he's much too frail to be only in his late sixties. From his stories, I know he's had a rough life and has always been a fighter. In fact, he was a boxer in the marines and he did not one, but two tours in Vietnam. I knew he had tons of war stories, but he usually focused on the ones about his boxing. I figured the war stories bothered him too much to talk about. There was no doubt in my mind that back in his prime, the paramedics would have been hauling that thief out on a board instead of him.

I cleaned the apartment and placed his possessions back the best I could remember. The last item was a picture of his deceased wife, which I lovingly set on the mantel. Mr. Thompson talked about her often, usually after his second glass of whiskey. He told me how they had met at the county fair, back before all the punks hung out there. He said it was a cleaner, more wholesome time. I have to admit, that time period has a certain appeal. He claimed she had the best legs this side of the Dixie line, and that no other woman could ever outshine her smile — she could light up a room brighter than a nickel-plated moon. Once he got to his third glass, the stories turned into tears.

I find it terrifying to think of caring for someone that much, and then losing them. I loved my dad before he passed away, but this type of love was different. This was the love between a man and a woman, a bond that is supposed to sustain itself through any of life's cruel tricks. I suppose the love they shared did last, until they were overtaken by the one thing we have no control over: the shadow named Death. We can never quite shake him. He is always lurking close by, watching, and waiting.

Chapter 6

Mercy General hospital is known for many things: crowded hallways, the homeless, local drunks, and the occasional psychiatric patient roaming the building in a flimsy, yellow gown. The cacophony of patients can be deafening at times, and it's hard to ignore the vile smell that seems to emanate from every corner. I can only imagine the variety of excreted human fluids causing that type of stench.

It's also a level-one trauma center, which means all major trauma calls in the area are transported there. Overworked doctors and nurses wander bleary eyed and disheveled amongst the sick and dying. Many wear bored expressions on their faces. The waiting room is constantly overflowing with patients complaining of anything from chest pain to a protruding projectile protruding from a limb. All of these people wait behind a heavy, pale green door that is guarded by a fierce ER nurse. It's her job to triage these cases, and unless the person is actively dying, unconscious, or barely breathing, they will not be given a bed.

On my next shift, we finally made it over to Mercy General where Mr. Thompson was recovering. As usual I had to dodge a psych patient roaming around unattended, and I narrowly avoided two highly-intoxicated gentlemen panhandling in the hallway. I nodded my head in the direction of one of the medics from Medic 12. He was in the process of unloading a regular whom Dave and I had transported last shift. The patient had a wide variety of ailments stored for our pleasure: abdominal pain, back pain, feet pain, and my favorite: "My damn hemorrhoids are about to hit the floor." I sure as hell wasn't checking to see if she was lying, which brings me to the number one reason for our repeat customers.

The most amusing and absurd rumor on the streets among our regular clients is that if they are brought in by ambulance it means instant bed and instant physician. This is not the case. In fact, suggesting this to your friendly neighborhood paramedic upon pickup will most certainly prolong your wait by at least an hour. We have an understanding with the triage nurse. Now, what if someone is actually sick and in need of immediate help? The individuals who are truly sick do not inform me that they will be seen faster if they arrive by ambulance. They're much too focused on their symptoms.

After a few rotations, I quickly learned the regulars by name, and how to tell if they were faking. We aren't only medics, but also detectives. Detecting bullshit is half of our job. A simple arm drop over a suspected fake seizure works flawlessly. Simply raise the individual's arm above his head, and if he controls it to avoid hitting himself in the face — bullshit.

The arm drop also works well on drunks, child attention seekers, and disgruntled girlfriends. However, I have an even more entertaining solution for the fake syncope. Simply place an ammonia inhalant in the palm of your gloved hand and pop the seal; then cup your hand and cover the person's nose and mouth. The real drama professionals might try and hold their breath, but eventually they will have to breathe. And when they do, back up and let the dramatic coughing fit and drool begin.

While Dave finished his report, I found Mr. Thompson's room number. The door was open. I stopped the nurse and inquired about his tests, and she immediately obliged. Being in uniform has its perks. The good news was Mr. Thompson's CT scan didn't show any bleeding in the brain from the head wound, but the bad news was that he had a broken femur. That would make it difficult for him to get up to his second-floor apartment.

"Hey, Mr. Thompson, how's it going?" I said, trying to speak over the screaming TV as I entered the room. I knocked on the door to get his attention. He smiled when he saw me, and with a shaky hand quickly lowered the volume. He had a cast around his right leg, and multiple bandages around his head.

"Tryke, good to see you. Come in, come in, have a seat. Hope they're not working you too hard out there."

"No, sir, not too bad. How are you feeling?"

"Like a brand new hundred dollar bill," he said laughing. "Okay, maybe a few ones wadded in a teenager's front pocket. Just this old darn leg finally broke after all these years of being intact."

I laughed with him, "Well you've done pretty well then. I broke mine when I was eight."

"I just hope that son of a bitch who robbed me felt some of the whacks I got in. Have you heard anything? Did they catch him?"

"No, sorry, haven't heard anything. If I see any police officers today, which I'm sure I will, I'll ask. I just came to check on you, and give you back your keys. Dave is waiting for me in the ER. Is there anything else I can do for you?"

"Hold on to those keys. If you wouldn't mind I would appreciate you watering my plants. They say I'm going to be in here a few more days doing that physical therapy stuff."

"I can handle that," I said. "Oh, and I picked up the broken things and placed everything back the best I could remember. If you need anything else, call me."

"Thank you for that, Tryke, but you've done enough. You take care."

"You too," I said. "And take it easy on these pretty nurses around here."

Hearing the nonstop traffic on the radio, I knew we were about to get a call. We'd been there over thirty minutes, and dispatch gets antsy. They would check on our status soon, especially if they were running out of available medic units.

Sure enough, Dave informed me that they had called a few minutes ago via the red ring-down phone at the nurses' station. The ring-down phone is a direct line to EMS dispatchers. Its sole purpose is for dispatchers to relay information to the ER from our units if we can't call via radio for some reason, or send emergency information as in mass casualties. And, of course, to check up on us.

"So, what's the damn problem out there. Is the city going to shit, or what?" I asked Dave.

He laughed. "Hardly. A city bus got rear-ended by a freakin' Prius, and you know what that means? 'Ouch, my check hurts, oh, I mean my neck'", he continued, pantomiming one of the bus passengers holding their neck with greedy fingers. "We're the only available unit now."

I shook my head in disgust at the thought of the uninjured people on the bus faking injuries so they could sue the city. I'm sure it's quite a spectacle to see ten to twenty people being taken off the scratched-bumper bus and placed in full C-spine precautions.

"That's such crap. A damn Prius versus a city bus. What the hell, I bet the ones in the Prius aren't being transported, are they?" I said.

"Nope," Dave said smiling broadly. After Dave informed the nurses and doctors that they would be getting ten patients from the "horrible" bus wreck, they began lining beds against the walls of the already bustling hallways. The greedy bastards would certainly be lying on the stiff boards in their confining C-collars for hours. Payback is a bitch.

• • •

A few minutes after we left the hospital, dispatch sent us on a call. The adrenaline Dave mentioned on our first code — the stuff that kept eluding me — was running full bore through his veins as I read the text that the dispatcher relayed to our MDT. The orange digital information read, "Chief Complaint: infant not breathing."

"Son of a bitch, this pisses me off," Dave said. "We have to go way across town because some moron is faking an injury on a bus, trying to get some free money and taking our rigs out of service! Medic three would have been right on top of that address. Now some baby could die!"

I understood the rationale behind his anger, but that wasn't what was going through my head. I had been waiting for the inevitable moment of the death of a human just born. The soul hadn't even had time to make itself at home, or adjust to its new environment in an infant. I wondered as we blew through lights, our siren wailing, if I would get to see the infant's soul. Would it be the same size as the infant, or was its growth process entirely different than the body?

I had heard many horror stories about the infamous pedicode, or pediatric code. Dead babies never evoke the same emotions as incidents involving adults with unfortunate endings. Tragedies involving adults are exploited. The more gruesome and horrific the call, the more attention one receives while describing it. When I was in paramedic school, my instructor loved telling one particular story he named, "The Wreck." I heard the story so many times that I can still recall the make and model of the car, along with the exact location where each body part was found.

The story goes like this…Apparently five years ago, some

guy was testing the speed of his new Ferrari on I-635, and lost control near an exit. His vehicle was the only car involved in the accident, but pieces of the wreck, along with pieces of the driver, were scattered for a hundred yards. The part of the story that always seemed to get people was when the instructor described the rookie medic who had the misfortune to find the guy's head, which had been severed in the wreck. He picked it up by accident, and dropped it once he noticed one of the still intact eyes was staring back at him.

Demented story, I know, but a person has to be slightly off anyway to see this crap everyday, and not go insane. I always wondered how the rookie could have mistaken the head for something else, but I never asked.

The pedicode is infamous for two reasons. One, kids don't die often, and when they do it's usually from some type of airway issue, as in choking or asthma. Only a rare few die from violent accidents. Two, most paramedics don't have an abundance of experience with kids, because again, kids don't usually die; adults do. Nine out of ten paramedics will tell you they'd rather code their own grandma than a baby.

Me, I think about all this a bit differently. Even if I did stay in this profession for the same reason as the majority of other paramedics, I still tend to look at things in a different light. I'm not God, nor was I the one who caused whatever incident we were dispatched to. A code is a code, and if someone is dead, then any action I take is more than the person had going for him.

I find it humorous when I hear other medics praise their own actions. Those who usually do this are, ironically, the God men. If you ask me, we're merely bystanders in His game, and for them to think they actually saved a life is blasphemy.

I had my expectations before we arrived on scene. The scenarios people have described to me were all very similar. I figured some distraught mother would meet us at the curb cradling her dead child. She would hand off the child to us as if in a game of keepaway, all the while yelling, "Save my baby!" The infant would most likely have died during the night, sometimes from SIDS. Rigor mortis would have already begun to set in, but we would perform as if the child were viable, even if we knew there was no way in hell we were getting them back.

I've heard of distraught parents pulling guns on medics for telling them their baby was dead and not attempting resuscitation. I imagine that parents lose all rational thought when it comes to their children's survival.

When we arrived, three police cars were parked along the curb. It wasn't odd that they beat us there, considering we came from across town. Police are automatically dispatched to every code in case of unexpected surprises, and for our protection if necessary. Dave was huffing and puffing frantically, grabbing equipment and tossing it onto the stretcher. As we marched up the driveway, I tried to place a hurried look on my face to mimic Dave's.

Grabbing our equipment from off the stretcher, I heard an adult female's distraught screaming voice through the front, partially-torn, screen door. Two cops were hovering around the infant on the couch, one rapidly compressing the tiny chest with two fingers while the other looked on, terror-stricken. He must have remembered his CPR class. Most of the cops I've met stay away from anything medical — it was a curse to them.

On the couch next to the dead infant, and oblivious to his surroundings, was a man who looked to be in his thirties. He was either in shock or seriously high. The mother turned around upon hearing us enter and immediately started tugging on my shirt, and cried out, "Help my baby! Save her!" She then slammed her fist into the wall behind her. I motioned for the cops to stop compressions and to assist her while we took over.

Dave's hands were furiously shaking as he fumbled through the pediatric drug bag. His adrenaline was now in full force. I needed some information, but it was obvious the mother wasn't going to be of any help, and the spaced-out man on the couch was stuck in his own world.

I opened the child's mouth to place an airway and quickly realized it didn't matter what information I could have obtained. The muscles of the tiny jaw were already beginning to stiffen. I made eye contact with Dave and signaled my hand over the jaw.

We began the motions of a courtesy code. I placed the tiny bag valve mask over the child's lifeless face while Dave began compressions. Out of the corner of my eye, I caught a glimpse of something along the arm of the man on the couch. It was a black tattoo with feathers and a beak. A crow. Mr. Thompson had mentioned a bird tattoo on the day he was attacked.

I kept my cool the best I could, continuing to squeeze the BVM pushing oxygen into the child's inoperable lungs. I didn't alert the officers as to my suspicions about the man, because I wanted to be certain before proceeding. Besides I wasn't entirely sure if I was going to hand him over to the authorities. He would just be out of jail in a few days. That wasn't justice for Mr. Thompson, nor for this dead infant whose death I felt confident this man had something to do with. I had no way of knowing if it was simply neglect or something worse, but first I needed to confirm his description.

We scooped up the child and made our way to the closest hospital. The mother rode up front with Dave. Her frantic pleas drowned out Dave's words of false comfort. Alone in the back of the rig, I stared down at the lifeless infant in front of me. I may have made a mistake taking on this profession. I wasn't any closer to understanding where my sister had gone. Why was this innocent infant lying dead in front of me, stiff and still? Why did my sister have to die so needlessly? I was helpless, drifting further into life's labyrinth of unanswered questions. The answers seemed to be eluding me as much as the adrenaline.

I began opening and shutting the drug cabinet beside me, catching myself after a count of five. I knew things were off when my OCD kicked in. As far as I know, I've managed to avoid counting repeatedly in front of people. I can't have everyone thinking I'm crazy. I don't think the public would take too kindly to a paramedic who has to tap his own shoulder five times before he can begin chest compressions.

I regained control and focused. I couldn't dwell on the unanswered questions for now, because they only left me vulnerable. For the time being I had another objective to occupy my mind. After delivering the infant to the ER, we stopped by Mercy General to pick up the backboard we had left there from another call. I paid Mr. Thompson a quick visit to ask for a detailed description of the man who had robbed him.

He confirmed the man's identity, right down to his greasy brown hair. He seemed excited that the police were following up, flares of future justice burning in his eyes. I felt ashamed for lying to him about that, but the information was important. I had a decision to make.

Chapter 7

Before the end of our shift, something peculiar happened to me at the hospital. Dave and I had dropped off a male in cardiac arrest, which turned out to be another failed "comeback."

It wasn't the patient that caused the confusion, but a female in the code room; an x-ray tech named Lesley. She was huddled in the corner next to her machine, waiting until it was her turn. The bemused look on her face indicated that she was in training. I imagined her attempting to put the chaos of the room in order. A cramped space invites madness, which is the reason I preferred to work in the field. The ER is a breeding ground for onlookers and rubberneckers. Every numbnut wearing scrubs will filter to the area and attempt to get a peek at the dead body that's being probed and scrutinized. Sure, bystanders on the streets gather at times, but hardly do they interfere.

I unattached the leads of my monitor to transfer to theirs, and began collecting our supplies out of the way of the mob.

After placing all of the gear on the stretcher, I wheeled it out of the room, and as usual, kept my head down to avoid eye contact with anyone.

She left her machine briefly, and held the door open for me. "At least you brought us a calm one," she said.

I lifted my eyes and looked up at her. She was grinning, and let out a soft giggle that brought back a fond memory of my sister. I hovered for a moment, entranced by this sound that was both eerie and refreshing. Normally I would have spouted off a somewhat witty comment in return like "You should've seen him last night," but for a reason I couldn't yet grasp, I only stared. I'd been caught off guard by the least likely of scrub-wearers in the room to make a comment to me. I moved quickly to leave, and inadvertently slammed the stretcher against the door.

Outside in the driveway, I dressed the stretcher and wondered what had just happened to me: suddenly speechless for no apparent reason, and overly clumsy. I didn't remember ever experiencing such a combination of irrational reactions.

While Dave wrote his report, I sat next to him in the small room, flinging a paper clip against the wall, still conflicted about the encounter. Just as Dave lifted his head and was about to put an end to my annoying act, there was a knock on the door, and she entered.

"Tryke, is it?" she said.

"Yeah," I said, much smoother now.

"Do you mind if I ask you something about the patient you just brought in?"

"Sure," I said. "Let's go outside and let Dave finish his report in quiet." Dave looked up at her, and then at me with a prying smile and raised eyebrows. He knew my reputation of avoiding conversation and sensed something was amiss, but people only see what they want to see, and she had many attractive features: night black hair resting just at her shoulders, eyes an entrancing deep blue, and skin a soft unblemished pale that outlined her round cheekbones delicately. But it was her comment and laugh that caught my attention, and that rarely happens. I was intrigued. Nothing more.

She introduced herself and gently shook my hand. She then proceeded to ask me very briefly about the patient. Smoothly, she changed the subject to more personal dialogue. I was oddly relaxed while talking to her, revealing more than I had with anyone in a long time, especially a female. I had to hand it to her: she was good with transitions. I didn't realize I was talking about myself until it was too late.

The unexpected encounter with Lesley lasted about thirty minutes. Dave interrupted us after he'd completed his report. We exchanged phone numbers, and I made it clear to her that I was only interested in friendly chatter, and that the reasons were my own. She looked at me with a sly grin, then we shook hands again and departed. I was pretty sure what was behind that grin. It was a friendly reminder that a woman's allure is more powerful than a man's will. But not this man, I told myself.

I had never been opposed to having a friendship with a female, but I knew of the potential complications that would eventually arise. Why not give it a try? I knew myself well enough and could put a stop to it, if necessary.

• • •

When I can't sleep at the station, which is quite often, I sometimes sit with the rig in the bay and absorb the quiet. I often ponder what it would be like to not be quite so normal, so mundane and repetitious, until the day my life ends. Human beings can't be here solely for the purpose of waiting for our ultimate demise. There has to be more than chaos, a more meaningful purpose. If not, it seems awfully wasteful to me.

There was no wind that night, and the heat wasn't letting up, even though its source was fast asleep below the horizon.

The weather report called for rain.

Rain was the one thing that seemed to make life less mundane. A sunny day is too normal for me, and there are way too many of them here in the South. While people flee indoors and change their plans with a frown, I smile and embrace the deluge. The drops feel good on my skin, and let me know there's more going on in the world than just me. I'll take a dark and cloudy day anytime over a bright, scorching one. Besides, the rain places my mood in the optimum position to sleep.

The man's tattoo kept flashing in my mind, and with it brought rage and a lingering question. Now that I had all the information I needed, what should I do with it?

The MDT beeped in the truck and interrupted my thoughts. We were about to be dispatched on another call. Dave often explains to me with great conviction, and quite often, how precious and dear to him the thirty seconds of sleep are between the information being transmitted and the actual alarm sounding.

I jumped into the passenger seat and waited for him to come stumbling out and perform his normal routine of buttoning his shirt, combing his hair, and adjusting his belt before stepping into the rig. He had to line up his belt perfectly with his zipper, and that can be quite an amusing thing to watch when he's really tired. As we sailed down the street to pick up a regular patron who frequently insisted on not taking her diabetes medication, Dave flew into one of his cursing tirades about people being idiots who lack personal responsibility. I was already on a first name basis with her, though I never used it. I prefer to address my patients with a Ms. or Mr. in front of their last names; it keeps things less personal.

It wasn't atypical for this particular patient's blood sugar to be in the twenties, or even lower. For the majority of the population, blood sugar that low would mean certain death, or at least a diabetic coma. But somehow the persistent medication avoider's body seems to adjust and tolerate. However, sooner or later the body will fight back and say, "Screw off, I'm done taking up for you." It was only a matter of time before we coded Ms. Dundee.

The rain joined the pursuit halfway to our destination. I smiled while Dave swore about how he was cursed. I laughed silently, and thought to myself how we were all cursed, not just by the rain or Ms. Dundee. There was something else out there waiting for us all.

Ms. Dundee was a sixty-year-old diabetic whom we visit at least once every three-shift tour. She lived with her mentally challenged twenty-five-year-old son, Karl, who saved her life on more than one occasion by calling us. She was lucky to have someone like him looking over her, but was hardly grateful when she woke from her near-death episodes. Several times we had to involve the police when she began throwing items and swearing at Karl. Once she even threatened him with a kitchen knife held to his neck. He may have been annoying at times, especially when he banged his head repeatedly against the wall, but he was still her son. There was definitely a dark side to that woman.

When Karl called us, he would usually travel to a pay phone a block away instead of using their home phone. I never asked him why, but I had my speculations. We caught him many times staring from the street corner at the rig's lights as if caught in some sort of trance. From that same payphone he also had a bad habit of making false 911 calls, but thankfully dispatch was used to them, and could usually filter the real from the fake.

Karl also had a weird fascination with Dave, which I find not only amusing, but also highly entertaining. He often pelted Dave with cheerful greetings, and usually by the end of a call, he was repetitiously chanting his name. The guy meant well. It was difficult to get angry with him, although I have heard Dave mutter a few colorful metaphors under his breath.

Karl wasn't in the house. I assumed he was watching the lights from the corner. Ms. Dundee was lying on her bed face down, wearing a long stained white t-shirt and light blue granny panties. Her shirt was drenched in sweat, as usual, and an overabundance of forgotten hair was protruding from her bikini line. It was a disturbing sight, and it brought to mind the Guns N' Roses song, "Welcome to the Jungle."

I placed an IV and injected her with an ampule of our concentrated form of sugar known as D50. All it took was five seconds of pushing the thick substance into her right AC vein, and she awoke from her diabetic slumber wondering who the hell we were, and how we got into her house. I always enjoy watching how fast the substance rouses a drooling, unconscious person to wakeful ignorance.

Dave went to the kitchen to make her a sandwich. We have a routine: I inject the meds and he makes the sandwich. The D50 is a quick fix, but it wouldn't sustain her for long. She needed sustenance or she would end up right back in a stupor — and we would end up having to do the whole thing over again.

Ms. Dundee always refused transport to the emergency room. This was fine with Dave and me, even though we had to at least give her a lecture about taking her meds, and try to persuade her to seek medical care. One of the conditions of allowing her to stay at home was that we had to witness her eating a meal.

After consulting with the physician via radio, and watching her slowly and methodically eat a peanut butter and jelly sandwich at 2am, I was glad to be heading back to the station as the rain steadily pelted the windshield. Hopefully, I'd be able to get in a few hours of sleep.

I exited the rig to help guide Dave back into the bay of the station, and as I was shutting the door, I heard the MDT beep again. Maybe Dave didn't feel like telling dispatch we were back in the station by radio, and instead pushed the in-house button on the keyboard. This wasn't an uncommon thing for him to do, because he superstitiously believes that if he presses a button instead of talking on the radio, it will somehow keep dispatch from sending us on another call. He imagines that it puts us in some form of stealth mode, undetectable by human dispatch eyes.

No sleep tonight. The reverse beeping alarm stopped as Dave shifted into drive. I opened the door to get back in and saw his never-ending nighttime sigh plastered on his face.

"Medic 15, this is dispatch," the radio amplified.

"Yeah, yeah, we copy. Place us en route," Dave answered and tossed the mic down. "Where're we going?"

I looked down at the address, and relayed the annoying information to him, "Back to old faithful, Ms. Dundee." I was irritated myself watching the rain steadily falling, and knowing that it probably wouldn't last for long.

"Are you serious?" He said. "Perfect, another restless night, and another argument with the wife. She'll ask me to fix something when I get home tomorrow, and I'll snap. It never fails. She'll have a whole slew of stuff that has to be done the moment I walk in the door after being up for twenty-four hours."

Dave was on a roll that night. I could tell the city was really getting to him. Not to mention his wife Claire. There was no telling what she had hidden behind that dark smile of hers, and I don't envy him during those times. I guess I'm lucky to be alone, with no wife to answer to or kids to watch. I can go home, drink a glass of Scotch in peace, and wake up whenever I want to.

Pretty good for now, I guess, though I am curious at times what it would be like to be married, to care and be cared for by another. At the same time, the thought of being around the same person every day makes me nervous. When I hear the guys talking at the station and hospitals, the word "care" is never used. The words "nagging" and "constantly," however, are used quite frequently. I'll join their brotherhood someday, but not anytime soon.

I didn't see her son Karl anywhere near the house when we arrived for the second time. It was strange for us not to see him at all.

"Your friend's not here again," I said to Dave.

"Lucky for all of us," he said. "I don't think I could handle him tonight, and I might just lose it."

"I wonder who called us if he didn't? You think Ms. Dundee called?"

"I doubt it, but who knows?" He shrugged, and knocked on the door.

The door was usually unlocked, but we have had to use a hydraulic tool on it at times in the past. Ms. Dundee has had to replace the lock several times, and I'm sure she blamed her son for it. She eventually began leaving the door unlocked, as it was earlier.

"Huh? That's odd, it's locked. We were just over here," Dave said.

"I'll walk around the house to see if she's in her room."

"All right. This better not be one of Karl's fake calls. Not tonight."

There was something else bothering Dave that he wasn't telling me. I'd seen him cranky before, but he'd never voiced it as much. If Karl did show up, staring in awe at the strobe lights and continually calling out his name, I'd have had to pull Dave off of him.

Thankfully the light was on in Ms. Dundee's room. I balanced on a piece of broken brick left from a forgotten flower-bed and tried peeking through the tiny holes in the blinds, but I didn't see anyone. The bed was empty. I looked again, this time lower, and I saw what appeared to be a man's head leaning against the bed. I couldn't make out if it was Karl or not. Every once in a while a strange man would be at the house, one of Ms. Dundee's gentlemen callers, as she liked to say in her 1950s lingo.

I headed back to the front door where Dave was impatiently waiting. "Someone's in there, a man I believe, but I'm not sure if it's Karl. They weren't moving. I'll get the tool."

"Great, son of a bitch," Dave said and sighed loudly. "All right, let's get this over with."

I placed the tool's teeth next to the dead bolt, and began cranking. After a few pumps the wood splintered, breaking the door open. "Ms. Dundee's going to be pissed at Karl if he called us, now that we had to break the door again," I said.

"Yep, hope he's not here," Dave said entering the house. "Ms. Dundee, you home?"

The house appeared messier, but how? We had just left there.

We made our way to her bedroom. The door was off the bottom hinge, and hanging loosely. I cautiously entered, and saw Karl lying on the ground with blood coming from multiple wounds on his head and face. I knelt down and tried to wake him. "Karl!" I did a sternal rub, with no response. "Shit, Dave, he's hurt bad. Throw me the airway bag."

Dave tossed the bag to me and did a quick sweep of the house for our safety. "There's no one else here," Dave said, returning. "Who the hell did this to him? The door was locked, and I didn't see any broken windows. You don't think his mom did this?"

"I wouldn't put it past her. Or maybe it was one of her gentlemen caller freaks. Who the hell knows, but we need to call dispatch and get the police over here," I said.

"Yep, on it," Dave said and radioed dispatch. He then placed an IV in Karl's left arm, and attached a bag of saline while I continued to work on his airway.

Karl still had a gag reflex, but blood was flooding his mouth. I quickly suctioned it out. "We're going to have to paralyze him. I can't put an airway down."

Dave pulled the vials from the drug box. "The Succs is ready," he said. He pushed 100mg of Succycholine and 30mg of Etomidate to paralyze Karl's airway so we could take control of it. I contemplated taking my time to see if

Karl's energy would reveal itself. Perhaps the teasing of the soul would make it appear. I could pause briefly, and still get the tube in with no harm done.

Karl's labored breathing halted when the medication set in. I slowly and methodically positioned the miller blade of my laryngoscope posterior to the epiglottis. I leisurely slid the tube through the vocal cords, hoping to get a glance of the elusive soul. I didn't pause long, but long enough for Dave to notice.

"Tryke, you going to give him some air or what?"

"Yeah, sorry… I thought I saw something in his airway for a second," I lied. Karl wasn't ready to go just yet. After securing his airway, I spotted a phone that was partially hidden under the bed a few feet away. Why the hell would the phone be under the bed? I had seen it on the dresser earlier. I looked behind me and saw pieces of sheetrock on the carpet where it had been ripped from the wall. With my foot, I nudged the telephone out from under the bed and saw that it was covered in blood.

"I found the weapon." I motioned my head toward the bloody phone.

Dave shook his head in disgust. "That's just wrong, and if his mother did do this, she should be put away."

"Or down."

"Yeah, that sounds better," Dave said.

We rolled all two hundred and fifty pounds of Karl onto our backboard and then onto the stretcher. The police arrived as we were loading him into the rig. We quickly informed them of the situation and relayed our suspicions about Karl's mom or one of her gentlemen callers being the attacker.

His condition didn't improve or worsen on the way to Mercy General. Dave and I both knew the usual outcomes of head injuries of this magnitude caused by trauma. If by chance Karl ever did resume consciousness, he would likely be even further mentally-impaired. Injuring the disabled sickens me, and even more so when I think about a disabled child's own mother committing the act.

I decided to stick around the ER until the CT scan was complete. I wanted to see the extent of damage Karl had suffered. Dave didn't object, realizing it would be futile now to try and get any sleep before the end of the shift. Besides, I could tell he held a soft spot for Karl deep down below the curses.

I watched as the doctor pulled up the scan on the computer next to the nurses' station. An oblong-shaped mass illuminated on the left hemisphere of the brain. The physician informed me that it was blood.

"What's next, doc?" I asked.

"He'll be in surgery within the hour."

"What are his chances?"

"I won't know until I get in there and see the extent of the injury, but I'd say he has a fifty/fifty chance of survival. Although, if he does pull through, returning to his former mental state is far less likely."

I placed my hand on his shoulder. "He's a good guy, doc, just got the short end of the stick in life. And now it's been shortened even more."

"I'll do what God allows," he said.

The doctor's last statement stuck in my head. I didn't know if it made me feel better, or worse.

Year Two

Chapter 8

I found myself at a crossroads with my memory. This certainly wasn't the first time for this to happen, but it was the first that involved passages I had written.

In my hands was a journal I had begun in the beginning of my career to chronicle the calls that involved a "comeback." There weren't many, so I began documenting every death that I encountered, writing down details of any extraordinary visual occurrences.

I flipped casually through the pages to the end where I had stopped writing. I was about to close it when I saw more words written past the blank pages. This was a section I didn't remember, but it was definitely in my handwriting. As I skimmed through, I knew what had transpired.

He was back. He never really leaves. I've managed to avoid his unyielding grip for far too long this time. I hold on for as long my mind allows, longing for any stage of sleep to enter, past the numbness and through the pain until I ultimately become submissive to his power.

He is Insomnia.

My profession only fuels his desire to return with each interruption during the night. Every call held the potential to precipitate my thoughts, continuing them throughout the night as if on a swift moving conveyor belt. I was obsessed with finding the human soul, and each failed attempt left my mind in disarray.

Over the years I have managed to identify usefulness within the pursuits of my arch nemesis. I find that my subconscious is more pliable when I hit the thirty-six hour mark. I interfere less with the process in my mind and have time to mull over its contents.

I've found solutions to confusing thoughts, recalled missing memories from years back, and even had the rare epiphany. But then there are times, such as this one, when I find myself staring into dark places within my mind, places I'd prefer to close up forever. I usually snap out of the trance just long enough to ponder whether the dark places were real, or merely figments of my imagination. For my sake this time I wished for the latter, but the more passages that I read in the back of my journal, the more real the dark became.

I was hoping to find some insight: How can I break the desire to see death, and just as important, how do I let the memories of my sister rest? But that was hardly the case. In fact, what I found seemed only to enhance the obsession.

The first paragraph revealed a lurking fury within me: *I am overcome with anger and frustration. Darkness has crept in, shadowing my once dimly-lit hope for mankind. I can no longer accept this way of being, lingering in the corner like so many of the bystanders I have pitied. I can no longer shy away from this world, sometimes fleeing, other times healing. No more.*

On the following pages were names, followed by the calls associated with them. Some were the actual patients, while others were family members, onlookers, or even hospital personnel. They were labeled with one or more crimes, all violent offenses that have avoided our society's so-called judicial system. Above each entry was a lone number that I couldn't yet explain.

I could feel the anger boiling inside of me as I read name after name. I began to recall the scenes and atrocities that took place. And I began remembering plans that I had formed.

A few months ago I had been on the brink of quitting my profession. I was left fuming and more confused by the end of each shift. I was out of answers. Death was way too unpredictable to follow around.

But I couldn't give up, I knew that much. I simply needed a new direction. It was all in front of me, just waiting to be unleashed. All was prepped for the voyage.

Why let so many of these obviously aching souls be trapped in their restricting organic suits? Why let them roam the world, free to inflict unbridled mayhem on the innocent? It all seems so terribly painful.

If my experiment worked, then the world would be rid of these pain-riddled monsters — at least a few of them — and I would get to see their true selves once they were released. We all win in the end.

• • •

It was an odd sight to see the space where my father had once toiled, now transformed into my own workspace and discovery center. It was a good feeling knowing the place wasn't completely dead and that the memory of my dad was still very much alive. My expectations about the venture were still up in the air, but that was the beauty of it — the excitement of the unknown.

I set my half-empty glass of Scotch onto the table, then made my way down the dark stairwell and out to the parking lot. It was a nice night; the humidity had dropped, leaving the evening's summer wind pleasantly warm. As I walked to my mom's house, I gleamed with excitement. I had accomplished the first step. I even whistled a few lines to

"Whistle While You Work" — I believe that's the name of it.

The kitchen lights were on, but I still knocked before placing the key in the lock so I didn't completely surprise my mother. Her brittle state could shatter at any moment. I found her in the living room, seated in my dad's favorite recliner and staring straight ahead. The TV was off and the only light in the room came from a dying candle flickering beside her. The house was spotless as usual. She had always kept a clean house, which was the only thing that hadn't changed.

"Mom, are you all right?" I said as I entered the room. She didn't answer right away.

"Tryke, is that you?" She asked, sounding as if she'd aged ten years since last week.

"Yes, mom, it's me." I sat on the quilt-covered couch. "How are things going?"

She continued to look forward. "As well as they're going to be." Another moment of silence passed. "How are things with you?"

"I can't complain," I said. "Not a lot to talk about. Work is pretty much the same."

"That's good." Silence again. "Your father would have loved to see you in your uniform. When you first were interested in becoming a paramedic, he told all his retired friends what you were going to do after you graduated. He couldn't have been more proud." I could tell she wanted to cry, but her eyes wouldn't allow it anymore. She turned her gaze to the window beside her.

"Well, I do my best every day at work for both of you." She would have normally smiled at my comment. She often called me her little comedian, knowing I was full of crap most of the time. It was harmless sarcasm for entertainment purposes. She didn't always get my humor. That wasn't surprising, considering I got it from my dad. She never got all his jokes either, and would usually shake her head while he smirked away.

She was still quiet. "Well, I need to get some sleep before my next shift," I said. "I just wanted to check on you. Before I leave, can I get you anything? Are you doing okay on supplies?"

"I'm doing fine, son. Thank you for stopping by. It's always good to see you."

Her monotone voice left me sad. I kissed her on the forehead before I left and locked the door behind me. She actually talked a little more than usual, which was a good sign, I suppose. I told myself that after I got situated in my new venture that I would dedicate some time to helping her get back to some sort of life. She deserved normalcy at the very least.

Not all women who gave birth to a child are allowed to call themselves mothers. One in particular comes to mind. After many nights in the hospital and two surgeries, Karl survived his phone beating. The police never found enough evidence to convict his mother or any of her gentlemen callers. And of course she never admitted to what she had done. But I knew the truth. It was smeared all over her haggard face every time we made a call on her after the incident.

Karl was left in a vegetative state and placed in a nursing home. It was a cruel fate for anyone to have to endure. Death would have been much more humane. Every now and then we'd make a call to that nursing home and I'd check in on him. I made sure he was being treated well. I also inquired about visitors, but he had none since being admitted. I personally didn't think Ms. Dundee deserved to see her son, but he needed to hear her voice. He had always been resilient in the face of her cruel ways, returning to her with unconditional loyalty, and ready to save her life one more time. But he will never hear her voice again, and not because of guilt. She had something inside of her lurking around — something dark — and I wanted to see it.

Chapter 9

My first catch had taken me only a few days to plan. During that time Dave was constantly suspicious of my behavior. I was livelier, he said. He actually caught me pacing around the station a few times. I blamed it on my ADD. The truth... I was "pumped," as Dave would have put it, and especially about the upcoming night. My attempt at shrouding my excitement had failed.

Lesley had noticed something off about me also, telling me I appeared nervous during our latest weekly drinking-and-discussion session on humanity's flaws. We'd become good friends and she'd acquired a rather impressive, yet annoying, ability to read me. Of course, I didn't let her in on that secret.

I couldn't believe it myself, an actual friendship with a female not involving sex. All the rumors were false, but I knew better. This was too good to be true, and eventually something would fail, but so far her sly smirk had yet to penetrate my defenses.

Dave was on the other end of the relationship spectrum,

desperately holding on to his marriage. Lately he had been projecting his own issues onto me thanks to everyone's friend: Denial. In the end, Dave would have to be dragged away from him by his feet while screaming and clawing the floor. Dave and his wife were now separated. It wasn't a surprise, to me anyway. Every phone call and text ended with long exasperated sighs, followed by a few curse words uttered under his breath. She slowly bled him until she was ready to leave. I saw it the first time I met her, through her wide joker grin.

Once I started the process, there was no turning back.

I made sure no one had transported Ms. Dundee to the hospital while I was on my days off, because that would have put a kink in my plan. I filtered through the reports at the station, and wasn't surprised to see that no other rigs had run a call on her. She reserved her sugar plummeting spells for two in the morning, saving them for our shift. I was flattered.

Dense clouds kept the moonlight at bay. It was a perfect shadow for my first time. I knew the house well, inside and out. I had been there enough times. I chose normal-colored clothing, not all black, which had been my first instinct. I didn't feel it warranted that type of stealth. Besides, how would I explain my burglar attire to the police if it turned ugly?

There was no car in Ms. Dundee's driveway, which meant no gentleman caller. Because of her medical condition, she didn't have a license. From the driveway I saw that the light was on in her bedroom. As I had to do many times in the past, I was going to peer through the small holes in the blinds to make sure she was home.

Standing on my favorite broken brick from a failed garden long ago, I caught a glimpse of her dark hair splayed across the stained carpet. She was either asleep or her sugar was taking a plunge yet again. I hoped for the latter.

I slowly turned the knob to the front door with my black latex gloved hand. It was unlocked, as usual. The wooden door creaked from the splintered wood that had been kicked and forced open countless times.

I entered the quiet dwelling.

A dim lamp lit the dirty living room. As many times as I had been there, there was no way to avoid the abundance of miscellaneous objects scattered around aimlessly. It was a minefield of dirty dishes and partially-eaten frozen dinners.

A half empty plate of Mexican food threatened my surprise as my left boot pressed against it. I gradually lifted my foot, making minimal clinking sounds from the fork smothered in dried refried beans.

I quickly scanned the house for anyone else, just in case. I didn't need any surprises. All was silent and clear.

Her bedroom door was cracked open. I nudged it with my foot, opening it just enough so that the creaking didn't wake her, if she was indeed asleep.

She was displayed on the floor as I'd seen her many times before: drool sliding down the left corner of her mouth, dirty oversized t-shirt drenched with sweat, and her glucometer beside her, surrounded by unused strips.

I placed the syringe of my mixture back into my pocket; there would be no need for it. She wouldn't be conscious until her body received glucose.

I lifted her dead weight from the floor, and as I placed her over my shoulder I noticed the phone was off the hook. My gut sank well below the nasty carpet as thoughts shuffled through my mind. "Shit," I said aloud. I hoped she didn't have the ambition to live and dialed 911 before passing out. I stood perfectly still, listening for diesel engines. It was unlikely, but things happen.

After a minute of quiet, I sighed in relief. My paranoia was getting the better of me. I wiped perspiration from my brow and continued to the front door, dodging the clutter.

Why the hell didn't I have the foresight to park closer? But I knew the answer: I was being overly cautious.

"Ok, Ms. Dundee, don't move," I whispered and sat her

against the inside of the front door so I could back my truck into the driveway. It wouldn't look right, me carrying a half-naked sixty-year-old lady over my shoulders down a dark street.

I jerked my head back and forth like a skittish rodent being hunted, attempting to remain calm and cool as I walked to my truck. Silence and darkness were a good sign.

During the entire drive to my personal lab, I kept glancing at the rearview mirror toward the backseat. Her snores made it easier to concentrate on the road, but I'd feel much better once she was on the table, secure and out of sight. Then I could work.

• • •

There's something to say about the quiet. It fits perfectly along the contours of my mind when I'm alone. Though I wasn't completely alone, the fit was still there. I felt good, on the brink of great discovery. The silent whisper of moonlight brushing my skin kept me going like warm sunshine does the masses.

Her extremities were secured with leather restraints, compliments of Mercy ER. Of course we carry restraints on the rigs — disposable ones — but they aren't leather, and leather is much more effective. Even a worn pair, like the ones given to me by a smiling nurse in the ER, were as good as a new pair. She still smiles at me shyly when I see her, no doubt wondering in her perverted mind what purpose I had for them. "If she only knew," I thought, smiling back at her.

I didn't predict Ms. Dundee would be struggling too much anyway, because her glucose was bordering zero by the appearance of her breathing. There would be no need to interfere after all. I removed my outer clothing, revealing my work uniform. I needed everything to be official. I soon had her attached to every machine in the lab, including IV access. The cameras were on, and the alarm was set on the stairs. And then, I waited.

I had to hand it to myself. The place didn't look too bad with all the medical equipment turned on and functioning. It was a one-man ER, complete with monitoring devices, cameras, and a mad-scientist paramedic — not to mention a security system and first-class accommodations. "Ms. Dundee, your own private room," I said. "You won't get that at Mercy ER. But I do have to insist on no visitors. This is an exclusive institution, for high-profile clients only."

The equipment was easier than expected to obtain. Thanks to recent hefty government grants, the training facility was well-stocked with an abundance of supplies. They would never miss the minute number of things I borrowed. I also took on the responsibility of ordering supplies at the station for all three shifts, a task that the other medics were happy to pass on. Yep, I was a regular ambitious Joe, ready to help out in any way I could.

I waited, and waited, and waited. I even waited some more. Her body was used to being glucose-deprived, and compensated well. Ridiculously well. It was getting late. The glucose monitor gave me a reading of twelve, and hadn't wavered in an hour. So much for not intervening.

I drew up the insulin and restarted the cameras. Moments later her snoring ceased and the monitor alarm rang as her heart quickly jumped from a sinus rhythm to v-tach. Seconds later it halted to a steady asystole.

I stared intently, never removing my eyes from hers. Nothing. I considered reviving her to finesse the soul, a little nudge, but not just yet. Her window for revival was narrow, and every minute I waited, her chances of survival dropped by another ten percent.

Three minutes.

I decided to give it five. That way she would have the same survival rate as the doctor gave her son — how poetic. I do surprise myself at times.

Four minutes. Still nothing.

I had the epinephrine ready. The sweat that had been

pouring from her pores had ceased.

Four minutes, thirty seconds.

"Come on, Ms. Dundee, show your true self, as dirty as it may be," I whispered. "I'm not judging, I merely want a glance. There's no reason to be shy."

Four minutes, forty-five seconds.

I pushed the epinephrine and knelt down on my thinking chair (now turned compression chair) and began chest compressions. I didn't intubate, or bag her airway. I wasn't that ambitious. I thought that compressions and epinephrine should more than suffice for a first run.

Staring at the monitor, I continued to press on her skinny sternum, listening to her ribs crack with each push. The sound of ribs cracking was always a good sign you were doing compressions efficiently. I can still hear my preceptor's words amplifying in my ear from paramedic school: "If you ain't cracking ribs, you ain't doing shit."

The monitor continued to show a steady flat line. I did three rounds of epinephrine and compressions without success, so it was failure on two counts: no revival and no soul. Her black aching spirit must have snuck out. It probably saw me coming, but there was always the possibility that my camera had caught it.

I grabbed a towel and dried my face. The room was warm with all the activity, and I made a mental note to remember a fan next time. I was sure the generator could sustain a little more voltage.

As I sat back and stared at the body left by Ms. Dundee, I ran the entire experiment through my head. I considered what I'd done and witnessed. It wasn't a pretty sight, but discovery was sometimes messy. I couldn't very well explore undiscovered territory without getting my hands dirty, though I couldn't take full credit. She took most of the walk, while I merely slid open the door. We were a good team on the first step of my search.

Next, I had to consider an obvious but over-looked issue

that had just crossed my mind. I had been so enthralled by the idea and strategy to get her there, I hadn't given any thought to what I was going to do with her body once I was done. How could I have been such an idiot as to not have a plan, now that it was over? I began racking my brain for solutions and nervously tapping an empty syringe on the arm of the chair. I didn't like not having a plan.

It wasn't long before the solution struck me. It wasn't the most genius of ideas, but it was cleverly simple. Take her back and leave her exactly where I had found her — dying on her bedroom floor.

• • •

I was home by four a.m., and had a few hours before my shift started. Sleep, as pleasant as it sounded, would not be allowed. Nor was it an immediate concern. Notes on Ms. Dundee were top priority, while the memories were still fresh. Once I viewed the footage, of course. Though I was impressed with the quality of the video, it didn't matter much without something to see. And as I suspected, the soul was a no-show.

• • •

Yawning, I slowly got up from my recliner and silenced the annoying alarm calling to me from the living room. I wasn't asleep — he wouldn't allow me the luxury at the moment — I was in that space between the world of the living and dream world, swaying on the edge of a cliff.

I had an alarm set in every room of the apartment, with two alarms on each, set twenty minutes apart for just this reason. I must have missed the first one. I still had my uniform on, but wrinkles weren't acceptable no matter how exhausted I was, so I grabbed a crisp one from my closet and set the coffee to brew. I always made time for coffee and a bagel. Coffee for initial waking, or in this case sustained consciousness, and the bagel for nourishment.

The drive to work was a terribly unpleasant one, as I had imagined it to be. I didn't like traffic. I left an hour early every day to avoid the bustle of everyday workers jostling for a better position in the bumper-to-bumper jam. Today, however, I had to join them. Thankfully, I had the exhilaration of last night still lingering on my tired eyes. When I recalled the failed but completely necessary events, the mental image gave me small bursts of energy.

The two medics turning over the shift to Dave and me both looked at their watches in unison as I entered the station.

"Holy shit, Tryke, your not an hour early? What the hell, did you pass out whacking it this morning?" Mike said. Mike was short and had eaten way too many cheeseburgers in his few years as a medic. He was mostly annoying and loud, but usually tolerable. His crude sense of humor was all he had going for him.

"Screw off cap-ass," I said. Dave laughed at my failed attempt at an insult, nearly spilling his coffee.

"Ass-hat is the term you were looking for," Mike said.

"Thanks, I knew you'd get it." I smiled as I walked away toward the bedroom across the truck bay to drop off my bag. It became a fun game to act like I was terrible at insults. It had come about completely by accident during my second week at work. The insult retort failed as it spilled out from my mouth. I believe I said something like "face-dick" when I meant to say "dick-head." The reaction I received began the game I have continued ever since. It's the simple undercover humor that's the best, I've found.

Two sips into my coffee and three sentences into the morning paper, the bell sounded, and Dave made his usual comment. "And so it begins," he said. I wasn't as disgruntled. I needed to keep moving that day. The more calls the better, until the evening when the lack of sleep would once again attempt a takeover. But I had no doubt my old friend Insomnia would intervene and slap me awake at pivotal moments.

When the address was announced over the speakers, I flinched, spilling hot coffee down my arm. It was a welfare call on Ms. Dundee.

Chapter 10

A welfare call is simply a request to check on an individual who hasn't been seen or heard from in several days. A neighbor or family member often places the call. These types of calls are usually reserved for Sundays, when grandma hitches a ride to church with family. More often than not, grandma is found stiff as the headboard of the bed she's lying on. However, Ms. Dundee's only family was in a nursing home and unable to speak, which meant either a neighbor had contacted us out of concern or one of her gentleman callers had a boner aching to be relieved.

I wasn't quite sure how this situation was going to play out. I began envisioning several different scenarios, and asking myself questions: What if someone had seen me? If so, who? And did they inform the police?

This could turn ugly.

Dave took his sweet time getting there, which made the trip even more agonizing, not to mention dispatch had just informed us that the police had a unit on the way. It wasn't unusual for the cops to be dispatched on welfare concerns, but it certainly didn't ease my anxiety.

"You all right?" Dave asked, watching my boot rapidly punish the dash.

"Yeah, sorry, just the caffeine. I didn't sleep well last night and I was on my fourth cup of coffee before we got this call."

"No more for you, then."

"I'm good till lunch." That is, if I'm not in prison, I thought. They serve coffee in prison don't they? Probably not. They don't need to be providing stimulants and creating any more tension behind those bars.

A police unit was already on scene, parked in front of the house, when we turned the corner onto the street. I sighed loudly as I unbuckled my seatbelt and then mumbled, "Here we go." Dave didn't comment. He was probably saying the same thing under his breath — only his words would be referring to annoyance, and not nervous anticipation.

The officer stared at me over his partially rolled-down tinted window as I exited the rig. He was wearing aviator sunglasses and had a toothpick, or maybe it was a matchstick, protruding from his mouth. He looked a little too much like Stallone in the movie *Cobra*. My hands were mildly shaking as I fumbled for the handle to shut the door. I quickly opened the side compartment door next to me and grabbed our hydraulic door-prying tool to keep my hands busy.

"Why do you have that?" Dave asked, looking down at the bag.

"Just in case," I said, with a nervous smile.

"Greetings, officer," I said clumsily. "Nice morning isn't it?"

He looked at me as if I'd just asked him for his daughter's phone number. "Yeah, I'm thoroughly thrilled to be here," he said, without expression. He followed us up the short path to the front door. "I did a quick sweep around the place. No doors forced open or any broken windows. I take it y'all have been here a few times by the information I received from my dispatch."

"She's a regular client of ours, a diabetic who likes to avoid her medication," Dave said. "The good thing is, the front door is usually left unlocked for us. She likes to prepare for our arrival a day in advance."

"I tried the front door and it was locked," the officer said. "The back door, too."

Crap. Of all the repetitious bullshit I do, why the hell did I have to be so paranoid and lock the door behind me last night? I should know better. Mistake number…hell, I didn't know, but I definitely had some improving to do before my next one. If there was a next one.

"Huh. Ms. Dundee is getting brave these days, unless she isn't really here," Dave said.

"Maybe one of her gentleman callers took her on a trip," I said.

"Doubtful. She's too much of a liability to take places. I'm sure they've figured that much out, seeing our rig parked in front every other day," Dave said.

The officer actually smirked under his gunslinger persona at Dave's comment. It made me feel a little better, but this was far from over. "So, uh, do you know who called this in, officer? Neighbor?" I asked.

"Yeah, it was a neighbor. Said they haven't seen her in two or three days."

"Any suspicions, or just missing?' I said. I felt like kicking the words back into my mouth the second they were out. I realized how suspicious I was sounding. Even Dave looked over at me when I asked the question.

The officer paused and looked down at me through his mirror sunglasses. I jerked my eyes away and opened the bag that held the hydraulic tool. "Just concerned, nothing else," he said smoothly.

"Oh," I said, and wedged the teeth of the tool against the lock. The door popped open after a few pumps. "After you," I told the officer, then stepped back to let him into the house.

I concealed my shaking right hand in my pocket after I lowered the tool back into its bag. He returned thirty seconds later with his aviator sunglasses in hand. He stared at me with his sharp dark eyes and said, "Your lady is back there all right, but I don't know what y'all are going to be able to do for her."

Dave hurried along the hallway to the back bedroom. I followed, glancing back at the officer who was now radioing his dispatch from his shoulder mic. He knew something. He had sniffed out my involvement somehow and was now calling for backup. I yelled silently to myself, "Get a hold of yourself, Tryke! No one saw you last night. No one suspects anything."

There she was, nicely placed back in the same position as I had initially found her. Only this time she wasn't diaphoretic or snoring, but cold and stiff. I stood in the doorway and stared as Dave knelt down and turned her over. More paranoid thoughts forced their way in. Did I remember to remove everything: The tape from her arm where I had placed the IV? The electrodes for the monitor? I quickly reassured myself that I did.

"It was only a matter of time," Dave said, looking up at me.

"What?" I asked in the most surprised voice I could manage.

"Can't you see for yourself?"

I took a deep breath and gazed down into her accusing eyes. They were screaming at me, cursing my intrusion. I shut my eyes and reopened them to clear the thought.

"You okay?" Dave asked. "You're sweating an awful lot. Maybe you should sit down for a second."

I wiped the beads of sweat from my forehead with my right hand. It was still shaking. I leaned against the wall and placed my hands on my knees. Why was I taking this so oddly? I rationalized that it was most likely because she was my first. I was a rookie once again. But the thing is, I was never nervous as a rookie paramedic. In fact, I had always been calm and methodical. I was sure this feeling would pass. Time has a strange way of making things seem familiar, and easier to deal with.

"We've been over here so many times, I felt like I knew her," I said, regaining my composure.

"Don't let it get to you. Sooner or later we all die, right?" Dave was patting me on the shoulder as if to comfort me by his words. It was a nice try.

"Yeah, sure," I said.

We walked back to the living room where the officer was waiting patiently for us. "She's all yours, officer," Dave said. I wanted to sprint past Dave out the front door to the rig, just to avoid the officer's glare.

"Thanks, I'll cherish the moment," the policeman said. I began to relax as he spoke into his mic and asked his dispatch for the coroner. "Wait, one second," he said, touching my shoulder just as I was about to exit. Dave was already safely out. I closed my eyes and sighed. I was done for, and ready to accept my fate.

I turned around and faced him. He lowered his right hand down to his holster and rested it on the butt of his gun. "You forgot your tool," he said, pointing down to the bag next to his boots.

I was in such a hurry to leave, I had forgotten the bag. "Whew, thanks. We might need that." He didn't say anything in return, only nodded. I grabbed the bag and coolly walked out the front door, holding my gaze straight ahead.

• • •

Back in the rig Dave began his rant, only this time it was his dark side being thankful we didn't have to run any more calls on Ms. Dundee. "She got what was coming to her. It was justice for what she did to her son," he said.

It was nothing, Dave, I thought to myself. You're

welcome. It was my pleasure. I nodded, agreeing with his words. If she had revealed her soul then I would have been celebrating the same as Dave. Although I did learn some things for the next time: cover all my tracks, including my demeanor around police officers. I was careful in my lab, wiping everything down with the kill-all solution that we used to clean the rig after each call. I was good at finding blood and fluids hiding in crevices. I also recovered all of the disposable equipment that had any DNA on it and placed it in a red biohazard bag. That bag was safely in our larger biohazard bag in the station, and would be picked up on Thursday.

All in all, job well done and complete. Every loose end was tied off and sealed neatly away. Though my head was heavy along with my eyes from lack of sleep, it was turning out to be a rather good day. A burden had been lifted from my chest, and to top it all off, the sky had darkened and released a welcome flow of water. I smiled as we backed into the station. I left the bay door open so I could enjoy the soft sound of the soothing drops. I knew I wouldn't sleep, but a man can dream, can't he?

Chapter 11

It had been nearly a week since my first experiment failed. The last few shifts had been rather slow for us. Unusually slow. Maybe everyone in the city had gotten in touch with their inner chi and took a vow of silence. Now if only I could get them to move to the top of a mountain and wear brown robes. Nah, then I'd be out of a job and potential specimens. The summers down here were never actually slow; the people merely migrated to other areas. The higher the heat index, the more calls we ran, whether it was our station or another across town.

GSW's also tended to increase with the heat, but if the good citizens got bored with shooting one another, they would surely find some other form of violence to entertain themselves. And that night I was betting on knives. It was a little game Dave and I played at times, usually payday weekends. We would often make wagers on how the citizens were going to off one another.

My phone vibrated next to me on the table. It was a text

message from Lesley. She wanted to visit with me at the station. It was an odd request, considering that she had never been to my station before, or showed interest. I didn't have an excuse to say no. Besides, I'd been to the hospital where she worked many times, though never out of uniform and off duty.

I was sitting on the picnic table in the rear of the station when she arrived. "So what's the occasion?" I asked as she exited her car. She was carrying a small blue gift bag.

"You really don't know what today is?" she said. I thought about it briefly, but nothing immediately came to mind. "It's your birthday, goofball."

That's right. It *was* my birthday. I really hadn't thought about it. My mom certainly hadn't been in a state of mind to celebrate anything over the last two years, and I wasn't one for bringing attention to myself. If my dad were still alive, he would have made sure to acknowledge the day. In fact, I would have had a horrible rendition of "Happy Birthday" recorded on my voicemail.

"I guess I forgot," I said.

She looked at me with sad eyes, giving the impression that it was a tragedy to forget such a memorable occasion. She sometimes surprised me with sentiments like that, especially when I recalled her usual comments on society and its tendency to over-do everything.

"I don't remember telling you my date of birth before. How'd you know?"

"I have my ways," she said with a devious smile.

I looked over at the window and saw Dave peeking out at us. "Oh, I should have known. Dave."

"It's not his fault. I bugged him until he told me."

"He's a sucker for beautiful girls," I said. She grinned and looked away. Then she sat down at the picnic table and I sat across from her.

"Open it," she said.

I removed the decorative paper from inside the bag and

lifted out a small wrapped box. I tore off the glittery black wrapping. It was a watch, but not just any watch. It was the same watch my dad had given me when I graduated high school, a dark tarnished metal timekeeper crafted by hand. I forgot I had told her the story of losing it during paramedic school.

"This is pretty great. Where'd you find one?"

"I ordered it online from a little shop in Italy."

"That must have cost you a fortune. Can I help you pay for part of it?"

"No, but you can wear it and tell everyone that I gave it to you."

"Will do." I slid the watch onto my wrist and remembered my dad's smile when he handed it to me. My mom was clicking away on her camera, attempting to catch a candid moment. My dad knew I had always admired the pocket watch that he carried to work each day. He purchased it in Rome on their honeymoon after my mom found it in a small shop. He told me he had worn it on his wrist until the band was broken while helping the stock boys unload a pallet from the morning delivery. He said it didn't feel right replacing it with just any band, so he kept it as a pocket watch. When I lost it in school I was devastated, pissed off for a month that I could be so careless.

"So," said Lesley, "do you want to celebrate tomorrow night?" She reached her hand across the table and rested it on mine. I instinctively jerked it away. By the time I realized what I had done, it was too late.

"I'm sorry, I shouldn't have done that," she said. She got up from the table and stared down at the concrete.

"Lesley, I didn't —"

"I have to go." She quickly walked to her car and drove off, wiping her eyes as she backed out of the driveway. I didn't know what to do. I wasn't the one who broke the rules, she did. But I wasn't mad. A little confused, but certainly not mad. I could get past it, though something told me it wasn't going to be that easy for her.

When I walked back inside the station, Dave was sitting in the day room watching TV.

"Don't act like you didn't hear what just happened," I said. "I know you were watching from the kitchen window like a little teenage girl."

Surprisingly, he didn't deny it. "Was that a first fight I just witnessed?" he asked.

"We didn't fight. But if you're referring to a disagreement between friends, then I suppose it was our first."

He didn't push the subject. "Well, if you want some friendly advice or just want to talk about it, I'm here."

"I'm good. It was just a simple misunderstanding. It'll blow over."

I was trying to convince myself, and Dave knew it. I could tell by the way he said, "Uh huh."

• • •

The rest of our last shift continued to be slow, and the next one started out the same. On any normal occasion I would be impatient, eagerly waiting for some idiot to spill a beer and spark a fight in a bar. But since the episode with Ms. Dundee, I couldn't get my mind off of my side work. My eagerness to learn more was exhilaratingly painful, so much so that I couldn't seem to concentrate on anything else. And of course, there was the recent incident with Lesley still lingering.

The slow spell would end soon and the people would migrate back our way. There was no need to worry about that, and there would always be plenty of death to go around. But I needed a distraction, and it didn't come.

Dave, being his overly-involved and helpful self, asked me over to his place for a beer the next morning after work. He was concerned about me, no doubt, and would attempt his own form of therapy and intervention. Partners in our profession spend a lot of time together, and it's hard to maintain complete privacy — one more thing I needed to keep in mind as I continued with my search.

I was good at manipulating conversations and changing the subject. A sly comment here or there can do wonders for any situation that may arise, and most people love for others to guide them, no matter how much they deny that fact or attempt to lead.

Before Dave got an opportunity to begin his failed attempts of friendly intervention, I quickly started the conversation when I entered his one-bedroom casa. "How are you liking the single life?" I asked. "Any new nurse prospects?" He lowered his head and closed the door behind me. Dave wasn't good at hiding anything. He had a wide array of animated features, and one was constantly plastered on his face, revealing more than he likely wanted others to see.

"It's lonely. I don't see how you've done it for so long."

"I prefer the peaceful silence. And don't forget, Sally visits pretty often," I said, making a shaking motion with my right hand. It made him laugh, so whether it was true or not didn't much matter. "How's your daughter? Brianna, right?"

"Yeah, she's doing well." He tossed me a beer.

"Thanks," I said.

I reminded myself that I need to sway Dave toward a more suitable drink than this cheap, watered-down beer. He needed something with bite, something that got to the point much quicker. I wanted desperately to introduce him to the great flavors of the island of Islay in Scotland. He might be reluctant at first, but once the smoky peat flavor hit his senses, he'd be hooked on Scotch.

Dave's apartment wasn't anything like I'd expected — saying it resembled debris after a tornado would have been a compliment. When he lived with his wife, their house was immaculate, museum-like, and as I suspected when I first met her, she was behind most of it. Though, for some reason he is still a fanatic about neatness at the station. I smiled, shaking my head as I looked around. After all his silent lectures, delivered by repetitively placing items in their proper assigned areas, he was a damn closet hoarder all along. And something of a slob. I guess we all have our secrets.

The walls were barren, containing no pictures or frames. I expected him to have at least some photos of his daughter around. He had plenty in his wallet and taped to his locker door, and he showed them to me on more than one occasion.

"I like what you've done with the place," I said, stepping over a pile of clothes to get to the balcony door. On a table to the left of the door were the missing pictures of his daughter, and also his wife.

"Sorry about the mess. I haven't had the energy to do much. The last few shifts I haven't been able to sleep."

"I know the feeling," I said.

I took a seat in one of the two blue-and-white striped lawn chairs on his balcony. He had his head held down, holding his beer as if praying to it. I had seen in his eyes when he first opened the door that he didn't call me over for my intervention, but his own. I felt terrible for not focusing on that earlier, and thought myself a bad partner. He had always been there for me, offering a shoulder to lean on, though I never took him up on it. It was my turn now, my duty as a fellow paramedic.

It was probably hard on him in the beginning, when I seemed to not need advice. He viewed himself as a mentor, a guide to everything paramedic. He most likely felt helpless when I sailed along smoothly and didn't act like a stranded damsel. I'm sure that when Dave was a rookie, his first partner kept him safely under his wing, and emotionally guiding him along.

He was only doing what he felt was right, what he was taught. I, on the other hand, take the "let's see what happens" approach to life. I do have to take some of the blame for egging on his ego every so often, but like I said before, it's the undercover humor that's the best.

I took a long swig of the cold beer and it pleasantly stung going down. I wanted to start out by saying, "So how's the treacherous bitch?" But that wasn't what he needed. He knew she was a cheating whore. Why bring up old news? It was time he moved forward and enjoyed the good life of solitude and silence.

"So, have y'all finalized everything with the divorce?" I thought I might as well start off with the second-worst thing to say, and work our way out from there.

He sighed, and then began speaking as if he'd been holding his tongue for years.

"I can't do it, Tryke, I won't do it. I don't deserve this crap. We're a family, dammit, and I'm not giving that up. I don't care what she did." I had to hand it to him, he had passion and conviction for his marriage. But what good is that when the other half is spreading her passion around town?

Tears slid down his cheek to his beer can and then to the concrete balcony below, forming a small puddle. Okay, now what? I guess I shouldn't have led with that one.

"What's she think about you feeling that way?"

From the vague expression on his face, I knew I had again chosen the wrong words. I'm too rational, too straightforward. He didn't care what she thought of him. He forgave her, and was willing to see past anything. But I saw it as a relationship that involved two people, and if one of them wasn't willing, then it doesn't matter what the other one thinks.

"She thinks she's happy with that asshole she found," he said, "but I know her better than that. I could see it in her eyes she wasn't happy. She was full of guilt." I wanted to yell to him the truth that I could see without even having to look at her. It was over, so move on, you crybaby. But he had experienced something I hadn't before: he was in love with this woman.

"How about another beer?" I said.

"Sure," he said, continuing to stare at his feet. I got up and trudged through his jungle of clothes on the floor to the kitchen. The refrigerator, like his side table, was a collage of family photos, there to remind him of what his life had once been. I pitied him and wanted to help, but I didn't know how. I was terrible with this stuff, though I was confident that having pictures of his wife displayed around his small apartment wasn't the right direction. He should reduce them to just his daughter. But how to tell him that? I was pretty sure it would just make him angry.

I handed him his beer and patted his shoulder as he'd done to me on so many occasions. "Well, I say go for it Dave. Fight for the woman you love, but if you see past that guilt and she still doesn't want to reconcile, you have to promise me you'll move on. I don't like seeing you like this."

I had gone in the totally opposite direction. I baffled myself with my own words, but they seemed to finally be the right ones.

"Sure thing, I promise," Dave said. "And me and you, we'll hang out and run the town together."

Whoa, pal, I thought. Slow down. One thing at a time. I have other ventures on my plate at the moment.

"Sounds like a plan," I said.

We finished off enough beers for me to drive five under the speed limit on the way home, just in case old aviator gunslinger was working traffic that day. I didn't need any attention from the police. I especially didn't need to be arrested for driving under the influence.

Dave would now think of us as a couple of old chums. I considered him a friend, but he had been a married man whose wife kept a tight leash on him. Now things were different, and that was my worry from the moment I agreed to go over to his apartment. I was being extra careful now with everything in my life. I didn't need anyone getting closer to me, visiting me unannounced, or wanting to tag along on the spur of the moment because they were bored or lonely.

Chapter 12

Another failed attempt at sleep resulted only in a dazed dream from the land of insomnia, and I startled myself back to awareness. It somehow felt as if it were an actual memory as I attempted to put the pieces together.

I was a young child strapped into a car seat in the rear of a vehicle. The driver was a blur, but from the voice and thick laugh, I knew it was a man. The passenger, I could see more clearly, was a woman whose face I had seen before, though I couldn't recall from where. She occasionally reached a hand back toward me in a playful manner. The shoulder of the seat in front of me slightly obscured my view of the windshield, but it felt like we had been driving forever.

Suddenly the car darkened, as if we had driven through a tunnel. I was slung back in my seat by an overwhelming force. From the darkness came a powerful light surrounding the car. I shielded my eyes with my hand. Once I removed my hand and squinted through the brightness, the sight was terrifying. Outside every window, all I could see were flames dancing violently up and down the outside of the car. Then came the heat. Thankfully, I woke up before being burned alive.

The dream left me with an overwhelming need to find the woman in the passenger seat. She was somehow the key to solving the riddle.

I couldn't stop thinking about it during my usual breakfast routine. After my third bite of bagel, it hit me: I had seen the woman in our family photo album. I couldn't quite place her, but I knew one person who could help me remember.

• • •

I was reluctant to peel back any unhealed wounds, but this I felt very strongly about. I needed to know the woman's identity. Besides, there were plenty of pictures of my dad still scattered around the house that could evoke memories.

After I finished my breakfast, I drove the short distance to my mom's house. I was intrigued to see what my dad had found so fascinating about short trips in a car. Nothing came to mind as I pulled into her driveway a few minutes later.

I used my key, knocking as I entered the back door.

"Mom, you there?" I said aloud. There was no answer. I walked around the short hall to the kitchen. "Ah, there you are. You had me worried for a moment." She was sitting with her back toward me at the kitchen table. She didn't speak. "Mom —" I reached my hand out to touch her shoulder. She flinched, looking back at me with wide and startled eyes, as if I had roused her from the depths of a terrible dream.

"Everything okay?" I asked.

She placed her right hand on mine. "Sorry... I was just... thinking."

"I tried knocking before I used the key. Sorry if I scared you."

"It's all right. I'm glad you're here, son. Are you hungry? Can I make you some breakfast?"

I noticed that her hair was down. That was new. I hadn't

seen her hair down in years. I was optimistic.

"No, thank you. I already had my bagel this morning." I sat down across from her at the table. "Mom…" I slowly began testing the water. "I was wondering if you wouldn't mind going through some pictures with me, from the old albums."

Her forehead wrinkled at the question. She looked up at me. The suggestion appeared to have sparked something.

"That's a good idea," she said. "Let me go grab them. Was there a particular year you wanted to see?"

"No, I'll get them," I said, getting up. "You stay here." She nodded and sat back down. So far, this was going better than I had expected. Maybe time spent looking at photos is what she needed to heal, remember more and forget less. I really hadn't given it much thought for myself, the healing part, though I do think of my dad often.

The back room was saturated with memories of him. Three cherry oak bookshelves held his entire collection of books, mostly westerns, but there were a couple of mystery novels that he was exploring a few years before he died. I found the albums in the cabinet, right where they'd been kept since I was a kid. They looked as if they hadn't been touched in years. Each was labeled by month and year, and took up three entire shelves — my mom's camera never left her hands. I picked up the three I needed and dusted them off.

I had set the albums down when one of my dad's books caught my eye. It was an old Sherlock Holmes hardcover that he had talked about often and carried with him everywhere. During the last year of his life, it almost never left his side. The cover was frayed and faded, just as I remembered. I had always wanted to read it, curious to discover what he found so appealing. But I never got around to it.

When I opened the book, I was confused by its contents. It was some type of journal, obviously hidden for a purpose. But what? Even more intriguing was the fact that the words were in my dad's handwriting.

As I began reading, my stomach rattled with nervous curiosity.

Day 1: I can't stop the thoughts from flowing. They tread freely in my mind without permission. They scare the hell out of me. I fear that I may lose control if something isn't done about them.

Day 2: The night was long. I hardly slept. The thoughts came and went throughout the night. When I did manage to fall asleep, I was scared awake by a nightmare that I don't feel much like recalling at the moment. I don't want to encourage my foes.

"Tryke, did you find the albums?" My mom was approaching from the hall. With my heart pounding, I quickly flipped to the middle for one more glance. I could read the rest later.

Day 45: The alcohol seems to help. The demon thoughts are lessened. I have convinced the thoughts to stay focused on me and leave my family alone. This is bearable, but I don't know how long I can hold them at bay.

I shoved the book down the back of my pants and picked up the three albums just in time. "I found them," I said, attempting to conceal the fright curdling inside me.

"All right," she said.

I sighed in relief and followed her down the hall, shrouding the top of the book with my shirttail.

"Are you looking for something in particular?" She asked, placing the tea kettle full of water onto the stove. The kettle made a soft sizzle as she placed it on the hot burner. "Tryke?"

"Sorry...I was just thinking about the dream I had last night." That is, until I came across the hidden journal. I had to focus.

"Did you want to talk about it?"

I wanted to run home and read more, but now I had to finish what I started.

"Yes, it's the reason I wanted to see the albums. I saw a lady's face I recognized as a relative, but I couldn't place it."

"Was it a bad dream?" She seemed to be probing, which

was unusual. It was unlike her to be curious of anything lately.

"As a matter of fact, it was." I was trying to decide if it was wise to continue. If it wasn't just a dream, but an actual memory, it could open up even more despair. But she seemed intrigued. Why stop now?

I told her the dream, including every tiny detail I could recall: the woman's face, the man's laugh, and the frightening flames. As I was describing the end, she appeared uncomfortable, fidgeting around in her chair. Maybe it had been a bad idea to bring it up.

She reached out her hand and placed it on mine. "That dream… was a memory. The man and woman in the car were your uncle and aunt, my sister Karen." Her eyes began to fill with tears. She got up from the table and grabbed a paper towel to wipe her nose.

"They were taking you home from your grandmother's birthday dinner. We were all going back to our house for coffee and dessert and they insisted that you ride with them. They adored you. I agreed, and your father secured you in the car seat in the back of their car. I didn't see the harm. We were following closely behind. A few blocks later, a car ran a stop sign. There was nothing your uncle could have done. They were hit so hard, they were pushed into oncoming traffic and then hit again. This time the car caught on fire. We watched the entire event unfold in front of us. Your father pulled the car to the curb and ran over. I'd never seen him react like he did that day, so fast, so determined. I looked on, horrified, as I tried to make it across the road that your father had crossed so easily. By the time I arrived, their car was engulfed in flames. Your father yanked you from the back seat and handed you off to me, and then, with burnt hands and smoke-filled lungs, he pulled my sister from the car. But it was too late for her, and her husband. Thank God you were okay." She paused. Her soft wet eyes hardened when she started again.

"The whole tragedy of the thing is that it didn't have to happen. The guy who ran the stop sign was from out of town and most likely drunk, but he fled the scene and they couldn't test him right away. He had been arrested for a DWI in the past and had warrants out for his arrest. Your father and I were furious when we heard about his short prison sentence. My sister's life was worth more than a few months."

I comforted her with a hug. I hadn't heard her speak that much since before my father passed. I was glad to see that she hadn't lost her passion, even if it was about a terrible incident. She wasn't lost in the mind's abyss after all. She continued to speak.

"You have a few scars, but I never told you the truth about them. That story about you falling out of your crib... it wasn't true. The scar under your right eye and the one on your back were from the wreck." The expression on her face was full of remorse. She felt guilty for hiding the truth, but what good would it have done to tell me? Besides, the scar under my eye was hardly noticeable.

"That's all right," I said. "I'd forgotten about them. But thank you for telling me now."

We flipped through the albums over the next few hours, remembering old times. We laughed at a few and she cried through some, but I couldn't get my dad's hidden journal out of my head. I kept picturing him across the table, carrying on and laughing, all the while battling voices in his head.

On my way home, I mulled over the new information. All of it. I had seen death at a much earlier age than I had thought, and my dad had a dark and secret world. The vehicle incident had left its mark on my subconscious as well as my body, while the other I had yet to uncover.

When I got home, I poured myself a stiff drink and began the journey through my dad's written thoughts.

Chapter 13

Lesley and I finally talked the other night on the phone and settled that the incident was a simple misunderstanding. We both apologized and agreed to keep our hands away from one another. Of course, words are easily said over the phone and without seeing her body language, I wasn't convinced. I was pretty sure she wasn't over it. She didn't make any plans to hang out in the near future, and her random text messages had stopped.

The story of my aunt's death and the discovery of my dad's journal kept my mind busy over the next few shifts at work. The journal had only revealed short passages of thoughts, and nothing tangible. I was left with many unanswered questions. I wanted to know my father's diagnosis, or if he ever received enough help to even get one. If they were only his thoughts, why write them down and then hide them away? And the question I was curious about most: Did he act on any of those thoughts?

I felt certain there was more, perhaps another journal.

The group of numbers I found written on the inside of the back cover — 32545/62 — only served to bolster that possibility. I might have ignored this latest discovery if my dad hadn't reminded me, almost daily, that "It's not worth doing something without a purpose." I flipped through the book, looking for any more numbers or clues, perhaps linking them to passages or page numbers. Nothing stood out. I struggled for an answer, and to make matters worse, I didn't have anyone I could discuss it with. I didn't think my mom knew about the journal's existence, and feared that in her fragile condition, showing it to her now could be catastrophic.

After torturing my mind over the numbers and the unanswered questions about the journal, I decided to focus on my mom's story about the car wreck. I wondered if this new knowledge of the accident had changed my feelings about death and the soul. Nothing immediately came to mind, but it did bring a potential new element into play — a very special one that could give me answers. I already had a plan forming.

While that plan developed, I encountered yet another specimen that would fit nicely into the current vacancy, waiting to be filled. I called him Mr. Crow.

Mr. Thompson had never fully recovered from the incident a year ago. After having the cast removed from his leg, and going through extensive physical therapy, he still walked with a limp. And his breathing worsened with the pain as he struggled to walk. Still, he was doing well enough until a few months ago, when he fell again and broke his hip. Just as he was finally adjusting to the first injury, another incident knocked him back down.

After enduring two surgeries, he was out of the hospital again and battling his new walker, as well as his long-term nemesis: the oxygen bottle. I helped when I could, bringing him groceries and accompanying him to the seemingly perpetual physical therapy sessions. It was the least I could do, seeing how he gave me something that this world so greedily keeps hidden — unselfish conversations and good Scotch.

I had gotten off work that morning and needed to sleep, but that wasn't happening. My body was now moving in known patterns, as if on a circuit board, only much more slowly.

I heard Mr. Thompson outside my apartment door arriving with a nurse who helped on the days I worked. With his meager retirement, he could barely afford her at all. I opened my door and greeted them with a heavy smile.

"Let me give you a hand," I said to Ida, taking the keys from her and unlocking the apartment door. Ida was a hefty black lady in her fifties. She was good to Mr. Thompson, and nice as could be, but she liked to talk, and mostly about her grandchildren. He would appreciate my saving him this morning from yet another story of three-year-old mayhem on the playground.

"Good morning, Tryke," Mr. Thompson said. "I thought you needed your sleep today. I didn't wake you, did I?" He probably noticed my struggling eyes and felt guilty. "I can't seem to keep this damn oxygen bottle from hitting the railing."

"Nah, I was still awake." He knew of my periodic bouts with insomnia. He had his own exhausting experience with it after the war. We both concluded that the only solution was time. And of course a stiff drink didn't hurt the process.

"You sure are lucky to have a good neighbor, and a paramedic at that, Mr. Thompson," Ida said. She winked and smiled at me like I was going to be her next meal. I smiled back, ignoring her harmless flirting. I took his arm from her, assisting him the rest of the way into his apartment.

"Thank you, Ida, for today," Mr. Thompson said.

"You're welcome. I'll see you next week, Sugar. You take care now," Ida said. "And you too, Tryke, honey."

"I will, Ida. Bye." I closed the door.

"So, how are things going? Any new developments with the son of a bitch who robbed me?" Mr. Thompson handed me his walker and eased down into his recliner. I think old Mr. Crow was on his mind, too, probably more than my own. He would never rest until the bastard was brought to justice. Mr. Crow would soon be caught, but not by the police. I was going to be the one doing the catching. I had never even relayed the information to the police, but had it safely written down in my journal. The police stopped looking for him soon after the incident, and there wasn't going to be further investigation. He was now part of a growing plague that evaded capture from the law.

I wanted to relieve Mr. Thompson's worries about injustice, but he wouldn't understand. "No, sorry, but those crack heads are like slippery leeches, from what I've been told. Until he attacks someone else, he probably won't be caught."

"It's a shame how those thugs get away with so much, he said." I nodded in agreement. "That reminds me, did I ever tell you about the time your father stopped a robbery at the store?"

"No, I don't believe so," I said. I liked hearing stories of my dad, and this one definitely piqued my interest.

As Mr. Thompson related the tale of my dad's heroic and risky act, I couldn't help thinking of my own twisted way of providing a form of justice. With each word, my stomach began filling with excitement about the future adventures with Mr. Crow. And I felt closer to my father after the story, like we were somehow on the same pursuit. Except that I wasn't being haunted by disembodied voices.

• • •

I may have drifted off for about twenty minutes, but I could never be completely certain. No sleep for the passionate. I filled my day by covering the basics for obtaining my new specimen. If my luck continued, Mr. Crow wouldn't need my assistance with temporary slumber, especially if his condition was anything like the one in which I'd seen him last time. Most of the regular drug addicts make it their number one priority to stay blitzed if they can afford to, and if they can't, they make visits to defenseless people like Mr. Thompson.

• • •

I watched Mr. Crow's house all afternoon, drifting in and out of reality under the shade of a thickly branched oak tree. I had driven by there a few times when I was deciding my route and I knew his rotation, not that there was much to it. He was a drug dealer, plain and simple, and worked out of his house.

I wanted to drag him into my backseat and begin the moment I saw him step out through the front screen door and flop down on a tattered, broken couch on the porch. I had to restrain myself. After all, this was research time, and there was no need to be hasty.

Cars pulled in and out of the driveway, their occupants looking like high school kids. They stayed in their vehicles while Crow quickly exchanged gifts through the window and then returned to his porch. I was expecting to see the previously screaming Mrs. Crow stumble out onto the couch and sit beside him. I was curious to know if she was still living there. Or maybe she'd sobered up long enough to realize how filthy her husband really was.

Nope. Moments later she came stumbling out, dressed for a nice crack dinner: loosely hanging stained tank top, no bra, and sagging boobs. If she'd had an ass, it would have been sliding out of the shorty shorts she was sporting, the word "Juicy" written on the butt. They really were a beautiful couple who shared the same interest. They both appreciated the wonderful art of white trash, and captured its essence perfectly.

I had gotten what I needed. I was ready. A day off and some rest was all that was standing in my way, though the latter was far off in a distant land, nestled deep in the pages of a fantasy world.

Chapter 14

Sitting alone in the dayroom, I thought about the next step I would soon be taking. It would take some time to feel comfortable on this new unpaved path I was currently stumbling down. I disliked change, so any deviation from my normal routine wasn't easily accepted. I enjoyed my manageable life, even though I often yearned for anything other than a mundane day. I was usually happy in my role as a bystander in the mayhem that surrounded me.

Dave was nestled snuggly in his sleeping bag for the night, despite the early evening hour. I often laughed when he attempted such a feat, especially after he'd failed so miserably, over and over again. He knew as well as I that it was futile to try and get any sleep before midnight, but he was determined to try. His persistence to beat the system was sometimes painful to watch. "It's all chaos," he repeated often, referring to 911 calls. That may be, but the odds certainly weren't in his favor. He's always had a close relationship with denial, but maybe he'd get lucky. We all deserve a break every now and then.

With Dave going to bed early, I was bored. I contemplated reading a book, but I didn't like interruptions. The air outside was too damn humid and there was no rain on the radar, so that ruled out sitting in the bay with the doors open — sweat *and* boredom didn't sound appealing at all. What I really wanted to do was scan through my dad's journal, but it was safely stashed in my apartment, and for good reason.

I decided on one of my least favorite activities to make the time pass. It wasn't that I didn't enjoy a good fantasy or action movie every now and then, but TV in general irked me. The news was the same most of the time, with some politician calling another a liar, or one pissed off citizen shooting another. Sitcoms weren't much better; they've just incorporated more sex and curse words over the years to rattle the desensitized audience. I flipped from channel to channel, unable to settle on any one show.

The bell startled me during a night-drift. *Night-drift* was just another name for a failed sleep attempt — they weren't worthy of being called naps. I glanced at my watch as I retracted the recliner. It was 2330 hrs. That meant Dave had managed to actually get some sleep. He needed it, considering his haggard appearance earlier.

I sat in the rig and waited for him to come out cursing. Two minutes passed and he still wasn't there. He was probably peeing. On calls in the middle of the night, peeing was top priority before leaving the bedroom. An hour-long call with a full bladder is not a fun experience.

After another thirty seconds passed, I went to check on him. I found him still sound asleep in the darkened and wind-filled room. It wasn't like him to sleep through a call. I flipped on the lights and tried waking him by nudging his shoulder. He jolted up from the bed, flailing his arms and screaming as if he were falling from a thirty-story building.

"What the hell!" He was slinging damp hair away from his

eyes, his nostrils flaring.

"Dave, snap out of it. We have a call. You slept through the bell."

After a few seconds of staring motionless at the ceiling, he returned to the living, throwing on his boots and racing out the bedroom door. I followed with a grin.

"I've never slept through a call before. Man, I was dead to the world. What time is it?"

"Eleven-thirty. Congratulations. You got in a couple of hours."

"I need about twelve more," he said, turning the ignition key.

Halfway down the street, he realized he didn't have a clue as to the address of the call. "Where the hell are we going, anyway?" he asked, stretching his eyes.

"I was just going to let you drive and see where we ended up," I said. "You're headed in the right direction, 210 Jordan Avenue, domestic disturbance. There isn't any other information."

"Great, now we have to wait on police. I hope they have a unit available. I really don't feel like being there all night." It wasn't unusual for the police to run out of units on occasion, and not surprising with the amount of crime and domestic crap that they have to deal with. At times, mostly at night, we would have to wait ten or twenty minutes for an available unit, especially on domestic calls. They milk things, just as we do, to get out of annoying situations. I can't really blame them.

We turned our lights off as we entered the street, just in case the police weren't on scene yet. If the assailant or anyone involved sees us, they may decide to come over to the rig. And you never know out here what they're thinking or what they might do. I keep most people in a general category: Crazy. That way I'll never be surprised or caught off guard.

We sat in silence and waited for the police. Dave and I are both usually quiet when awakened abruptly, which is probably one of the reasons we get along so well.

He told me stories of a past partner who made "perky" look like a narcotic overdose. Sure, Dave can be dramatic at times and embellish an event, but when it came to late nights or early mornings, everything slowed to a nice simmer. We understood each other in that regard.

A few minutes later, a police car pulled up from the other end of the street. "Good, that didn't take long," he said.

We gave them a minute to assess the situation before we headed in. As we walked up to the residence and opened the screen door, a male's voice amplified from the rear of the house.

"Why the hell did you call the cops? Dammit!"

A woman's shrieking voice yelled back, "You wouldn't stop! You wouldn't fucking stop!"

We rounded the corner of the living room, following the raised voices, and ended up in a child's bedroom. Several posters of superheroes were scattered along the far wall and Lego pieces littered the floor. There were multiple holes in the sheetrock the size of fists around the room, and many more areas that were poorly patched. Someone had been tossed around in there a few times, I thought.

An officer was attempting to calm the couple whose voices we had heard.

When the man saw Dave and me, he became enraged. "Why the hell are the paramedics here?" He looked directly at me with deep angry eyes, as if accusing me of wronging him. It was obvious misdirected rage, but why? What was he hiding? He outweighed me by at least a hundred pounds, but it was mostly sagging man breasts and belly. I started thinking about tactics, just in case he decided to charge past the police toward me. I made it a habit to keep exits close and my clipboard handy. The sharp edge of a metal clipboard can be very convincing.

"Get them the hell out of here!" he yelled again, eyes still fixed on me.

"Shut your damn mouth," the officer said. "They'll be here as long as they're needed."

Although the man reluctantly obeyed the officer, his fists remained clinched, and his nostrils continued to flare as he tried to catch his breath. His face and ears eventually settled on a dark shade of crimson. With any luck, I thought to myself, his plaque-filled coronary arteries would clog and shut his overly loud mouth for good. I've been yelled at before, and even spat on, but never experienced the feeling I had going through me at that moment. There was more to this than just domestic fighting between husband and wife.

I heard the voice of a crying child coming from another room.

The officer pulled Dave and me into the hallway while the couple continued to argue with each other. "There's a female officer in the other room with a little boy. We need you guys to check it out." He pointed us toward the room, and at that moment I suspected that the call was about to take a turn for the worse.

We entered another child's room. This one was a little tidier, with only one visible dent in the wall. But the shelves lined with stuffed animals most likely hid more scars. The child's crying had softened to a painful mumble. I knelt down slowly and faced the frightened four-year-old. He was covered in a Scooby-doo blanket, shaking, lips trembling. The female officer whispered some words in my ear that made my insides boil with anger.

She eventually convinced the boy to let us see what was underneath the blanket, and he lowered it, revealing that he was wearing only a pair of Spider-Man underwear. There were so many dark bruises and whelps covering his body, I didn't know where to start. Not to mention old cigarette burns along both legs and the top of his feet. The beatings had obviously been going on for longer than that night.

As I continued to stare at the injured child, I couldn't breathe. I suddenly became dizzy. A palpable fury was building inside of me and I wasn't sure if I could control it. But I knew I had to, if only for the little boy's sake. His eyes didn't need to witness any more violence. I took control of my breathing and slowed the rolling boil of my blood to a calm simmer.

But I needed to get outside.

The female officer carried the boy for us. He had already become attached to her. His aching whines as she lifted him were heart rending. Before we left, I noticed a baby carriage holding a sleeping infant across the room. How he was able to sleep through all of the yelling was beyond me. For just a moment, I was envious.

"What about the infant?" I said.

"The baby's fine," said the officer. There aren't any marks or injuries on him." She motioned for the other officer to send the mother in to watch the infant. I was sure that I would have lost it if the baby had been injured. The mother passed us in the hallway with eyes plastered to the floor. I didn't know the facts yet, but I felt certain she wasn't completely innocent.

As I passed the next room, the man was still yelling at the police. I stared at him, wishing he would step into the hall and try to stop us from taking the boy. I wanted him to look into my eyes and see that I knew about his cowardly beating sessions. I wanted him to know that someone was now hunting him. He didn't budge, staying safely sheltered behind the officer. At least for now.

I was thinking that I might take a brief detour from my original, unsettled plan. I'd been naïve to think that anger wasn't going to enter sometime during the journey. I had always been good at suppressing my emotions, but certain situations trigger things I have trouble controlling. Abuse of the helpless or feeble, for example.

• • •

On the way to the hospital, I was able to get some more

information from the female officer. The man was the stepfather of the boy, and the police had been over there numerous times in the past for the same thing. Mostly he would beat the little boy, but on occasion the wife would have a few bruises, too. Always, she would lie about how she got them.

"We've tried and tried to get the mother to tell us about the stepfather beating the boy and her, but she never does. I'd shoot him myself if I could."

I smiled. "I'll get Dave to turn around if you want."

"Nah, but I will Taser that SOB if he ever gives me a reason."

"I'd like to watch that," I said. "By the way, where's the biological father?"

"He died a few years ago. Cancer I think, or something."

Even better. Not that the father was dead. That was terrible, but the idea that the father had passed away and the mother let this happen to her kids only further fueled the burning anger inside of me. The boy had no one to protect him. For me, that was enough justification for my next plan of action.

Maybe the mother wouldn't allow the man to go so far as to kill the boy, but she would never stop the beatings. Mr. Crow was going to have to wait one more turn. There was a soul in immediate distress, aching so badly to be released that it had to take it out on a defenseless child.

Chapter 15

I didn't wait long. I wasn't sure how much more abuse the four-year-old boy could handle, and I happened to be off from work the following night. As I sat in my truck and stared at the house, I thought about why I was there. It was an impulsive move that had to be controlled in the future. I needed to regulate my emotions. Slow down. If I didn't learn to be methodical and smooth, I wouldn't survive.

Ms. Dundee was a fluke that happened to fall into place. This one, I feared, wasn't going to be that simple. I also had the same reservations about Mr. Crow, but at least I had finally figured him out. I didn't know anything about this latest guy, other than that he liked to beat children. Still, if there was any way to conduct my impulsive experiment that night, it was going to happen.

An hour later, he emerged from his front door and got into his tiny, beat up convertible Miata. It was quite an amusing sight as I followed him. With the car's top down, he bore an uncanny resemblance to Donkey Kong from the

Mario Kart video game. At least that thought kept me entertained until I found the piece of the puzzle I was searching for.

I followed him around for a couple of hours. He visited two fast food joints, three gas stations and a pawnshop, before returning to his neighborhood. I didn't find anything that I could use, and considered just winging it that night for the little boy's sake. It was a rather exciting concept, *winging it*, but still dangerous and stupid. I needed a way out, a place to put him after the deed was complete. Not thinking things through would be a mistake, one I'd already made and didn't intend to repeat.

I was back under the shade of another oak tree and yawning, about to leave for the day, when he raised the garage and dragged out a push lawnmower. I watched him drench his wife-beater lawnmower attire with dirty sweat as he repeatedly yanked the pull-cord to get the stubborn mower to start. An idea hit me. I recalled him tossing cigarette after cigarette onto the pavement, nearly going through an entire pack. It wouldn't be out of the ordinary for an overweight smoker who'd exerted himself in the hot southern sun to die of a heart attack during the night. There would be no need for an autopsy, so no one would find the cocktail of chemicals I was going to introduce into his cardiovascular system.

• • •

I ended up winging most of it, after all.

The only thing I had going for me was his chain smoking. I didn't recall the house smelling of cigarette smoke, which meant he would eventually go outside in the middle of the night to keep his nicotine levels from dropping below saturation.

The house sat on a corner lot, which benefited my stealth, thanks to the vantage point and a trusty pine. The inside lights went out around 1230 and sure enough, thirty minutes later, I saw the spark of the cigarette lighter on the front porch. Thank you, nicotine.

I eased my truck forward and pulled into the driveway, making sure to keep the headlights off. I didn't want to attract the attention of any nosey neighbors who might be scurrying about. Thankfully, there weren't any streetlights near the house.

A truck pulling into your driveway at one o'clock in the morning would spook a normal person, but not a brave soul like him. His curiosity got the better of him as I rolled down my window and called out in a friendly voice, "Hey, Laurence, how's it going?"

After hearing his name, he decided it was okay to approach the truck. Good boy, take the bait. He took another puff and arrogantly blew the cloud of smoke toward my rolled down window. I tilted my ball cap downward so he couldn't see my face. He stepped closer, stopping just a few feet from me.

"What the hell?" he said, looking down at the window seal. He must have spotted my black-latex-gloved hand resting on the door. I couldn't reach his neck with the syringe in my right hand.

I shoved the door open, knocking him to the ground. He clumsily fell on his side, sending the lit cigarette into the air. I bolted from the truck and lunged toward him.

The overwhelming smell of cigarette smoke and filth filled my nose as my head was forced into his dirty robe. He flipped over onto his stomach, clawing the damp lawn with his nicotine-stained fingers.

My right hand was almost in position to strike, but then he swung his heavy arm back. His elbow missed my head by inches. I took advantage of the miss and slid the syringe up to his neck. His hands relaxed, slowly releasing the fistful of dirt and grass. He wouldn't be moving again until I allowed it.

• • •

After the strenuous haul of Mr. Laurence up to my lab, I made a mental note to not choose heavy specimens until I found a more efficient way of getting them upstairs.

After he was secure and prepped for release, I took a breather. I was tired, and still had residual anger flowing through my veins. I removed the navy blue overalls I was wearing over my uniform and placed them on the back of a chair. They were easier to disrobe and to put back on in a hurry, if needed. Wearing them was part of my ongoing plan to be more cautious.

I stood over him, peering down at his flabby exposed chest and hairy shoulders. I examined the rest of the wasted body suit, furious at the thick arms and stubby fingers that had struck too many young limbs, and the yellow stained teeth and narrow lips that had no doubt spouted too many curse words at innocent ears. And then there were those dark, rage-filled eyes that were now closed, resting and perhaps preparing to absorb more violence soon. But they wouldn't be opening again. They had witnessed their last injustice.

A high dose of Epinephrine was a sound choice for the situation. He was used to a rush of adrenaline from beating and burning children, so it seemed fitting to give him a little extra.

His heart rate increased instantly, sounding the alarm on the cardiac monitor. The faster and narrower the rhythm, the more calm I became. Whatever the outcome of the experiment, there was one thing for certain: he would no longer be able to hurt another child. I wasn't going to attempt resuscitation. I wanted the experiment over quickly, so visualizing the soul became secondary. Putting an end to the wasted puke was what mattered most.

After his heart cycled through a multitude of rhythms, it finally settled for the flattest one. When the monitor alarm bell signaled that it was over, I hadn't seen anything that resembled a soul leave his body. There was no flash of smoke or howling of gratitude from a spirit that I was certain needed to escape. I was mentally exhausted and wanted him out of my lab. Anger and anticipation wear heavy on a man's soul.

• • •

After dropping Mr. Laurence back onto his front porch with a lit cigarette in hand, I went home and quickly scanned through the video, but there was nothing to see. I wasn't disappointed. Not on this one. The journal entry was short and to the point. I made sure to put emphasis on the words *impulsive* and *dangerous* to remind myself of future caution.

I had veered off track. Though I had stopped a nasty individual from causing more mayhem, I needed to stay on a particular path. Mistakes are made on whims.

By now, the rage had finally subsided. I lay my head down on the cool pillow and begged my enemy to give me a break that night, to just this once let my eyes shut for more than a wink.

Chapter 16

The following morning, I felt better about the Mr. Laurence situation. I managed to sneak in a few actual naps during the night and I even went out for a jog, something I hadn't done since Insomnia began his draining session. I even anticipate coming out from under his spell soon, but I can never be sure.

The next two shifts at work went by relatively fast and smooth. I felt better than I had in weeks. Of course, there were still the unexplained numbers in my dad's journal that I had yet to decipher, but I wasn't going to let that interrupt the rare moment.

It was Friday, the last shift of our three, and I was tenaciously hanging on to my good mood. Mr. Laurence was no longer a burden and I was back on track with Mr. Crow. And as an added bonus, Mercy General was full, out of beds, and it was only three in the afternoon. I was ready to begin pelting the other hospitals with our regulars.

Dave didn't share my enthusiasm. In fact, he was usually

more annoyed than the nurses and doctors. He preferred simple routine, especially nowadays since he seemed perpetually tired. Heck, I was beyond tired, but I'm an opportunist.

Normally the nurses and doctors at the other hospitals weren't nearly as friendly and receptive to us as they were at Mercy. Maybe it was the number and variety of patients Mercy staff receives that makes them easier to consort with. They understand our perspective and are willing to accept our way of handling patients. I've always felt there was an unspoken camaraderie among those deeply saturated in life's raw medical mayhem.

Corvine Hospital's staff, in particular, is flooded with more douches than the rest. Let's just say they have a bad habit of staring down at the less fortunate with wry grins. I've never been prejudiced when it comes to pointing out a moron, but these guys are very partial to themselves. They trash everyone.

"Hey, you know what sounds good right now?" Dave asked. His voice was oddly calm just seconds after yelling at some idiot who cut us off and then slowed down to ten under the speed limit right in front of us.

"What?" I said, knowing the question was rhetorical. I was distracted anyhow, pressing the buttons on the keyboard as if to send a desperate message to dispatch requesting they send us on a call.

"A barbecue sandwich from Nick's."

"We just ate two hours ago," I said. I guess I shouldn't have been surprised. He'd put on a few pounds since the separation from his wife, slowly deteriorating from his once slim-shady appearance. It's annoying how much our emotions control us. One second, we're planning out our next venture, and then out of nowhere we're hit with some asshole who likes to beat children.

"Yeah, I know. I'm doing the eat-every-few-hours diet thingy. Can't you tell?" He patted his stomach, almost proudly. The MDT beeped. "Tell me that's just a message for all units and not a call," Dave pleaded.

I glanced down at the screen. "It's a call. Sorry." I said it in the most irritated voice I could manage, all the while concealing my delight.

"Son of a bitch, we were one block away from Nick's." Dave flipped on the lights and siren and stomped on the accelerator. His hunger rage was engaged. He blared on the horn, nearly running over the guy who, moments ago, had cut us off in his tricked-out Geo Metro. The other driver swerved to the right lane and flipped us off as we zoomed by, sirens blaring. I shrugged my shoulders and pointed at Dave as we passed by.

"Why do you always do that?" asked Dave. "You should have flipped him back off."

"I just couldn't resist," I said, and laughed. He softly laughed back and punched me in the shoulder.

"Where're we going anyway, and to what?"

"411 Park Street. Domestic stabbing."

"Well, at least it's not another damn seizure. But knowing my luck, this son of a bitch will be seizing with a knife hanging out of him."

"It's a female," I said.

"Well, then, *she'll* be seizing with a knife hanging out of *her*."

As we pulled up to the address, two officers met us at our rig. "Man stabbed his wife in the leg for burning his dinner," one of the officers said. "Doesn't look too bad."

"Serves her right. What the hell was she thinking?" Dave said, smiling. But somewhere in that joke there was some truth. His demeanor had definitely taken a turn toward the cranky side. He was still dramatic, but he'd added a few more curse words along the way. The officer didn't reply to his failed humor. "What the hell is his problem?" Dave whispered, as we followed the officers up to the house. I shrugged.

The smell of burnt food was overwhelming when we opened the front door. The husband was in handcuffs on the couch and the wife was sitting on the floor with a bloody towel wrapped around her lower leg. A cigarette hung loosely from her lips. He was a frail man, nearly half her size. Why is it that the skinniest guys end up with the biggest ones on the block? I don't think I'll ever figure that one out.

"Is that burnt chicken I smell?" I asked, casually bending down to examine her leg. The comment rekindled the smoldering fire in the room.

"Yep, it sure as hell is," said the husband. "Burnt as black as her damn soul."

"Keep your mouth shut!" the officer said. I concealed a smile as I unwrapped the towel from her leg.

"Ma'am, can I have your date of birth and age?" Dave asked, starting the paperwork. "Or if you have an ID, that will work also."

"I lost my ID, but I'm 45 years young," the woman said, batting her wrinkled eyes.

"Don't lie to the gentlemen," her husband shot back. "You're 62 years old, and a devil woman."

She jolted up from the ground, leaving me with the bloody towel in hand. The wound in her thigh was slowly seeping down her leg. She lunged toward her husband in a rage.

"I should've killed you long ago, you little bastard!"

The other officer moved between the two of them and placed her back on the floor. "Let the paramedics do their job, please, or I'm taking you to jail right along with him." She flicked her lit cigarette at her husband, but it missed, landing on the soiled carpet.

Hearing her alleged ages — 45 and 62 — instantly brought to mind the numbers from my dad's journal. They were the last four digits, separated by a slash — 32545/62. The distractions of recent events had caused me to push them aside, but I knew I couldn't avoid them entirely. I mentally added the frustrating mystery back to my list.

Returning my thoughts to the situation at hand, I asked the officers where the weapon was. One held up an evidence bag. It was a medium-size kitchen knife. Non-serrated.

"Well, it looks like the knife most likely just nicked a vein," I said to the woman. "But you'll still need to go to the hospital and let a physician look at it. Are there any other wounds?"

"Just a bruised arm where the son of a bitch grabbed me."

"What hospital do you use?"

"Mercy. We don't have any insurance."

Perfect, I thought. My first customer to unload.

"They're on diversion right now," I said. "Would Corvine be okay? It's the closest. And don't worry about the insurance. They bill Mercy, and they'd be happy to have you."

"Corvine it is," she said, insisting on limping without help to the stretcher. The smell of cigarettes and cheap beer saturated the air as she landed on the small cushion.

Corvine Hospital is always my first choice to pummel, but there was another reason I blurted it out so quickly: Lesley worked there. Subconsciously, I must have been thinking about her. But why? I knew it would most likely be an uncomfortable encounter. We hadn't seen one another since that day at the station. I thought briefly of diverting to another hospital, but that was childish. We were going to run into one another eventually.

Chapter 17

After listening to the soft, sarcastic tone of the nurse taking my patient report over the radio, and answering a wide array of unnecessary questions, we arrived at Corvine Hospital. The questions were a last, failed attempt to divert us elsewhere so they didn't have to take the patient. After explaining, slowly and thoroughly, that the wound was superficial, I had gotten them to give in. It never ceases to amaze me, the amount of effort people will put forth to avoid the inevitable.

As I was helping Dave remove the stretcher from the room, I saw Lesley standing at the nurses' station talking to one of her female colleagues. At some point I overheard the phrase "funky chunky hair," and I laughed. She turned around and smiled when she saw me. I smiled back, timorously, still unsure of our situation, and pointed to the small room where we write our reports. What was I going to say now that I had initiated a one-on-one? I still lacked experience when it came to resolving awkward moments with the opposite sex.

"So, you two make up yet?" Dave said as he entered the room. Lesley hadn't yet arrived.

"What do you mean by make up?" I asked. "We were never fighting. It was just a misunderstanding, remember?"

"Yeah, yeah, whatever. Where is she?"

"I motioned for her to come in here a few minutes ago, but she was in the middle of a conversation."

"Oh, well, I'll just be leaving then so y'all can talk about the misunderstanding," Dave said, making those annoying hand quotes in the air.

"Hey, Tryke," Lesley said after knocking on the open door and entering the room. "Hey, Dave."

"Lesley," Dave said nodding. "I was just heading over to vending. Either of you want anything?"

"No thanks," we both said. Dave looked back at me from the door with a double thumbs-up. I shook my head and mumbled, "Whatever." He has a bad habit of being corny at times.

"Haven't heard from you in a while," she said. "Anything new?"

Well, lets see. I now have my own lab of sorts, where I do experiments on live specimens in search of the human soul. Other than that, not too much. And you? "Not really. Just doing a little soul searching, trying to figure things out."

"Whoa, deep thoughts," she said playfully.

"Yeah, I guess," I said laughing. "What about you?"

Not much. Trying to wean off some guy who won't leave me alone after one date."

I knew I shouldn't care, but something inside of me twitched when she said the words "guy" and "date."

"Need some help with him?"

"No, I can handle it. Besides, he's not stalking me. At least I don't think he is. Just persistent. So what's this about soul searching?"

"Nothing, really. You know, the usual who-the-hell-am-I-

and-where-am-I-going routine."

Lesley and I had talked about such things many times. In fact, most of our conversations usually led to some philosophical unanswered questions or beliefs.

"Have you come up with anything new or interesting to discuss?" she asked. "It's about time for another one of our all-night conversations."

I was perplexed by her obvious dismissal of our last encounter. She was acting as if nothing out of the ordinary had happened. I suppose I should have been glad that things seemed to be back to normal.

"Maybe a few things," I said. In truth, I had more than a few ideas and stories that could entertain our minds for many nights.

"So how's Dave doing since the divorce? He looks like he's put on a few pounds."

"He's just separated. No divorce yet. I don't think he wants one. Either way, I'm about to put him on a diet. He's moving a little slow lately, and making me work harder."

"That's too bad. Not the weight, but about him still lingering on her. Tell him I have a couple of friends he can hang with if it doesn't work out. And don't worry. I'm not talking about Jessica."

"Good. I'm sure Dave would appreciate that, especially if he knew her."

Let's just say Jessica was known for quick relationships. A lover here and a lover there, usually involving a hangover and a lot of regret the next morning. Though with that much experience, I wonder how she could still have regret. Maybe what most women consider repulsive and pointless, she finds appealing. Or maybe she likes the adrenaline rush she gets from gambling with STDs. Who the hell knows? All I knew was that Dave was too damn sensitive and vulnerable for a soul like hers.

"Code blue, room 235. Code blue, room 235," a woman's voice blared from the speaker system in the hospital. Lesley pulled the beeping pager from her scrub pocket and silenced it.

"I gotta go," she said. "I'll call you." With that, she walked swiftly down the hall toward the deceased occupant of room 235.

"Okay," I yelled back as she turned the corner.

Dave returned and threw me a soda and a candy bar. "Thanks," I said. "But I didn't want anything."

"I know how you get after seeing her. You need some energy."

"You're delusional. We're just two people who enjoy viewing the world differently together. That's all."

"Sounds like a love story to me," Dave said.

"Whatever."

Before leaving, I waved to everyone at the nurses' station with a broad, sarcastic smile and said, "I'm sure we'll see you soon with more Mercy Hospital patrons." They didn't look up from their computers, but I was pretty sure one or two mumbled, "Go screw yourself." Lesley has never explained to me how she tolerates working around so many self-absorbed jerks, but I have a few speculations. I suspect she's doing her own experiments, observing lesser species that have somehow mastered the art of being both abusive and apathetic.

Once back in the rig, I asked Dave, "Still in the mood for Nick's?"

"Not really. Besides, it's after four o'clock and it's Friday. I don't think I can handle another disappointment without inflicting some damage to that damn computer in front of you."

While Dave tapped his thumbs on the steering wheel to the beat of an eighties rock ballad, I couldn't help but wonder why I felt weird when Lesley mentioned that she went on a date. Was I jealous? Did I have feelings for her? Of course I did. She was a good friend, but this was different. Friends don't get jealous over another guy.

• • •

That night, while lying on top of my sleeping bag and listening to the whirring of the fan, I thought about Lesley. What if I had subconsciously grown to have stronger feelings for her? What if I were to let down my guard long enough for her to sneak in and infiltrate?

I had to get ahold of myself. I was in control of my feelings. I could and would stop the friendship from going further. I did a good job of that on my birthday, though that was never the intention. But could I do it? Could I put an end to our friendship if I really had to?

Lesley had many attributes and quirks that I found appealing, and would certainly miss if we never saw each other again. There was her never-ending wit, and those light-hearted snide comments that initially drew me to her. And our late-night conversations, and her views on the world. She's delicately rebellious to society's norms, and pleasantly beautiful to speak to. And we agree about life's darkness on humanity.

We even had this silly notion one night, after consuming a few too many, about the soul. We made a pact that I had forgotten about until now: If one of us ever discovered that there was more to human existence than this fragile body, we would have to confide in each other, and explore it together. It was an intoxicating prospect, to be able to share my latest endeavors. But I couldn't risk it at the moment. Besides, I didn't think what I was currently exploring was what she had in mind that evening.

She saw something in me that I also saw in her — someone who sees things differently — views the world from a few steps back. I was wrong that day, thinking she was confused by the chaos in the code room. Though she was in training, she saw the room for what it was: a crammed space packed with sardines alive and flopping around, while the patient, calm and dead, waited his turn to be released. She told me that if she could put the chaos to music, it would be a symphony masterpiece that Mozart himself would be proud to have written. She grasped the humor of the situation, and even added an artful twist to it.

And I certainly can't forget about that laugh of hers, riddled with remnant poetic lyrics of my lost sister. If I ever decide to embrace the relationship aspect of my life, Lesley would be the perfect fit.

Chapter 18

My repetitive counting fetish was pissing me off the next day. I was snared by my own mind yet again. The encounters are more than frustrating at times; they're exhausting, and make me feel as if I'm a stubborn magnet stuck to a refrigerator. The counting worsened when I didn't want a circumstance to be altered, when I didn't want a kink in my already formed plan. It was pretty bad the night of Mr. Laurence, the moment I knew I was going to sway from my path.

Excitement, or simple elation about an event, was also to blame at times. Too many positive things happening at once could only mean something terrible was waiting its turn. There's no way this world would give excessive goodness. That's not compatible with life. We have to endure the inevitable trials, right? Or, to use the word I prefer: *torment*.

The counting may have been triggered by the knowledge that in just a few short hours, I would be giving Mr. Crow a visit. Or maybe it was caused by another failed attempt at deciphering the meaning of the numbers in my dad's journal.

I had visited the post office that morning, hoping that the numbers might have represented a postal box. I even visited the public library, desperately asking the librarian for assistance — was there a book that had such a reference number? All proved to be dead ends in this incredibly difficult and frustrating scavenger hunt.

I had to endure many of his games as a teenager. For instance, after I passed the driver's test, he hid my newly-acquired license and made me hunt for it before I could drive. The riddles weren't usually hard to decipher, but every once in a while he would throw a twist at me, as in the rogue numbers I was currently faced with. Now, I was on the brink of giving up, thinking that the numbers were simply numbers, and nothing more. Maybe I was being delusional, thinking they meant something important.

And then there was this faint, but persistent, feeling that my repetitive counting may have had something to do with Lesley. It wasn't an irrational idea. If it were she, it would definitely be the stress aspect. Jealousy wasn't exciting, was it? Not in a constructive way.

• • •

Twilight: a time for kids to come in for dinner and time for the ambitious to prep for breakthroughs and discoveries. I was on the verge of something great, and could feel the energy flowing and urging me forward. That night, it was especially powerful. I was energized to be back on track once again, on the path I had created.

It was still early, so I kicked back in my recliner and closed my eyes. I wanted to let the silence blanket my mind. Maybe that would help me organize the massive number of lingering issues I needed to figure out.

It lasted for thirty minutes.

My cell phone startled me, interrupting the quiet by vibrating loudly on the wooden table next to the recliner. I saw a familiar name illuminated: Lesley.

I listened to each short vibration, conflicted about whether I should answer. Once again, I didn't know what to say about the dilemma of our relationship. I decided to let it go to voicemail. If it was something urgent, I'd call her back right away. If not, I would call her tomorrow after I'd had more time to think. Besides, I had obligations that needed my attention.

A few seconds later, the phone let out another short pulse, alerting me that a message had been left.

"Tryke, it's Lesley. Sorry I had to hurry away at the hospital. I'm excited to hang out. It's been too long. Besides you... you looked like something was on your mind. You looked tired, and I'm worried about you. Anyway, call me when you get a chance. I'll be up a while. Bye."

We'd only seen each other for a few minutes. How could she tell that much about me? Was I revealing too much? I'd been exhausted lately and running on temporary adrenaline fumes. I knew she had always been good at reading me and seeing things about me that I tended to neglect. My careless hair, at times, or a curled-up collar that needed to be straightened. Now she spotted my fatigue. Of course, I could blame it on work — always an easy alibi, and not completely untrue. But the part I was worried about was the pause in her voice. That meant she had spotted something else.

• • •

Before my impulsive venture with Mr. Laurence, I had thought about how risky the Ms. Dundee incident had been, and how lucky I was that she slowly drifted away into a diabetic coma, although that outcome seemed like a sure thing. I couldn't rely on such luck with Mr. Crow.

As I had watched the cars move in and out of Mr. Crow's driveway during my initial research — before Mr. Laurence distracted me — an idea hit me. I didn't know why it took me so long to figure it out, but like most things lately, it was probably caused by lack of sleep. I followed one of the cars after the swift exchange of goods, choosing one of the most easily-conned species on the planet. High school girls were suckers for a handsome smile and a few compliments. A story about scoring some dope and a twenty got me the number I needed.

Now I just had to wait for an opportune moment. I'd send the text and Mr. Crow would come right to me. I could only hope that he wasn't low on supplies and out on the road again, beating old men for money. He had yet to wander onto the porch, and no cars were coming or going. If he didn't show that night, no matter how badly I wanted to do it, I couldn't go searching for him. I would have to reschedule.

With Mr. Laurence, the experiment had been a waste, but the end result was satisfying. Dangerously satisfying. I vowed to not let that happen again. I had to be patient and let my plans unfurl, even if they took unexpected turns.

I glanced at my watch: 0230. It was time. I eased my truck forward into the driveway and turned off the headlights. I rolled down my window and peered out along the dark and desolate street. I was thankful the moon was away for the night, tucked neatly behind thick clouds.

I typed the message into the phone and pressed Send. My latex gloved hand lowered the phone onto the seat, and then waited patiently beside me. I kept my other hand hidden away this time.

Thirty seconds later, he emerged from the shadow of the porch. If nothing else, this drug dealer was prompt. What a pleasant surprise. He trudged toward my truck, sleepily, with goods in hand. He didn't look up as he said, "Fifty." I didn't say anything in return. I just stared at the one thing that was staring back at me in the reflection of my truck's side mirror: the crow.

This take-down went much more smoothly than my tackle of Mr. Laurence. I was more deliberate with my moves, but it was also easier because I had an already-doped and half-asleep opponent.

Midway to our destination, the medication began wearing off. I should have known he would need a larger dose. No doubt his cell receptors were already saturated, and were unable to take in any more. He squirmed around with tape-bound extremities and asking clichéd questions: what, why, and who the hell are you?

This was the first one who had woken up and seen me. I wasn't in the mood for lecturing or playing a bargaining game. I was irritated at this lowlife in my backseat who dealt drugs and beat old men. And I could never forget the most disgusting of all his crimes: the killing of his own child by neglect. He didn't deserve the right to speak anymore.

I was doing it again. I was getting angry and personal, which was something I had hoped to avoid. My intention was to have the same impersonal relationship with the specimens as a research technician has with his laboratory rats. As I pulled him from my back seat, I realized that this plan was no longer possible. I had already planted the next specimen in my mind, and it was *very* personal. The memories that it would dig up would most certainly evoke anger.

• • •

I had the lab prepped and ready to go. After performing a quick second check on the equipment, I sat back in my chair to think.

This was number three, the third trial in my quest to find the human soul. I pondered a dilemma that had surfaced as I was buckling the restraints. What would I do after I saw the soul? Post it on YouTube and count the hits? Would I be satisfied with just seeing the soul? And then would it be over? Probably not. I had ventured far too deeply into this to even think of quitting.

I really wished Mr. Thompson could be there, to be the one to perform the release. We could witness the spectacle together and then enjoy a nice glass of Scotch, while he regaled me with more tales of my dad. This, of course, was only a passing thought. As angry as he had been about the situation, not many people would have the stomach for any of the stuff we do on the streets, much less the type of work I was now attempting. I was sure that he'd be more than satisfied with reading the obituary in a day or two.

Searching Mr. Crow's shirt, I found a mega-dose of his favorite mind juice. It was loaded into a syringe and wrapped in a paper towel in his right front pocket. I decided to serve him his breakfast a little early.

I imagined a dreamy sigh sliding across his unconscious face as I administered the entire syringe, along with gratitude seeping from his pores as his body accepted the all-too-familiar visitor.

It didn't take long for the substance to work its magic. A few moments later, his respirations began to dwindle and his oxygen-saturation plummeted. By instinct, I was tempted to intubate him. Repetitious training — the urge to *save* the person's life — automatically tries to take over. I would normally be pushing Naloxone to reverse the narcotics. I did have my uniform on, but it was for show only. There would be no hospital visits and no official report. The only evidence of this event would be the notes in my journal, and the video.

I reached up and silenced the alarm bell on the monitor. His heart rate was beginning its descent; the body was prepping for the release. My own heart rate and breathing were increasing, too, as I waited. My anticipation and intrigue were back.

He began to seize, flopping the crow-tattooed elbow rapidly against the table. I couldn't help but smirk as the bird attempted to take flight. The seizure lasted for a few seconds, and then the monitor alarm started beeping again. As I reached up to silence it, I heard a door slam from below.

My excitement rapidly changed to fear.

I quickly glanced over at the monitor and saw that he was on the verge of release. Seconds later, the alarm bell on the monitor beeped yet again. He had flat-lined. Suddenly, a different alarm sounded.

"Shit," I whispered aloud. "This can't be happening." Something had triggered the stairwell alarm. I quickly made my way over to the closet that housed the small generator and switched it off. The room instantly fell into darkness... and silence.

"Really?" I noticed that the reserve battery on the monitor hadn't kicked on when I shut the generator off. I bent down and looked through the small hole in the blacked-out window beside me. I scanned the store's bottom floor from one side to the other. Nothing. I moved to the door and pressed myself against it to listen down the stairs. No footsteps.

It could have been a rat or a stray cat that had triggered the alarm. But that still didn't explain the slamming of the door. I couldn't continue with the experiment until I made sure no one was lurking below.

I fumbled around in my shirt pocket for my "just in case syringe," but it wasn't there. I must have dropped it when I leaned down to turn the generator off. Inching back to the closet, I felt around on the floor.

"Whew," I whispered when my hand brushed against the syringe.

I was trying to move slowly and quietly, but a loud bang from downstairs made me jump again. It sounded like another door slamming, this one much harder than the last. I wiped the floor grime from the syringe and made my way back to the door.

I tried squinting down the dark stairwell, but it didn't help my vision. Then I remembered the cameras. I could use the thermal imaging. I placed the syringe into my front shirt pocket, making sure to button it this time, and pulled one of the cameras from its tripod. I pointed it down toward the bottom of the stairs. The stairwell was empty.

Slowly, I made my way toward the bottom, camera in hand.

Halfway down the stairs, thunder rattled the building. It scared me, but also provided some relief. Maybe it was only the wind that had caused the door to slam.

At the bottom of the stairs, I panned the open empty grocery area with the camera. A lone possum scurried against the far wall. All clear.

Next, I cautiously nudged the door open behind me that led to the back lot. I scanned the parking lot as the deluge of rain punished the failing aluminum awning above my head. The steady lightning veining through the clouds illuminated the ground just enough for me to see that there was no one there.

I took a few deep breaths. It was just the weather.

Back in my lab, Mr. Crow was as calm as expected. I flipped the generator back on. The monitor revealed a steady flat line across the screen. I was pissed. All of this wasted effort. All my work destroyed, with nothing to show. I was now back in experiment mode and justice was second in line. I slid my back down the wall and sat with the palms of my hands massaging my temples.

After a few minutes of sulking I remembered the other camera, and some faint hope returned. I looked up at its blinking red light. Though nothing had been revealed during the last two experiments, there was always a possibility. It was the reason I had gotten the cameras in the first place. And it was what kept me going.

Removing the camera from the tripod, I flipped open the display screen and played the recording from the beginning. I watched myself move in and out of view, always making sure not to reveal my face. Then, from behind Crow's body, I saw something move across the screen. It was a dark blur. Probably my shadow, I thought, but the hair on my neck and arms was saying otherwise.

I pressed Rewind and watched again. The blurred image moved so quickly that it was difficult to tell what I was seeing. From the way the lights were facing, it couldn't have been my shadow. Chills of excitement and exhilaration covered my entire body as I kept watching. The door slammed below and the monitor beeped. Next I heard the alarm sound. The room went dark, followed by my scampering around on the floor.

That son of a bitch triggered the alarm!

I sat the camera down and took a deep breath. I had to think. There had to be a logical explanation. What about the lightning, could it have caused an electrical surge? I hadn't heard the thunder until after the alarm sounded. Most importantly, an electrical surge didn't explain the dark blur.

This was it, the exciting moment I had been anticipating. The breakthrough.

I pressed the Rewind button again and slow-motioned the image. It stayed the same, a heavy black blur. There was definitely something there, something dark and moving. It didn't look anything like what I saw hovering around my sister's body long ago, and that was a good thing. His soul was filthy, saturated in guilt and deceit. Of course, if it wasn't *his* soul, it was probably an even darker apparition from the underworld, one that had been waiting patiently for him to die.

We would all have to eventually face this in the end, I imagined. Some will go screaming frantically, in a hurry to escape their former prison. Others will accept it for what it is, and walk away in peace, lesson learned. I wasn't sure which one I'd be, just yet.

My phone vibrated, reminding me of the time. I had stayed longer than I wanted to. It was time to get Mr. Crow's body back home so that the living could find it. I doubted he'd be searching or longing to be anywhere near it again, although I did wish he could've helped me with it down the stairs. It was the least he could do for me, after I had released him.

• • •

I checked Crow's phone before turning onto his street to make sure no one had been looking for him. I was sure his wife was pleasantly plowed by then, and wouldn't be waking anytime soon.

"All clear, Mr. Crow," I said. "No messages." I erased the text I had sent earlier and placed the phone back into his pocket. I was getting good at setting bodies back onto porches. I should get my own corpse route.

Both confused and excited, I returned home and entered the new information into my journal. I was filled with intrigue, and even more questions as I wrote. The latest sighting didn't slow my search, but actually fueled it. After finishing the entry, I thought about my next very special — not to mention personal — venture. There was much planning to do, much more than any so far. But for now, it was time to relax and celebrate my accomplishment.

Chapter 19

When I was fifteen, my grim and lonely dreams occurred much more frequently. Curious about death and the possibility of a life afterward, I often turned to my parents for answers. That very next Sunday, we were back in church. The last time we'd been there was Christmas Eve. We were what people referred to as "Holidayers."

My parents thought church was the best place to find answers to the questions they weren't comfortable with. But no one there ever seemed to give me a straightforward response to my most basic of inquiries. Every adult and priest replied in much the same way: "Let God's will guide you" or "Pray, and the answers will come." I never sensed conviction in their explanations. Most of the parents — mine and others — seemed just as confused as I was. I felt they were trying to convince themselves of something they weren't really sure about.

I tried speaking directly to God for a long time. He never responded, and over time, as the dreams persisted, I drifted farther and farther away. I began venturing onto paths less traveled and trampled on. I was on my own. But I never completely gave up hope. This world is much too odd and unpredictable for such rashness. If there's anything history has taught me, it's that there are no absolutes. Always question, but never forget.

A favorite book I had found during my initial searching was about a man who claimed to have traveled to another dimension where everyone existed in soul form. He was unsure of how many dimensions were actually out there, but he claimed that if you were to look down on them from above, the scene would resemble the hall of mirrors at a carnival.

The man's story was so convincing that after each reading, I had to look around the room a few times to make sure I hadn't stumbled into another dimension. But I liked the idea. It left room for endless possibilities to be realized, and countless doors to be opened. Things in our world seem so overused and crowded. It felt good to know there was hope of untainted territory, just waiting to be discovered.

A pounding headache made me glad that it was my day off. After a dose of aspirin and a large cup of coffee, I sat down to reread the book. I was hoping to find something that might shed some light on the events of the night before. Throughout human history, so many people have claimed to have seen apparitions, and other things they couldn't understand. Multiple dimensions would certainly make those mysteries a little easier to explain. A soul could avoid us — or reveal itself — by slipping in and out of our dimension. The simplicity of it blows my mind.

As I read the book, my mind drifted. I pondered what it would feel like to exist in soul form: no legs to impact the ground beneath, no flesh to contend with or nerves to cause pain, and no joints to ache or skin to break. It was an attractive idea, but everything on earth falls victim to some type of predator eventually. Even the soul is prey to the human body. Who knows what predators lay waiting on the other side?

Once one passes over, how does one know where to go? If the evil souls are stuck, where do the righteous ones go next? Is there a GPS, or a map implanted in the soul's genetic makeup, leading it to the next destination?

I had countless questions, most of which wouldn't be answered until I witnessed my own death, and I wasn't ready for that just yet. Of course, I could just yell out to the next specimen as they released, and hope for an answer. Then again, maybe the point of not knowing is the mystery that keeps us going. It prevents our mundane human lives from being unbearably boring. Who doesn't love a good mystery?

• • •

The next morning at work. Dave asked me an odd question. Well, odd for him. It was after our first call, as I was finishing up a report and enjoying some of that hours-old hospital break room coffee.

"Do you feel numb inside?"

I was initially caught off guard by his question. What I had heard was, "You feel numb inside, don't you?" I was briefly panicked, wondering if he had been following me and seen what I had done. It was just my own paranoia, but his question still seemed strange.

Dave saw my confusion. "What I mean is, do you look at your patients as not being human? You know, to get past thinking of your own mortality, or letting your emotions take over."

I relaxed. I assumed he was talking about coping with the dead, erasing emotion as to not be swayed from your duties. Performing as a robot, blocking out the crying family members and the dead that you had just covered with a yellow blanket.

"I guess so," I said. "I assume we all do that to an extent. Otherwise, how could we do this job?"

He lowered his Styrofoam cup of charred coffee, and his brow tightened.

"Yeah, but mine has gotten out of hand. It's taking over every part of my life. I've become cold, emotionless. Even toward my daughter the other day, when I had her for the afternoon. She just wanted to spend more time with me, and I snapped at her for no reason."

I didn't exactly know what to say to him. I understood what he was talking about, but I didn't have kids, so I'd never had to deal with that situation. I was good at managing the impact of others' emotions, able to filter when needed. I didn't have to struggle with myself to accept major change, as he'd been doing.

"I fight with it at times," I said, "trying to change myself back to normal when I get off work. You have to learn to relax, man."

"You make it sound easy. I wish I could have your life for just one day."

"Come on, Dave, you have a daughter who loves you. And you're a good guy. You just need to find a hobby. To get your mind off everything."

He sighed, gulped the rest of his coffee, and tossed the cup in the trash. "Maybe you're right."

Life was getting to him, but I imagined that it was mostly his shaky marriage. He never asked these questions or looked so drained and out of shape before Claire cheated on him. In fact, I couldn't recall him ever mentioning any sport or hobby before. I hadn't either, but at the moment, mine was a bit sensitive.

It was odd that we never talked about extra-curricular activities. Most medic partners do. They play golf together or go fishing on occasion. Maybe I'll try fishing one day. It seems like it would be relaxing.

"What do you like to do?" I asked. "Golf? Fishing?"

He gathered the clipboard and started toward the door. "For the past year, I haven't been doing much. Other than sleeping and drinking beer." He placed a copy of his finished report on the counter at the nurses' station.

"Okay," I said. "But before that, what did you like to do?" What I wanted to say was, "Before the whore ripped your heart out through your gut." But that would have only further depressed him.

Now we were inside the rig.

"I like traveling," he offered. "But that brings back too many memories of Claire. I always wanted a boat, but she never liked the idea. And she never gave me a reason. Only her repetitive No Boat speech."

"Then that's what you should do. Get a boat."

"What about Claire?"

"What about her? You can't live in the past. She's obviously not."

"You're right. It *is* a good idea. That is, if things don't work out between Claire and me, I mean. I convinced her to have dinner with me next weekend." He didn't sound as passionate as he had that evening at his apartment, when he talked about reconciling with his wife. Maybe he was finally beginning to see what was so clear to the rest of the world.

He was looking over at me for a positive nod. I couldn't do it. I knew it was going to fail. I shook my head in disapproval. "All right," I said, reluctantly. "But if this dinner doesn't work out, the boat it is."

"Okay," he said. I could see the glimmer in his eyes when I mentioned the boat. I don't care how much he said he wanted his marriage to work out. The truth was just across the lake, and a boat was the vehicle to get him there.

The MDT beeped and I looked down at the message on the screen. "MVA, eighteen-wheeler versus car," I said.

"Whoa, that doesn't sound good. Where is it?"

"I-635 near the I-30 exit."

"Dispatch, we copy the call," I said, keying the mic. "You can place us en route."

We were only a few miles away. Seconds later, dispatch

announced the call over the air.

"Dispatch, this is medic 5, we're right on top of that. We'll take it for medic 15."

Normally, taking a call for another medic unit is a nice gesture, but we all know how it really works. If it were a seizure or a febrile child call during the middle of the night, no one would have been so eager to take the call for us, closer or not. We all like our sleep. On the other hand, no matter what our individually morbid tastes happen to be, everyone wants to be part of the worst of the worst, whether it's to help or merely watch the mayhem unfold. It's almost humorous to listen to the honorable radio chatter of medic units when a potentially horrid call comes in. Medic 5 was providing a perfect example of that behavior right now.

Dave grabbed the mic and said in a sarcastic tone, "Dispatch, place medic 15 back in service. Thank you so very much, medic five."

Dispatch said, "We copy medic 15... To all responding units, we're getting reports of two people trapped and there are now flames visible from the vehicle."

"Okay, now we're going," Dave told me. "They'll need our help, regardless." He keyed back up the mic, "Dispatch this is medic 15. Place us back on that call with medic 5, please."

"Dispatch copies, medic 15, we'll place you on the call." Dispatch didn't argue with Dave. Nor did our supervisor, Jerry. He would occasionally ask us to switch channels on the radio, and then question the situation. But not on calls like this one.

I could see the dark smoke billowing into the cloudless blue sky as we blew through the next intersection. As we approached the interstate entrance, the police cars parted to let us through. Medic five and the fire department were already on scene.

A police officer guided us to the front of the wreckage. The eighteen-wheeler still had flames shooting out from under its damaged hood. Apparently, it had rear-ended a small four-door vehicle, slamming it into the middle concrete barrier. Two firemen were knocking the truck fire down with one hose while another team was gathered around the smoldering smaller vehicle.

Jerry met us as we exited the rig. He's a chubby, middle-aged man with a full head of grey hair and the demeanor of a suppressed nun. I didn't loathe him, as Dave did, but his micromanaging of scenes was annoying.

"Hey, guys," Jerry said. His words left his mouth faster than usual. He seemed shaken. Something was up. "Medic five has the driver of the car in their unit, along with the front passenger, husband and wife. The eighteen-wheeler driver said he's fine and doesn't want to be transported. That leaves us with your patient. The fire department is working on cutting them out as we speak. Grab your Pedi board."

Dave had an "oh shit" look on his face, and nearly knocked me down as he hurried to get the equipment. Pediatrics, as I've mentioned before, can turn a normally calm medic into panic-stricken Mona. And the drama medic, as Dave can be at times, a total wreck. I very seldom get worked up, but hurt children do leave a distasteful feeling in my gut, a very uncomfortable form of acid reflux.

As we neared the vehicle, I wondered where our patient could possibly be hiding. The trunk was sitting where the backseat should have been. Standing next to us with an anxious right leg, Jerry relayed that the patient was a five-month-old. While he spoke, I caught a glimpse of what was left of the car seat as they peeled back the roof of the car. The firemen had trouble getting the hydraulic tool wedged into the tight space to spread the seats apart.

I couldn't look away as they finally managed to free what was left of the tiny body. It was an awful sight, revealing enough that I knew we weren't going to be transporting. Thankfully, both parents were already on their way to the hospital. No parent deserved to witness such horrible violence, especially when it involved their child. I felt sad for the first time on the job. Still curious, but sad, as Jerry quickly covered the body and carried it toward our rig.

I looked over at Dave and said, "I got it," meaning that I would wait with the child until the coroner arrived. Dave had enough going on in his life. Normally I would have ulterior motives behind this voluntary act, but not this time. Not entirely, anyhow. He nodded his head gratefully, failing at an attempt to hold back tears.

As I sat with the lifeless infant in the back of the closed rig, I couldn't help but wonder when his little soul had departed. I hoped it was before the eighteen-wheeler had caught fire. No child deserved that pain. I am convinced, though, that the child's soul had been softly guided away when it did leave. It hadn't had time to absorb the evil that saturates this world. The choices of children are very limited, unlike those of the specimens in my journal. I couldn't help but think that one of them would have made a much better fit, rather than the dead child in front of me.

Most of the medics I knew were spooked around dead children. None would have sat in the back with one, as I was doing, unless ordered to. And even then, some would damn right refuse. As terrible and sad as the occasion was, I found it somewhat soothing, being in the presence of a pure, unscathed soul. Or at least the physical body where one had recently dwelled. It felt cleaner and more breathable than the room did, the other night, with Mr. Crow.

• • •

After the call, the rig was painfully quiet. I was left with only my thoughts, as Dave was immersed deep in his. I thought about Mr. Crow and the morning paper, most notably the obituaries. I hadn't seen his address on the log the last day or two, which meant that either the police had cancelled us when they arrived, and called the coroner, or his wife was so blitzed out of her mind that she hadn't noticed her husband decomposing on the porch.

Chapter 20

On my way home from work, I stopped at a gas station and picked up the morning paper. I thumbed to the obituaries and smiled. Halfway down the page was Mr. Crow's small black and white picture. He had the same faint expression on his face as he did that day on his couch. Not only was he guilty of beating old men, but his neglect had led to the death of his own child. Neither of which were mentioned in his short eulogy.

The dried blood from a gash on the head of Crow's child was indicative of a fall from a crib. Unfortunately, I've had to see many of them. Child neglect and abuse are common. Disgustingly so. I recalled one of the police officers telling me on scene that the mom, between her fits of rage, insisted that the baby had no prior injuries. And also that she found her on the floor, not breathing, when she got home.

The officer explained to me a disturbing truth. Even though it seemed that the wife had sealed her husband's fate with her words, it wouldn't matter. Sure, they'd be investigated, but nothing would come of it. The wife would defend her husband until the end. He's her supplier of more than husbandly love.

And nothing *had* come of it. Until I got involved.

After I knocked on Mr. Thompson's door, I could hear him struggling with his crutches down his short hallway. He mumbled a few curse words when his oxygen pack hit the doorknob, then greeted me with bright morning eyes. He was an early riser, much like the rest of the older folks around.

"Good morning, Tryke. What do I owe for the pleasure of your company so early?"

I handed him the paper that I had rolled up in my hand. "Flip to section three, the obituaries, and look halfway down the page." I managed to keep a straight face. I wanted to surprise him. He swung the oxygen bottle over his shoulder to free his hands.

"Justice served, I see. What happened to the son of a bitch? Did y'all make a call on him, finally?"

"No, but an officer friend of mine told me he overdosed. Wife found him out on the front porch with an empty syringe lying next to him. She didn't even realize he was dead until that night, near midnight, when she needed another hit. She told the officers that he sometimes slept out on the porch, and she didn't think anything about it. Anyhow, that bastard won't be visiting you anymore."

"The world has a way of handling business in its own way," he said. "I've always believed that, and more times than not it turns out to be true. It took some time, but he finally got what was coming to him."

I thought Mr. Thompson would have been more excited, but it had been a year since the incident. I suppose I wanted some form of gratitude, a job-well-done handshake. My work was going unrecognized, but I knew it had to be that way. Undercover humor, remember? Now meet undercover gratitude. It would have to suffice.

I did have to admit to myself that the undercover gratitude

felt good, even if it wasn't directed toward me. It was fulfilling to see the hope in humanity sparkle in Mr. Thompson's eyes, after being told that his attacker was now paying life's ultimate price. I hoped he could rest a little easier at night.

• • •

That afternoon, I sat staring at my phone as it lay peacefully beside me. I was hating its very existence. Why did it have to sit there, so smug and easy to use? If it didn't exist, I would have had an excuse for not calling. I swear, the little bastard was staring back at me, taunting me to dial Lesley's number. It even had it prepped and ready on speed dial. I didn't know why I was so conflicted. I was merely returning her call.

After a few more minutes of failed arguments with myself, I dialed the number. As it rang, I repeated in my head, "Don't answer, don't answer. Go to voicemail."

Third ring. "Hello?"

Dammit. "Lesley, it's Tryke."

"Hey, I'm glad you called me back. Just one sec. Sorry, I'm at work." I heard the hospital intercom announcing Dr. Forrester to extension 1022. "Okay, what are you up to?"

"Just woke up from another failed nap."

"Lucky. Wait, you said failed. Sorry."

"It's okay. I'm used to it," I said.

"Used to what? Me saying —"

"No, no. I meant I'm used to failed sleep lately."

"I'm just giving you a hard time," she said. "But I am sorry you couldn't sleep today. I was thinking if you weren't busy tonight, we could go have a few drinks, catch up on things like we used to. But if you haven't slept, I understand completely if you'd rather do it another night."

I had inadvertently given myself a way out. How good am I? But I actually did want to hang out with her. It was exactly what I needed.

"No, I'm fine. Seriously. You know I get these bouts of insomnia at times. I wouldn't be sleeping anyhow. A few drinks sounds good. Where to? Our old hangout?"

"You read my mind," she said. "Seven thirty okay?"

"I'll see you then," I said, and hung up. I felt relieved. It's always the anticipation that's the hardest to overcome. Now that I had finally returned the call, I was glad that we were going to be hanging out again. I needed someone to talk to, someone who understood me.

Sure, Dave was fine and all, but our conversations led mostly to me trying to console him, which oddly enough I didn't mind doing. Somehow it made my life feel a little saner, hearing about all of his issues. Besides, he trusted me now, and I might need him in the future for something. Give and take — the old one-two work together. My dad said that often.

• • •

I wore a hat that night and slipped on a pair of old boots and jeans along with a t-shirt. I didn't want Lesley to think I was looking to get hitched. That was my usual drinking attire whenever we'd hang out. Not to mention, it was Texas, so I'd blend in with the crowd. I didn't need any unnecessary attention or changes at the moment.

Joe's Honkytonk Café and Bar sat alone near the edge of town on Willard Street. From the outside, you'd think you were entering an 1800s saloon. It even had the double saloon-style swinging doors. The inside was up to date, but still had that old western feel. A withered, ornate piano sat in the corner, looking as though no one had played it in years. The bar didn't have stools lined under its long brass railing — standing or leaning patrons only.

Charlie, the bartender, didn't like people eating at the bar. It was meant for drinking, and if he'd had it his way, he would only serve shots of whiskey. The food was good and the place was mostly quiet, except on Saturday nights. That was when the "honkytonk" part of the name took over. Lesley had tried to get me to go on those nights, but I don't

dance, not even the country version. It just seemed too…
well, personal to me. Not to mention that with my rhythm,
I'd probably look like a drunken zombie attempting to
pantomime the birth of a child.

It was Thursday, and if they still had the same specials, it
was burger night. They made the best burgers across two
counties, charred to perfection with just the right amount of
grease sliding out along the sides of the soft bun and down
your chin. And the fries were cut into wedges and doused
with garlic butter. It was truly a perfect harmony of goodness,
but I could enjoy it only on occasion, because of my family's
history of heart disease.

I asked one of the waitresses one night how they got the
meat to taste so fresh. I had never paid attention to the field
of cows just a hundred yards behind the restaurant. The
owner Joe was a butcher before he decided he wanted to
work for himself, and this is what came of it. I was glad he'd
decided to take that route.

Lesley introduced me to Joe's. She said she had stumbled
upon it one afternoon while she was driving and thinking —
something she did often to clear her head. She had been
hungry and the place looked unique, so she pulled in and ate.
She fell in love with the food and the atmosphere, and now
I'd grown quite fond of it myself. I enjoyed the feel of the old
west.

I didn't see her car as I pulled into the gravel parking lot. I
looked down at my watch. Seven-twenty. I was a little early,
so I decided to get a drink and wait inside. The aroma of
grilled burgers and garlic butter fries filled my nostrils and
evoked hunger pains.

Charlie was working. I greeted him and he served me my
usual Scotch. I sat at an empty table in the corner, just far
enough away from the jukebox and the door. It was a table
Lesley and I chose when it was available because it gave us
the best view of the place if we decided to people watch.
There were always a few "characters" around to keep us

entertained.

Twenty minutes later, Lesley arrived. There were only a few small groups of patrons, but they all stopped what they were doing and stared as she walked toward me. She had that effect on a room. Her looks demanded attention from all in attendance. It wasn't her fault. She didn't dress to provoke, as so many women do these days. In fact, I think she tries to prevent the looks, viewing the whole thing as more of a curse. She doesn't wear much makeup, and chooses shoes that are comfortable. I admired that about her.

"Sorry, my relief was late, as usual."

I stood as she approached and waited for her to sit down. It was a gentleman thing that my dad would do for my mother. I noticed how pretty Lesley looked and I wanted to tell her, but I wasn't ready for that move just yet. She looked delicately enchanting, and it felt weird to have these thoughts move so smoothly across my lobes.

"I haven't been here long," I said. "I went ahead and ordered us a couple of burgers. I hope you don't mind."

"Of course I don't mind, silly. The smell nearly knocked me over when I was coming in the door. I haven't eaten since breakfast. I'm starved."

"How about a drink?" I said.

"Sure."

"Port, right?"

"Yes, thank you."

If I were to drink wine, it would be port. It has a sweet taste, with the kick of brandy.

I returned from the bar with her drink and set it in front of her.

"Thank you," she said, softly taking a sip from her glass. "So, how have things been? How's your mom?"

"I think she's doing better. I went to see her recently, and she actually spoke more than a few words."

"She seems like such a nice woman. I could see it in her eyes when I met her. She'll find her way, in time." She had met my mom a while back, one evening after we had hung out. I could tell my mom liked her right away.

Lesley reached out her hand to touch mine, but caught herself, retrieving it. She obviously remembered the response the last time she tried the touching act. Jerking my hand away had never been my intention. It was more of a reflex, and I started to explain that, but she had already moved on to another subject. I turned the conversation back to her.

"How are things with you?" I asked. "Still thinking of switching over to pathology?" I took the last sip of Scotch from my glass. The pathology route had crossed my own mind a few times. It was an appealing career, especially if dead bodies and human tissue samples make you giddy. Lesley said her interest in the field was rooted in a love of mysteries, and the challenge of solving them. Maybe she wasn't as morbid as me.

"I've been taking classes," she said, "but I still can't decide if I want to spend four years in medical school."

"That's a long time. But it's what you want. It's all you've ever talked about."

"You really think I should? It might mean moving away from here, depending on where I got accepted." The thought of her having to move for school had never crossed my mind. I was always one for going after something that you wanted. As my dad always said, "You can do anything you put your mind to." Still, I don't think he would approve of my latest endeavor.

I paused a little too long and that's all it took.

"You don't want me to leave, do you? Tryke Harper… would you miss me?" She said it playfully, smiling broadly and entrancing me with her deep blue eyes.

I wanted to say yes, but I didn't have to. The heat rising from my cheeks said it for me. "Of course I'd miss you. You're a good friend." I was thankful to see the waitress coming toward us with the burgers. It was a well-timed diversion. I could feel my face returning to its normal paleness as I asked the waitress for some ketchup.

"Well, if I do decide to go, I would love for you to help me pick a school," she said. "It would mean a lot to me if you were involved."

"I'm flattered, but what do I know about medical schools except that they're expensive and long-winded?" I was halfway through my burger when I noticed she hadn't touched hers.

"Aren't you going to eat?"

"Yes, but first I want to ask you something, and I need you to be honest with me. No sarcastic undertones or snide, avoiding comments of any kind, please."

She had my attention now. What was this? She was suddenly serious. The last time I had seen this look on her face was when she told me that her dog had died. But this was a question, a personal question, not information about a tragedy. Bad news, I could handle, but a serious and personal question was on a completely different plane.

"All right, I can be serious," I said, pretending to be cool. "Lay it on me. What's the question?" She tilted her head and pursed her lips, awaiting a second acknowledgement from me. "I *promise*."

She bravely touched the top of my hand with hers. Her skin was soft, and it felt good to be touched. It was something I had avoided for a long time, but now that it was happening I didn't know how to respond. I forced myself to leave my hand right where it was.

"I want you to move away with me," she said.

Chapter 21

I was speechless. Did I hear her correctly? I reached for my drink, but it was empty. I would have chugged it at that moment, or anything to avoid an answer to her off-the-wall comment. The swinging entrance doors opened and two ladies walked in. I wanted to slip out through the narrow opening before it fell shut behind them. But I didn't. I bravely stood my ground and cleared my throat.

She spoke again before I could respond. "I know how it sounds. It's completely absurd, nuts, all those things. But we have something, Tryke. Something different and I —" She stopped. Her eyelids were full, ready to spill over. Her lips were trembling. I was in a near panic and wondering what to do.

I spoke softly, thinking that it would help the situation. "Shouldn't we go on a date first? You know, to see if that's really what you want?" The tears that had been eagerly waiting now slid down her perfect pale cheeks. Crap, what did I say wrong this time?

But then, out of nowhere, right when I thought her whole world was about to shatter, she grabbed my hand again and smiled, agreeing with my idea. "That's all I wanted from you. I'm not asking you to move in with me, nor am I moving away yet. But if I have to move, I want to at least know we gave this a chance. I apologize for all the antics. I just didn't know how else to approach it with you. I was so scared to ask you, afraid you would say no."

"I would have asked you sooner," I said, "but I'm not really good at it. Your way was much better, and more entertaining." We both laughed, and I handed her a napkin for her tears.

Women's emotional ways of handling things baffle the heck out of me, but I was relieved by how things turned out. There was no more talk about romance, other than when our first date was going to be. We had another drink, finished our delicious burgers, and people watched.

Lesley found an old man with a rather large belly that extended well over his dinner-plate-sized belt buckle. He was wearing a t-shirt that was much too small. He was making crude gestures toward an older woman, whose rather obvious wig and heels screamed "broken hip before the end of the night." With his hand, he drew slow circles around his well-pronounced belly button while the woman, entranced by his mating ritual, smiled back at him just enough to reveal the last three of her thirty-two teeth. There was definitely a romantic comedy forming, brought to you by your local trailer park. We even named it, "No teeth, No problem."

It wasn't inevitable, my dating Lesley, only probable. She was right: we did have something, but I still wasn't quite as ready for it as I made out to be. I had complications in my life at the moment. She'd managed to nudge me forward, anyway, using her female mojo.

• • •

On the fourth of July, Dave and I were put on special duty to cover the evening of fireworks. It wasn't a bad gig. For a few hours, we got a break from transporting the inevitable kid who'd split his hand open by throwing a lit firecracker at his friend. Those fuses can be misleading bitches at times. And I can't forget about the hero dad showing off for his family, proudly kneeling beside his hundred-dollar firework cannon extravaganza that he had just purchased. He's flinching, nearly falling over with his lighter as he nervously misses the fuse over and over again. Finally he gets it lit, but his legs are now cramped. The cannon misfires and explodes next to his head, bursting his eardrum and burning his face.

They take their fireworks seriously down here in Texas, and I have to admit it's usually quite a show. Lesley wanted this to be our first date, but I was already scheduled to work. I most likely could have found someone to take my shift, but I was still procrastinating, which is what I usually do when it comes to things that make me uncomfortable.

We backed the rig up near the exit to the festival grounds and hopped into our mini rig — a custom gas-powered golf cart ambulance, complete with four-wheel drive and off-road tires. Dave and I usually have a coin toss for who gets to drive, but this time it wasn't necessary. During the last event we covered, his driving was disastrous.

We'd worked an outdoor concert, and midway through it started raining. We received a call that a woman had fallen off a parked motor home. On the muddy trail over to assist the woman, we stopped in front of a monstrous puddle of water blocking our path. Instead of going around it, Dave decided that it was shallow enough to travel through. The cart started to sink, and after I warned him of our impending doom, he gunned it. All four tires spun in place, slinging muddy water in every direction, and soaking us in the process. When we finally got some traction, the cart shot out of the hole at full speed. Once we started sliding on the wet grass, he couldn't control the thing and we narrowly missed a beer-tent and two bystanders. Then we toppled over and landed in a shallow ditch.

Thankfully, the woman didn't have any injuries. We were lucky ourselves that we hadn't ended up on backboards. Later, we told Jerry that some kid had stolen the golf cart while we were eating and taken it for a joyride. This evening, before we left, he reminded us about the incident at the concert. It was hard for me not to laugh right into his serious grey mustache as it flickered while he lectured. The whole time, I was thinking of Dave's animated face and the variety of curse words he spouted as he was losing control of the cart. "Oh shitfire," he'd said. "This ain't good."

"Let's check out the food situation before it gets dark," Dave said. I knew that was coming. Like Dave, I also looked forward to the carnival food, but I only trusted the corndogs and funnel cakes. Meat on a stick could mean anything. And the ones I'd seen always seemed to resemble a small, skinned rodent. I prefer to not eat rat if I can avoid it.

On our first pass around the food arena, Dave couldn't take any more of the fried batter aroma. He was done with planning and was ready for his binge. "First I'll have a hamburger, then off to the corndog booth. Next we'll head over to the fried Twinkie stand. And before we leave, I have to have a funnel cake. What do you want?"

"Why don't you just purchase your own booth, fatty?"

"Come on, Tryke, I'm a growing boy." He massaged his belly. "I promise, I'm going on a diet next week. For the ladies." Meanwhile, he continued to molest his own stomach.

"Yeah, right. Planning to capture you a big one, huh?"

"More cushion for the pushin'."

"Whatever," I said, shaking my head. "Just a corndog for me."

"Suit yourself, you skinny bitch," he said. "Hey, is the radio turned on?"

"Yeah, I checked it earlier."

"Well, I don't expect to hear a bleep out of that damn thing, anyway. This is our relax time." A superstitious paramedic would have slapped him for saying such a thing, jinxing both himself and his partner. But I for one am not superstitious, and Dave didn't give a shit anymore. His attitude toward most everything had changed since the separation from his wife.

We began Dave's food booth tour. Parents and children waved at us as we passed from booth to booth. I had to do the waving back, along with the smile greetings. He was way too caught up in the burger that was dripping grease on his light blue uniform shirt. When I threw him a napkin, he snatched it in mid-air and used it to smear the glossy sheen across his chin.

"I'm heading to the corndog stand," I said. "Is that all right? Your gobbling is making me hungry." He waved me forward, continuing to pat his shirt with the napkin.

"Medic 15 portable, this is dispatch."

"Did you hear something?" Dave asked.

"Nah, probably just someone saying hello to us," I said, feeding Dave's humorous denial.

"Medic 15 portable, this is dispatch."

Dave responded with a mouthful of burger.

"Medic 15, go ahead, dispatch."

"We have a report of a male choking near the south entrance of the festival."

He released the mic. "How the hell did dispatch find out before us? The police and staff know we're here working this event. They're supposed to contact us on tac channel one." Dave was irritated. He wadded the rest of his burger up into the wrapper and placed the mic back to his mouth. "We copy, dispatch."

I flipped on the mini light bar and blared the tiny horn across the festival grounds, hitting every bump I could in order to splatter Dave with any condiment willing to participate.

A skinny elderly man, wearing a sagging staff shirt and Wranglers tucked into his cowboy boots, frantically directed us toward the victim. Our view of the patient was blocked by the crowd that had formed, and we had to push our way through the people. A middle-aged man, weighing no more than a hundred and forty pounds, was being repeatedly lifted and yanked from behind by a woman twice his size.

I would have sat down and enjoyed the sideshow fun, but his face was turning cyanotic.

"I got this one," I told Dave. He grabbed the airway bag and began preparing for the worst. I noticed a half-eaten corndog slathered in mustard on the ground as I took over for the adrenaline-filled, hysterical woman. I placed my fists above his bellybutton and thrust upward. I tried a second time, but nothing expelled from his mouth.

I glanced over at Dave. He already had the equipment prepped and ready. The small man was giving up, becoming limp. We were losing him. I thrust a third time, and nothing again. I was frustrated.

Repositioning myself and spreading my boots a little further apart, I thrust a fourth time and finally heard the pop. The man took in an enormous deep breath, which returned color to his face, and hunched over with both hands on his knees. After a minute of deep and thankful breathing, he lowered himself to the concrete. The small crowd clapped and cheered. I nodded briefly to the bystanders, avoiding eye contact, and then bent down to examine the man.

It was an odd feeling having someone cheer for your work. I didn't expect or desire any form of gratitude for what I had done. I was getting paid for my job. Many medics would bask in this moment, looking for a podium to give their acceptance speech. There's an attention seeker around every corner. But I prefer the shadows.

As badly as I wanted to visualize the human soul, this man wasn't one who interested me. He didn't appear dirty like the others.

The woman who was determined to remove the man's innards by jerking him around like a limp puppet turned out to be the same vendor who'd sold him the corndog. Dave and I thanked her for assisting, while the man signed the transport refusal paperwork.

The man's three-year-old daughter hugged me before we left, and that sent chills up my spine. I had never seen or been given such pure gratitude. Her hug held no ulterior motives, only a very long thank you for giving her dad back to her. "I'm just a bystander in this life, kid. We all are." That's what I wanted to say to her, but I didn't. Why ruin the surprise?

"Still want that corndog?" Dave asked me as we loaded the cart with our bags. I didn't answer him right away. I was staring at the little girl who was staring back at me while hugging her dad. I saw in her what I had longed for: another chance with my own dad. I quickly snapped out of the dreamy fantasy when Dave repeated the question.

"Tryke? Corndog?"

"Of course. I've worked up an appetite, and seeing that half-chewed piece fly through the air only made me hungrier."

"I'm glad we think alike," Dave said. "Full speed ahead to the corndog stands!" Dave was yelling and holding out his fist as if flying, all the while blowing the pathetic horn that sounded like a sick dog farting. It lost its power on the way over to the call. We both held wide grins all the way to the food booths while adults stared and children pointed.

• • •

It was now past twilight and the fireworks were about to begin. People were heading over to claim their spots, lying blankets down and setting up chairs.

I gladly accepted the hot crispy corndog and began pumping stripes of tangy yellow mustard along the outside. The next time I would get one wouldn't be until fall, during the fair. Just as I was about to chomp down on my first bite, I felt a tap on my shoulder. I lowered the corndog from my eagerly salivating mouth and turned around. There was a policeman standing behind me.

"What can I do for you officer?"

"We have a situation brewing by the grilling section," he said. "We may need you guys, if you don't mind easing that way. But discreetly, please. We're trying to keep people away."

"Sure no problem. What is it?" I said.

"I'll leave it a surprise for now, but you'll know immediately when you get there. Do y'all know where that section is?"

I laughed and pointed at the grease stains down Dave's shirt. "He'll show me." The officer smirked and shook his head.

"What was that about?" Dave asked as I got back into the cart.

"There's something going on over by the grilling section that may need medical attention. He didn't tell me what it was, but judging by his tone, it should be interesting."

"Interesting usually means more work for us," said Dave. "By the way, did you get me a corndog?"

"Sorry, the officer distracted me. Here take this one." As I handed it to him, I bit a chunk from the top, but that didn't slow his reaching hand.

"Do you think we need to contact dispatch for a run number on this one?" I asked.

"Let's just see what it is first. No run number, no paperwork."

"True."

Another small crowd of intrigued onlookers was already gathered next to the blue grilling section tent, while the police were trying to keep their craning necks away from the opening. I could hear a female voice yelling from inside as we pulled the cart up next to the tent. My Spanish was rough to say the least, but thanks to a Puerto Rican medic acquaintance, my cursing in the language was fluent. And the woman inside was yelling every one I knew.

From a hidden opening on the side, an officer motioned for us to come in. He explained the situation. "She started yelling at the cashier after she got her hot dog and threw it back at him. She then climbed over the table and began flinging wieners at everyone in the tent. She's been behind that table since we arrived. She has an arsenal of wieners at her disposal, along with a variety of chef knives that thankfully she hasn't used. We're waiting on an officer who speaks Spanish to try and talk with her before we use other means."

"All right, then," I said. "We'll wait over here, out of wiener reach." I leaned over toward Dave and said, "Is she a friend of your future ex?" Despite her blonde hair, Claire was part Hispanic.

"Yeah, probably. One of her new friends, anyhow." He didn't comment on my slip of the words *future* and *ex*. Maybe he was subconsciously letting go?

After a few hundred more curse words and numerous hot dogs hitting the side of the tent, the Spanish-speaking officer showed up. Dave and I watched from a safe distance as he and the woman conversed in a rapid-fire exchange. A few sentences into their dialogue, the officer was hit with an array of uncooked wieners. Unlike the other police officers, this guy wasn't taking any shit from the woman.

I heard him say 'bitch' in Spanish, and then he drew the Taser from his holster and fired it toward her chest. Seconds later, the wiener-slinger was down for the count.

"That's how you take a motherfucker down," Dave said a little too loudly while patting me on the shoulder. I had to admit, the Taser was a rather efficient tool. It looked painful, but she had it coming. They handcuffed the woman and brought her to us.

"What do you want us to do with her?" Dave asked.

"Just a quick medical assessment before we haul her ass to jail, if you wouldn't mind," the Spanish-speaking officer said, in English.

"Sure," I said, and took a quick set of vitals from her before she woke from her electric nap. One of the officers pulled a bottle of pills from her front pocket as they patted her down for weapons. He tossed them to me.

"Lithium," I said. "That explains a lot." He tossed me two more from her fanny pack. "Prozac and uh —" The writing was partly scratched off, but I could make out enough to decipher what it was. "Valium, which she obviously hasn't taken lately." I removed the BP cuff. "Her vitals are fine at the moment," I said. The small lady was still snoring deeply, and drooling. "Anything else we can do for you officer?"

"No, thank you for your help. I just hope she stays calm for the ride."

"Good luck with that," Dave told him. The officer lifted the woman from the ground, and as he did, she woke just long enough to call him an asshole in Spanish.

"Pendejo," she mumbled.

Then she fell back into a slumber. Dave and I both laughed.

I finally got my corndog. The next few hours were calm, and the fireworks were loud and colorfully bright, as we'd expected. But my mind was elsewhere. I couldn't help but think of my dad when I saw the psych medications. Did he have his own array of prescription drugs hidden? Would I ever be able to fill in the missing gaps from his journal? Would I ever know the full truth about my own father?

Chapter 22

We were off the weekend after the fourth. I didn't have anything planned and was still mentally avoiding my date with Lesley, though she had managed to corner me on the phone Sunday afternoon to set a time and place. There was no getting out of this one.

It was late Monday afternoon, and Dave and I were back at work. We were attempting an everyday process that families across the nation accomplish flawlessly without giving it a second thought. Few paramedics have prevailed at it, but we hoped to be one of the exceptions that evening. I was determined to finish the meal — Dave's fall-off-the-bone, spicy barbecue-slathered ribs. Surprisingly, he'd agreed to make them, texting me back late Sunday night. We were both sick of fried chicken and hamburgers.

The morning and early afternoon hadn't been very eventful, at least not for us. A few chest pains and some minor wrecks. Death wasn't in the air that day, though I was sure it would be along shortly. It never stayed away for long.

I guessed that Dave's dinner with his wife had gone better than expected, judging from his higher than normal energy level, including his willingness to cook. Now I would have to wait for Claire to drag him back under in order to show him what she had been doing to him.

"Last night went well, I'm assuming," I said.

He finished another rib, completely annihilating any speck of meat that had resided on it, and placed the bare bone next to his building pile. After wiping his hands on a towel and gulping down a hefty swig of soda, he began. I immediately sensed sarcasm.

"It went great. I took her to the Mexican restaurant where she first told me she was pregnant. I thought it would be a happy place to remind us of our daughter. I ordered my usual, two tacos and a cheese enchilada, and she ordered pork quesadillas. She hates pork and would never eat it while we were together. Anyway, I didn't say anything about it. Later, while we were waiting for the check, and after we had discussed our relationship, including things that could have gone a little better — of course, I didn't mention the obvious one, *fidelity* — she started crying. I wanted to console her, but I couldn't."

By now he had finished an entire bowl of potato salad. From his deep sigh, I could tell he was about to reveal something big. "I felt angry all of a sudden. I wondered why the hell she led me on, making me believe we were going to work out our differences. She was still deceiving me. I could see it in her lying eyes."

He inhaled deeply through his nose, and with an odd smirk, he began again, "I had this sudden clarity. I got up, flung two twenties on the table for the check and told her to take a damn taxi home. She didn't say a word. She was in shock. I had finally stood up to her. I turned around and walked off. I watched from the bar, sipping on a beer as she paced outside on her cell phone, no doubt talking to her new lover. And now, here we are enjoying her potato salad recipe that I know you like so much. Just my way of thanking you for helping me see through her deceit."

"You knew it all along," I said. "I only nudged you. But what's next?"

"I'm taking your advice and buying a boat, that's what's next. And then you and me are going to take a trip to the gulf." That didn't sound like a bad idea. I had always dreamed of living near the ocean and sailing blue-green water into open freedom.

"I'll take you up on that offer."

"Want to go with me to look at boats?" Dave said.

"When?"

"Our next days off."

"Sorry, I can't on the days coming up. I have to handle some things with my mom. Bills and stuff. I wouldn't be much help, anyway. I've never owned a boat, and I've only been on one a few times."

I didn't completely lie about our next days off. I was going over to my mom's house, just not for that reason. I had more pressing matters. Research to be completed. Dave pushed his empty plate away and sat back in his chair.

"I was hoping you knew more about boats than I do. I did some research a few years back, but Claire put a stop to it, and I didn't get very far. Oh, well. I'll figure it out."

"I'll go with you next week, if you haven't bought one by then."

"All right," Dave said, and got up from the table. He started cleaning up.

"I got it," I said. "Go relax before the bell goes off. The citizens let us eat, but I doubt we'll get much more of a break."

"You're probably right. Thanks."

I cleaned the kitchen and washed the dishes. Home-cooked meals were a rarity in my life, and when they came around I was always grateful.

As I'd anticipated, five minutes after finishing the dishes, the bell sounded. I didn't complain. We had achieved a great feat that day. We were now among the few paramedics who'd ever finished a warm meal at the station table.

The call was for a thirty-two-year-old male having stroke symptoms. A stroke, or CVA, is a rather common call for us. What's not so common is a guy in his early 30s experiencing an actual stroke. There are many non-life-threatening physiological sensations that can mimic stroke symptoms. For example, prolonged hyperventilation from anxiety causes numbness in the hands and feet that some of our brighter citizens interpret as a stroke. And then there's my favorite. A few months ago, I made a call in the middle of the night involving a female who woke in a panic, relaying to our dispatcher that she couldn't move half of her body. When we arrived, we figured out that she had slept oddly, which caused her left arm and leg to fall asleep. I thought Dave was going to have a stroke himself as the woman explained her situation to us at three in the morning.

As for the man in his thirties, anything was possible. He could have had a congenital disorder. We were about to find out. As we entered the apartment complex, Dave asked, "What's the number?"

I looked down at the screen. "101B."

"First floor, good," he said. "I don't think I can haul anyone down stairs after what I just ate. But this is probably bullshit, anyway. How old did they say this guy was?"

"Thirty-two."

"Yep."

I knocked on the apartment door and a males voice yelled from the other side for us to come in. Dave opened the door cautiously. Even though it was still light out, evil always keeps one eye open and grabs a prey every now and then.

A heavy-set black man was seated on the edge of the bed. His lower body was covered with a white sheet, while on top he was wearing a stretched white tank top. The apartment was dimly lit and quiet.

While placing our bags on the floor, I noticed that the man was leaning oddly to his left. "What's going on this morning, sir?" I asked, kneeling down to get a set of vitals.

"My head began hurting all of a sudden. Then I couldn't feel my left side, like it was sleeping or something. When I tried to stand, I fell, so I called 911."

Down here in the south, I could usually count on a few constants by first glance at an overweight patient: hypertension, diabetes, heart disease, just to name a few. Add smoking and swollen extremities with pitting edema, and the list grows dramatically. This guy had many factors against him. He told us his medical history, and I was off by only one.

Blood pressure was highly elevated, 240/148. I checked his blood sugar, 86, which was fine. A low blood sugar can mimic stroke symptoms. It was always worth checking, especially with his history.

"Mr. Brown, what were you doing when the symptoms started?" Dave asked as he lowered the stretcher and handed him back his ID.

He didn't answer. A black female in her twenties, wearing a red silk robe, came from around the corner and stood silently against the wall. She looked as if she had just finished a wrestling match. "We were uh…you know…getting it on," he said finally.

"I understand," Dave said, managing to keep his composure. He looked over at the girl. "Will you be meeting us at the hospital?"

She looked at Mr. Brown for a long few seconds and then said, "I'll have to get dressed. I'll come up there after."

Dave and I exchanged peculiar looks. We knew this wasn't a subject they wanted to discuss with two strangers in the room. I noticed his wedding ring and her lack of one. It wasn't hard to put two and two together.

• • •

In the back of the rig, I started small talk as usual, and asked him what he did for a living. Mostly, it was a way to keep the patient's mind off the situation.

"I'm a reverend," he said. His speech through the oxygen mask was slurred. Ah, a reverend. Interesting. A man of God trespassing in another's bed. Was I about to witness justice in its most pure form?

Sitting up on the stretcher, he now had a more pronounced lean to the left. The seatbelts, already struggling and screaming for help, weren't going to hold him up for much longer. I slid beside him and straightened him on the stretcher. "I can't see," he said, in a calm but barely discernible voice.

I suspected he had a bleed, in other words a hemorrhagic stroke. He was deteriorating quickly. We would soon have to intubate and breathe for him. I looked through the side window and saw that we were two minutes from Mercy.

There isn't much we can do for a stroke in the field, other than give him oxygen and protect his airway. If he did have a bleed, he would need surgery — that is, if he survived that long.

I had to admit, this guy sitting a few feet from me piqued my interest. I didn't feel he warranted my form of justice, but I was curious about another's intrigue. Would his God or his Devil collect his soul?

We were now one minute away. His breathing had become labored, but as close as we were to the ER, he wasn't going to release in the back of the rig.

My back cursed at me again as I pulled the stretcher out and lowered the wheels. "He's definitely on his way out," Dave commented from the other end of the stretcher.

When the nurses saw the man's obviously lean and labored breathing, they immediately got to work and motioned toward Dr. Reed for assistance.

Dr. Reed was a tall, skinny, red-haired man who took life way too seriously. All of my witty or not-so-witty comments had slid by him every time. I suspect he was merely ignoring them, but I've never stopped trying to get a rise out of him. I'd decided today would be the day. We transferred Mr. Brown to the bed in med room 12.

"Dr. Reed," I said, nodding. He nodded back.

"What's the story?" he asked in his usual monotone voice, arms crossed, waiting for us to move the patient into the bed.

"Apparently Reverend Brown here was 'getting it on.' His words not mine. And now he's getting his stroke on."

There was no sway in his emotion. No smile, no flinching in disgust — only head movement toward Dave for more answers. "Hypertensive thirty-two-year-old male complained of sudden headache while having intercourse," Dave said. "He began having left-sided weakness. He has been rapidly deteriorating since. Last BP was 250/158 taken just before we pulled up."

He didn't thank Dave. I smirked at another failed attempt, then wheeled the stretcher out of the room and into the hallway.

"You know he's going to report your ass one of these days," Dave said.

"Probably. But it's still funny watching his expressionless face. How the hell does he do that? It's like there's a tiny robot in his head moving him around."

"He *is* a little off," Dave said, smiling.

I watched the symphony from the hallway, waiting to see if Mr. Brown would depart anytime soon, while Dave took the stretcher out to the rig. The patient was unconscious and Dr. Reed was attempting to intubate him as the heart monitor let out a long beep. A small female nurse leaped onto the bed, straddled Mr. Brown, and began compressing his chest. All she got for her effort was a lot of twitching, as if his chest was telling her to quit tickling. Seconds later, one of the residents took over.

I was now watching intently.

After a round of meds, they got a pulse back. "Damn," I

whispered. They wheeled him hurriedly out of the room down the hall to CT, or computed tomography. Since he wasn't leaving just yet, I was still curious about the results of the CT scan. I wanted to know if my suspicion of a bleed was correct. I took my time writing the report, and waited.

"Why are you stalling?" Dave asked, returning from stretcher duty and staring down at my half-done report.

"I wanted to see the CT," I said. "He just coded on them, but they managed to get a pulse back."

"Yeah, he had that 'coming to Jesus look' when we wheeled him in." A "coming to Jesus look" is a phrase heard often in our department. I don't say it, but a few of the others have become attached to it and use it often. It essentially meant the patient was about to code.

I finished my report and placed it on the table in the room where Mr. Brown would be returning after his CT. The room was a disaster, as most are after a code. Scrambling nurses, doctors, and techs don't worry about tidiness during the event. I had to hand it to myself: my lab may not be state of the art, but I do manage to keep a clean and orderly workspace.

Ten minutes later, Mr. Brown was wheeled back down the hall, intubated and with a full team surrounding him. I imagined all were anticipating the inevitable moment when he would code again. It was only a matter of time.

I made my way over to where the CTs were displayed and watched from a distance. Dr. Reed was sitting in front of the black and white screen and would most likely not be offering me any information after my smart-ass report. He clicked the mouse and the images appeared.

I knew the scans were bad the moment Dr. Reed placed the palm of his right hand on his head and let out a heavy sigh. The images looked very similar to Karl's after his phone beating. Same area of the brain, too, only Mr. Brown's bleed covered a much larger area.

I waited a while so I could witness the release, but Dave

was being impatient, insisting we leave. I didn't argue with him.

As I walked past med room 12 and out the double doors to the ambulance bay, I was curious if something was watching the reverends last moments — greedily waiting to snatch him up.

• • •

The next few shifts went by much too quickly, and I knew the reason. I was in denial. I glanced at my watch before getting into my twin bed at the station, 0130. There was more than one foe barricading the entrance to dream world that night. The next evening, I'd have my first date with Lesley.

Chapter 23

Medical school students spend an entire semester dissecting cadavers. During paramedic school, we visited the anatomy lab at Mercy General's Medical School for a *one-day* crash course on gross anatomy. In other words, we're hardly doctors out on the streets, but all too often the citizens like to think we're their personal physicians.

It wasn't a usual occurrence in most paramedic schools to get to poke around on a cadaver, because they were reserved for medical students. But our teacher happened to be friends with the anatomy instructor at the school. It was a unique experience, and in retrospect I'm even more appreciative to have had the opportunity to view an empty body from the inside.

The anatomy lab was on the third floor of the school. The medical students were off that day, so the lab was all ours to explore, under the direct supervision of our teacher, as well as the anatomy instructor, Dr. Ross.

The room was huge, big enough to hold twenty metal

tables that faced a large chalkboard. Each table was big enough for it's own cadaver. I thought at the time how gracious the once occupying souls were for such a donation. That is, until I actually viewed the aftermath.

Dr. Ross had our cadaver sprawled on top of one of the metal tables. It was an elderly white female whom the med students had already partially butchered. To put it mildly, it didn't appear human. In fact, it was hard to imagine the cadaver as a once living human being, now emptied of its life-blood and sliced up and layered like a buffet of pulled pork.

Two female students had to leave the room when Dr. Ross passed a kidney around for us to handle. I eagerly took their place in front. I had always been impressed with the human body, but to actually see and place my hands around the organs was a surreal experience. It was fascinating to see the inner workings of the human body, how fantastically complex and perfectly assembled it was. Every tiny vessel, ligament, and tendon methodically arranged, each cell programmed to perform a specific function, and countless chemical processes taking place simultaneously. It's a beautiful, intricate system, erected for the single purpose of keeping the prison operable until its prisoner was ready for release. The soul had to appreciate its organic suit.

While I watched Dr. Ross describe the pulmonary system, my mind began drifting. The metal tables and the bodies reminded me of a very interesting study conducted by a doctor in Massachusetts. He had placed six dying patients on scale beds in order to measure any differences in weight, before and after death. That difference, he theorized, might represent the mass of the human soul.

Though many have criticized those tests, the doctor did get some peculiar results. He concluded that the human soul weighs twenty-one grams, which is equivalent to approximately twenty milliliters of liquid. The amount is minute, but makes sense considering that an apparition can glide above the surface of an object, essentially floating. But what force is it that keeps the soul afloat? That is one of the many mysteries that I hope to solve someday.

• • •

I didn't sleep well that day after getting off work. I was too nervous. It was five-thirty and I had to pick Lesley up in an hour. I combed my careless hair and put on a nice shirt, along with my boots. No self-respecting Texan leaves the house without his boots.

I'd suggested a quaint Italian café not far from her house. I had driven by it many times and it was often busy. That was usually a good sign that the food was at least edible. The patio faced an open grassy area with a rustic gazebo in the center. Both the patio and gazebo were lined with soft white lights that were turned on once they started serving dinner. It was a nice afternoon, the humidity had tapered off, and there was a slight eastern breeze.

"I've always wanted to try this place," Lesley said. "I pass by it all the time and see people waiting. It must be pretty good." We took our seats on the patio. I pulled her chair out for her — another helpful and appreciated tip sent by my dad from beyond the grave. She seemed surprised by the gesture and thanked me with her eyes. Our table was perfectly secluded, near the steps to the stone pathway leading out to the gazebo.

"I hope it is, or I'm in trouble," I said.

"Yeah, big trouble," she said. Her remark was punctuated by one of her devilish smirks, which I suddenly found charming, for some reason. I hadn't given them much more than a forgetful glance in the past.

I watched from across the restaurant as an older man pulled the chair out for his wife before sitting. It was refreshing to see others showing respect for those they cared for. Some would call this an amorous act, but I never thought of myself as a romantic. And the word *chivalry* didn't suit me at all. It was just simple courtesy.

Twilight began its farewell wave, allowing the soft white lights and flickering candles on the tables to illuminate the area. I needed to settle my nerves, and was craving a drink. I felt awkward and didn't know what to say, now that things had changed between us.

"What should we order to drink?" I asked

"I was thinking maybe we should try some wine tonight. Are you up for it?"

I needed something stronger. "Okay," I said, "but I don't know much about wine." I turned the menu over to the wine section. Chardonnay, Merlot, Cabernet, Pino something — I was lost. But put me in the world of Scotch and I could tell you the exact place in Scotland where it was put into casks.

"I'm not an expert by any means," said Lesley, "but I think you'll like Merlot."

"I'll give it a try."

A few minutes later, our waitress returned with our glasses of red wine. I took a sip as Lesley watched, anxiously awaiting my response. I tried drinking it smoothly, but I accidentally took a big swig and puckered my lips. It was pleasantly bold and slightly tangy.

"So, what do you think?" she asked. "Are you on the path to being a wino?"

I took a few more sips and felt my lips loosen with each one.

"I don't know if I'll ever be a wino. But it *is* growing on me."

"It took me a while, too. You have to acquire a taste for it. Merlot goes better with meals than my port."

"Definitely," I said.

About halfway through the meal I began to relax, somewhat back to a tolerable self, with the help of the wine and Lesley's addictive charm. But the nervousness returned as we made our way out to the gazebo, our third glass of merlot in hand. Wine couldn't save me this time.

This was a much more private area, where we couldn't

distract ourselves by watching others. There would be no changing the subject because I'd spotted an odd pair of diners nearby, no dessert menu to peer at if I didn't want eye contact. We would be alone under the soft lights of the rustic gazebo and the stars above.

I could only hope that a couple was already there and making out, so we would have to turn back. But no such luck; it was empty and seemed to be awaiting our arrival. We sat and calmly sipped our wine. I fell quiet, unable to find words.

"So what's been on your mind lately?" she asked, breaking the silence. There it was, the question I'd been waiting for. Dinner had been way too normal. There was no way it could remain that easy. It wasn't a casual question, like "How's your day going?" or "What's going on?" This line of inquiry meant that Lesley had seen something in me — a hovering entity clouding my mind.

"What do you mean? Just busy at work, lack of sleep, the usual."

I knew I sounded nervous. Paranoid, even. Maybe it was the alien wine, but I knew better. I was avoiding, as usual.

"Come on, Tryke, I know you better than that. What's really bothering you?"

Well, it was worth a try, but she was too smart and perceptive to let me get away with the normal excuses. If I were to confide in anyone about my latest endeavor, it would be Lesley. I wanted to tell her, to spill what I'd done and accomplished, and share the experience. But what if she was disgusted and appalled by the realness of it all? And what if she decided to turn me in? I trusted her, but this was different. I couldn't tell her anything yet.

I paused for believability. "I'm worried about my mom. Mainly her mood, and the pile of bills that were left after my father's funeral. I've been trying to help her with them, but I can only do so much." I wasn't lying. I was truly worried about my mother. What's wrong with a little added drama?

She scooted closer to me. "I can help some, if you let me.

With money or just visiting with her. I'm sure she could use some woman talk."

"I can't take your money," I said. "We'll be fine. I just have to get her on a budget, at least for a few months."

"Then what about visiting with her? Can't I at least do that? I mean if she wouldn't mind, of course. I want to do something. I feel helpless."

How was I going to divert this one? Visits with my mom would most likely lead to further commitment. My mom may even guilt me into further involvement. Think, Tryke, think. And quickly, before she catches you thinking.

"Let me talk to her about it first. I don't want to throw anything at her unexpectedly, with her fragile state and all." Quick save, but Lesley won't forget about it. I'll have to face it again, and soon, no doubt.

She set her wine glass down and hugged me, resting her head on my shoulder. It felt awkward at first, but after a few seconds I gave in and hugged her back with my free arm. I was still a little apprehensive about the touching.

And then something happened that caught me completely off guard. I didn't know how to respond. She kissed me. It was warm and soft and it felt really good. Sure, I'd kissed girls before, but none had been so real and passionate. Her lips meant everything they were doing. I wanted to return the favor, a meaningful and passionate touch, but I wasn't sure how. I had never been in the situation of actually experiencing something more than lust. I felt terrible, confused, and embarrassed. I slipped away, dropping my glass on the gazebo floor and spilling the red liquid.

"I'm sorry," she said. "I didn't mean to come on so strong. This night was just… so perfect."

"No, I'm sorry," I said. "I didn't mean to —" She stopped me.

"I understand. We'll take this a little slower."

We sat quietly under the glow of the gazebo's lights, her head gently resting on my shoulder. Sometimes the silence says enough.

• • •

The drive back to her house was again quiet. I was glad she didn't live far away. I felt completely helpless, but somehow she understood. At least she said so. I didn't know if I had screwed up my chance with the only girl I could ever see myself with, long term. I hoped I was just being paranoid again.

I walked her to the front door. "I'm sorry about the gazebo thing," I said. "I hope you'll forgive me."

She hugged me. "There's nothing to forgive. We're just starting this between us. It takes time." She kissed me on the cheek and went inside.

My drive home left me with a lot to think about. Why was it that I could see people in total mayhem and operate calmly and efficiently? How did that come second nature to me, while dinner with a beautiful woman was mysteriously difficult? I didn't recall ever being baffled by a woman before this one. I had always kept it straightforward for a reason.

But Lesley had me stumped, for the first time in my life. That meant something, right? It wasn't an epiphany or anything, but it certainly made me think. We would go on a second date, and a third, but then what? If she did get accepted to medical school, she would probably have to move. And the invitation she used to lure me in would be reinstated. I felt overwhelmed.

Chapter 24

I walked to my mom's house around five-thirty. She told me dinner would be ready by six and to come over whenever I wanted. My plan after we ate dinner was to find out all I could about the man who had killed my aunt and uncle, and nearly me. I knew I would have to do further research, but it was at least a start. Besides, a visit with one another usually did both of us some good.

My mom greeted me at the door with a hug, and the aroma of savory beef and mushroom gravy cooked to perfection over many hours instantly brought back memories of Thursday supper with my parents. Those were pleasant times that I was always glad to relive.

The hug was an odd but welcome sentiment. She hadn't been the initiator in a long while, and the unexpected affection made me smile. But I didn't celebrate just yet. Her eyes were still far away from bright and colorful, occasionally-off-tune, whistling rainbows.

"It smells good," I said, taking a seat at the kitchen table.

"It was your father's favorite, too. I could always count on making my men happy. On Thursdays, anyway."

"You made us happy every day, Mom," I said.

"Charming, just like him. That's how he hooked me, you know. We met at the supermarket. Do you remember the story?"

"Faintly. Remind me." I would on occasion pretend to have temporary amnesia, knowing she wanted to talk about him. Of course I remembered the story, but it seemed therapeutic for her to tell it again.

She began to describe how my father had mesmerized her with his broad smile. And how she eavesdropped on him during one of his generous moments spent helping a customer. As she told the story, I noticed that she still had a place set for him at the table. I didn't think it was a healthy thing to do, but I hadn't said anything about it yet. I assumed in time it would pass, and she would let go of the physical part of his world.

"Perfect, as always," I said, taking a bite of the steaming, savory tender roast. The gravy was my favorite, and a good companion to the soft, buttery yeast rolls.

"Thank you," she said. The plate she had made for herself sat untouched in front of her.

"Aren't you going to eat?"

"I'll reheat it and eat it later," she said. "I had a big lunch." I didn't press the matter. After my dad's funeral she'd lost a few too many pounds, but thankfully she had slowly gained most of them back.

"So," I began. "I've been thinking about the story you told me. About your sister and her husband. The car wreck. I'm sorry to bring it back up, but I had some more dreams. I think I just need some closure."

"What would you like to know?"

"You said that the guy had warrants out for his arrest. Do you remember what they were for? Is there anything else you can tell me about him? I guess I was just wondering, really hoping, that he had showed some remorse for what he did."

"I was too angry and upset at the time to go to his trial, but your father went. He came home disgusted at the way the man handled himself. Mainly his arrogance. But your father told me something that was even more upsetting. He said that the man had a grin on his face when the sentence was read."

"It doesn't make sense," I said," how the world works at times. How some people are."

"No, it doesn't." Her mouth twitched and she made a fist with her right hand. "He'd been in jail a few times before. He'd killed others in similar accidents. But there wasn't enough evidence to convict him, supposedly. More of our judicial system failures." She sighed and unclenched her fist. "But what's done is done, I suppose. There's nothing left to do but move on."

Though she had calmed down, there was still an angry flare in her eyes that told me she was never going to completely let it go, no matter how self-assuring her words were.

"Do you mind if I take a look at the article you cut out?"

"I don't mind," she said, "but I don't know what you hope to find."

"Closure," I said. "Time to move on, right?"

"If it will help you, then sure. Just a moment and I'll go get it."

She returned a few minutes later with the newspaper article. I scanned it, making an effort to linger. I wanted to appear as though I were really searching for closure. There you are, you bastard. His name amplified on the page. The article read: *Steve Horning was the driver of a vehicle that, according to witnesses, collided with another after his vehicle swerved into oncoming traffic. Two adult occupants in the other vehicle were killed on impact. A baby, seated in the rear seat, survived and was taken to a nearby hospital with minor injuries.*

The article went on to say that Horning was from

Shreveport, Louisiana. That was only two and a half hours away. Not terribly far, but it did cause a small problem. How was I going to get him here to my lab? And was he even still alive?

"I've seen enough," I said. "I think I'm good now."

"He'll get what he deserves one day, don't you worry," she said, placing a hand on my shoulder and squeezing. Yes, he will and very soon, I thought to myself. I had managed to rekindle some stored away fury in my mom once again, but it was necessary.

"I know he will," I said. "It all works out in the end."

She continued to squeeze my shoulder, silently staring forward. After a few moments, I broke the silence. "I need to get going."

"Okay," she said, slowly releasing her grip on my shoulder. "Thank you for the visit."

"Thank you. And thanks again for dinner. It was great, as always."

"Before you leave, give me a second so I can make you a plate to go."

A minute later, she handed me a paper bag with a plastic container full of roast. I kissed her cheek and said good-bye.

• • •

The Internet is a giant pool of knowledge waiting to be examined. You can find anything, or anyone, if you know what you're doing. And thanks to a couple of acquaintances in college, I knew just enough hacking tricks to get me through the security of a midsize city driver's license bureau. If Horning was still alive I wasn't even sure if he would still have a license, considering his record. Then again, he had slipped through the system before.

After a few well-placed keystrokes, Steve Horning's face appeared on my computer screen. He was a bald man, 51 years old with a colossal dirt-brown mustache. He appeared haggard, worn from taking too many innocent lives, I imagined. His soul would be grateful when it was all over.

• • •

I spent most of my last day off planning out the trip to Shreveport. I had only been there a couple of times with my dad when I was a teenager. It would be fitting to bring Mr. Horning back here. Besides, I didn't feel comfortable performing the act on the road. I needed it to be right, and for that, it would have to end where it began.

When I pulled into the station parking lot, Dave was smiling and polishing his new prize with an old t-shirt. It was a twenty-three-foot white Bayliner with a blue stripe across the bow, and I had to admit it looked good on him. He'd be back to his old, structured self soon enough.

"You did it and did it right," I said, closing my truck door and slinging my duffel bag over my shoulder.

"Yeah, she's gorgeous. Now comes the hard part: naming her."

I had thought of this scenario before, what it would be like to own a boat. I even had a name picked out. *Soul of the Sea.* Maybe one day, who knows?

"What have you come up with so far?" I asked.

"Nothing really. I thought about naming it Claire just to spite her, but I'm moving on. Besides, knowing how vain she is, she'd think it was a tribute to her."

"Yeah, probably best not to use her name," I said. The bell sounded. I didn't hear what the call was or to where, only the words "medic" and "fifteen." I hurriedly changed and hopped into the rig, where Dave was patiently waiting and staring out the front glass with a dazed grin. He was obviously still in his heavenly state, daydreaming of the day when he would be taking his new boat out on the water.

"Can't take your mind off her can you?" I said.

"Nope," he said, and sighed dreamily. "So where're we going?"

I looked down at the screen as I was buttoning my shirt. I

didn't recognize the address, but I knew it was near my neighborhood. The comment at the bottom of the screen cleared it up quickly. Usually the dispatcher would place a comment under an address if it were a well-known structure, like a mall or an office building. I stared at the four bold words typed out under the address. Speechless, I took a deep breath and read them again: ***abandoned Peter's grocery store.***

Chapter 25

After my brief moment of shock, I read the remaining information about the call: 42 y/o male assaulted in parking lot. I felt a slight wave of relief brush over me, but I wasn't celebrating just yet. The police were dispatched on all assault calls.

I began running all of my cautious habits through my head and making sure I hadn't skipped any. I carefully wiped down the entire lab, usually twice, and meticulously removed and disposed of any biohazard materials. I covered the equipment with an old sheet, keeping the appearance of an abandoned business.

Still, the situation was unnerving. If the equipment was found, they could trace it back to the training facility and everyone who had access to it. I didn't officially have access, but enough snooping could call attention to me. I had been out there often, being my helpful self, while planning my venture.

We were supposed to wait for the police to clear any

scene, especially on an assault, before we proceeded. I was willing to risk ignoring policy, but I also had to convince Dave to push past the rules. That could never have happened with the old Dave.

"Heading over to your neck of the woods," Dave said cheerily, obviously still dreaming of his boat.

"Yep," I said. "Hey, what do you say we get there first and head this guy off before the police convince him that he needs to go to the hospital?"

Avoiding a report or a trip to the hospital was always a convincing argument, especially now, since his new boat was waiting on him. It was obvious he didn't want to leave her so soon.

He was twisting his lips, contemplating my suggestion.

"Your boat looked awfully lonely as we pulled out of the station," I said.

"You have a point. Let's get this over with." I smiled nervously as he flipped on the lights and punched the gas pedal to the floor.

When we arrived on scene a few minutes later, the police hadn't arrived yet. The parking lot was mostly empty, except for a few crumpled boxes and a rusted grocery cart. Okay, now where was the man who had supposedly been assaulted? Maybe he had gone home to sleep off the beating. Wishful thinking.

"Where the hell is this guy?" Dave asked, shifting the rig into Park and shutting the light bar switch off. He picked up the radio mic.

"Dispatch, this is Medic 15."

"Go ahead, Medic 15, with your traffic."

"Do you have any other information for us? There's no one in this parking lot."

"That's all the information the caller gave us," the female dispatcher said. "Is a police unit on scene yet?"

"Crap," Dave said. "Now what do I say to them? They know we're supposed to wait for the police. Oh, well."

"Medic 15?" dispatch repeated.

"Police not on scene," Dave said. "We're going to drive around to the rear of the building and see if we can find anyone there."

"Dispatch copies, Medic 15. Use caution."

"Whatever," Dave said to me. "We'll just say we thought we saw a police car across the parking lot when we arrived."

"I saw one, I swear," I said.

We drove around to the back of the grocery store, stopping at the dock where the eighteen-wheelers delivered their loads, as do I on occasion. A man who looked to be in his mid-forties was seated under an awning with his back pressed against a door. His suit was torn, and there was blood smeared across his nose and ears. More disturbing to me, behind that door were the stairs leading to my lab.

"Over there," I said, pointing toward the man.

I rolled down my window as Dave pulled up next to him. "Where is the person who did this to you?" I asked. "Are they still around?"

"They ran that way," the man said, pointing east with a bloody handkerchief wadded in his hand.

I got out to check on the man while Dave radioed back to dispatch that we'd found the victim. "Where are you injured?" I asked, as he struggled to remove his jacket.

"I'll be all right," he said. "They just punched me a few times, took my wallet, and jacked my car. Couple of lucky punches before I could reach the gun under my seat."

"Here, wipe your face." I handed him two 4x4 bandages. He leaned up away from the door. "The police should be along in a few minutes," I said, and slyly stepped behind him and nudged the door open. I glanced up the stairwell to make sure that the door at the top was still sealed shut. "Were they hiding in here when they attacked you?" I asked.

"No, they jacked me by the street and dumped me out back here." I was temporarily relieved, but I still didn't want the police snooping around so close to the entrance to my lab. I walked him around to the front while Dave followed in the rig. "The police can find us easier here," I told the man.

A few minutes later, a police unit pulled into the parking lot. I greeted the officer at his car and relayed the situation, hoping it would help expedite his report so he could get the hell away from the area. The officer seemed to like my idea of hurrying the call. The police dislike filling out reports even more than we do.

"Are we good?" Dave asked when I got back in the rig.

"Yeah, he's all right. And he's their problem now."

"How about some lunch? What's good around here, any home diners or hidden gems?"

I averted my gaze from the side mirror, where I was anxiously watching the grocery store parking lot fade slowly away in the distance. I glanced at my watch. "It's only ten o'clock," I said. I worried the police might move around to the back to reenact the crime. My paranoia was getting the better of me again. This wasn't some TV drama where they examine every minute detail. As I looked from my watch back to the mirror, I saw that they were still in front of the building.

"I didn't eat breakfast," Dave said. I didn't reply. He took my silence as disbelief. "Honestly, I haven't."

"Right," I said, smirking. I couldn't manage a laugh at the moment, not with my nerves still poking at me. "Take a right on Milton Street here. There's a place called "One Flew Over" on the left, a block up."

"They don't have a flock of psych patients cooking the food there, do they?"

"No, but the pie will drive you nuts. Trust me, it's good. That's what they're known for."

• • •

The diner was busy for a weekday, mid-morning. I pointed to the pie case before we sat down at the bar. Dave's greedy eyes grew wide at the variety. The strawberry had always been my favorite since I was a kid, when my dad took me there on Saturday mornings. He always had a slice of banana cream pie after his grits and toast. He adored the pie so much that he even let me indulge in a piece for breakfast. Of course, we never revealed our secret to my mother.

Dana brought my pie and Dave's order of scrambled eggs and grits. I had forgotten how good pie was in the morning, and savored each bite of sweet, creamy goodness.

"Tryke, what're you doing over here this time of morning?" Dana asked in her grainy smokers voice. She fit the typical diner waitress stereotype. She's thin as a rail with vein-ridden hands that were constantly wielding a cigarette. She's only in her fifties, but the years have hardly been kind to her, and give the impression that she's on her way out.

"Some guy got punched a few times," I said, "and his car stolen. Right down the street."

She shook her head in disgust. "That stuff never used to happen in this town. Since those damn punks started leaving the city and migrating here, it's been going downhill."

As I continued to enjoy my pie, I noticed a peculiar man enter the diner. He wore narrow shades under his dark brown cowboy hat, a suit jacket, jeans, and boots. At first glance, you might think he was a detective or some sort of lawman, but not me. He slowly made his way to the bar stools and stopped a few feet away. I lowered my fork and looked up at the man. He removed his shades, revealing worn brown eyes and well-developed crow's feet.

"How are you, Tryke?" he said placing a gripping hand on my shoulder.

"Good, Uncle Frank, how are you?"

"Can't complain. Heard the assault call on the radio a few minutes ago. Damn assholes around here get worse everyday." My dad's brother Frank was a police officer in the city for fifteen years before making detective and going into homicide. He claimed to be retiring soon, but I doubt he would. He loved the long hours even before his wife died.

Also, retirement would mean that he'd have to give up his "brown horse," as he referred to the Crown Victoria police issue vehicle that he drives. He still thinks it's the 1800s and he's Wyatt Earp.

"Just coffee, honey, black," he told Dana.

I introduced Dave to Frank. They shook hands and Dave managed to get out a short greeting between mouthfuls of grits. "You have to excuse him," I said. "He doesn't stop eating for anything." Uncle Frank grinned and took a sip of his coffee. Dave patted me on the shoulder with an extended middle finger gesture, a response to my comment.

"So how's your mother doing?" Frank asked.

"She's doing better," I said. "I visit her pretty often."

"You're a good son. She needs that." I felt sorry for him at times. He and his wife could never have kids. He was a strong man, but he would have appreciated a son or daughter to talk to, especially after his wife died.

"You should go by and see her sometime," I said. "She'd like it."

"It has been a while. I'll make it a point to stop by next week sometime."

I'd heard those words before. He never follows through and I thought I knew why. My mom and the house remind him too much of his brother. The four of them played cards every Friday night, laughing and clanking poker chips until the early morning hours.

Frank unhooked his radio from his belt and listened to the chatter. I turned to Dave. "Are you full yet?"

"I will be after that poor, lonely chocolate pie is in my stomach. You did say I had to try the pie here." Dave sounded as though I were accusing him with my stare. His eating habits had brought on paranoia.

"Yes, I did," I said.

Uncle Frank got up and put a dollar on the counter. "You boys want to tag along? They might have that vehicle that was stolen from the call y'all were just on. They're in pursuit right now."

"Dave, how 'bout it?" I could tell the chocolate pie monster was tugging at his stomach, but he also loved anything to do with police chases. The dilemma was too much for him, so I stepped in. "Dana, can you box him a piece of chocolate pie up real fast? We have a call."

"Sure thing, honey," she said, hurrying to the pie case.

Dave thanked me as we walked out to the rig, vigilantly guarding his small white take-out box. "We'll follow along until we get a call," I told Frank.

"Okay," Frank said. "They're on Second Street about to approach Church." He turned around before getting into his car. "Oh, one second, Tryke." He handed me his detective card with a cell phone number printed on it. "I know you have my number, but this is a reminder to keep in touch. Let's get your mother out of the house. We'll go out to dinner one night. My treat."

"Sounds good," I said, but I didn't believe a word of it.

"You drive," Dave said. "I feel sick."

"And you were about to eat that pie?"

"Yeah."

Before I got into the rig, I glanced down at the card Frank had just handed me. The phone number wasn't new to me; I even had it saved in my cell phone. But as I sat staring at the card the number suddenly screamed at me in 3D: 325-4562. Remove the slash and add a dash and you have a phone number — how cleverly simple of my dad. It was an exciting revelation. That is, if it actually turned out to be something, and my uncle doesn't direct me to the psych ward.

• • •

We followed Frank's brown horse back toward the city. I knew it would only be a matter of time before dispatch sent us on a call, but I was being optimistic. I wanted to see the chase and the ending result. Not to mention, I was eager to confront my uncle about the numbers.

We entered the toll way a few hundred yards behind the pursuit that was taking place. Frank galloped up to the five police vehicles that were following closely behind the fleeing compact car. The thieves' vehicle was somehow holding together and moving quite fast, despite two blown tires.

"They're determined to make this last," I said.

"This is freaking awesome," Dave said, gaining back some of his lost momentum. "Those bastards are going down. I just hope they either shoot them dead or not at all. I don't feel like transporting anyone right now."

From the way the police cars were jockeying around, it looked as if they were getting ready to try the "pit" maneuver. The police use their front bumper and press it against the rear side of the other vehicle to cause it to turn sideways. They can then box the car in and hopefully make it stop. But as my uncle explained to me, that maneuver doesn't always work, and if the assailants have guns, things can escalate into a messy, close range-shooting battle.

"There's too much traffic for them to try that pit thingy they do," Dave said. "Hopefully they'll wait till they can control the traffic, and block some entrances to the toll-way."

"We're about to find out." We passed another on ramp and sure enough a police car moved ahead to block oncoming traffic. "Now lets see what these thieves decide to do," I said.

"I bet they keep going until they run out of gas," Dave said

"Here's their chance to exit," I said. Herndon Street was the next exit and it would be very crowded this time of day. "Hopefully, one of the police cars will block them, if they do decide to go that route. It's way too busy of an area to take this chase there."

The thieves' vehicle looked to be edging toward the exit. One of the pursuing police cars pulled past the car in an attempt to dissuade them from taking the Herndon exit. They weren't going to be manipulated, though, and jerked the struggling vehicle to the right, ramming the police car and causing it to flip onto its side. It slid down the toll way, sending sparks into the air.

"Whoa, now that's fucked up," Dave said, as the police car finally came to a sliding halt. "Dammit, now we have to stop and check on him. We're going to miss the rest of the chase." The thieves took the Herndon exit, after all.

"Not if it ends here," I said. We stopped at the top of the ramp and watched. There were two eighteen-wheelers at the light at the bottom of the exit ramp. "They have nowhere to go unless those trucks move." The car wasn't slowing down. "Those idiots think those eighteen-wheelers are just going to automatically move for them?" We watched as the car plummeted into the rear of the truck in the right lane. The hood of the car crushed like an empty soda can.

"We're going to need another rig here," Dave said, and radioed dispatch. I walked over to check on the officer, who was already out of his vehicle. He waved me off, telling me he was fine. Cops don't typically want us to assist them unless they are unconscious. Not that they don't trust us, but they don't want to appear weak in front of their comrades.

Once the police had secured the scene, my uncle motioned us to approach the vehicle. We pulled the rig down the exit ramp to the wreckage. As I opened my door, Frank said, "I don't think you boys will be transporting either of them to a hospital." I knew what that meant: a good ole DRT.

Frank was right. As we approached the mangled car the smell of radiator fluids and burnt tires filled my nostrils. The hood of the vehicle was reduced to an eighth of its regular size. Luckily, the door was off its hinges and I could get in. Not that it mattered at that point.

Blood was splattered along the dash and the back of the eighteen-wheeler's doors. There were two men in the front seat. The passenger's head was sunk halfway into the dash and his right arm was dangling out the window. The driver's neck was bent completely to the left side and part of the windshield was sitting in the center of his head like a hood ornament. I checked the driver's pulse on his wrist, because there was no way I was finding his carotid in that mess. Dave checked the other guy.

I radioed dispatch to cancel the responding unit and to put us back in service. We only had one yellow blanket left on the rig, which I used to cover both of the bodies in the front seat. It would have to do until the coroner arrived. Besides, it wouldn't hurt for a few citizens to view justice, as ugly as it was at times. The police should've snapped a photo and plastered it onto a billboard as a deterrent.

Before we left the scene and while Dave was in the rig on his cell phone, I walked over to my Uncle Frank. He was seated in his car entering something into his cell phone. The driver's side door was hanging open. I was about to either unlock a hidden code or sound insane.

"Did my dad…?" He didn't look up as I stumbled for the right words. I cleared my throat. "Did my dad leave something with you, something for me? I found these numbers that turned out to be —"

He stopped me with a raised hand, not needing further explanation. He put down his cell phone and looked up at me with a stern, unwavering face. He sighed and reached over to his glove compartment and pulled out a sealed worn envelope. He handed it to me with a grin. "I don't know what's written in there and it's none of my business. Your father instructed me to give this to you if you ever came to me with questions."

I held the envelope in disbelief. The numbers were real. I wasn't insane after all. The only thing I could manage to say was, "Thank you."

"You're welcome," he said. "Your father was a good man. Don't you ever forget that."

"He still is," I said.

Frank smiled, and tipped his cowboy hat.

• • •

Despite my growing anticipation I didn't open the envelope at work. I had no idea what it held, and most importantly, how I would react. I kept it folded in my back pocket.

When I got home the next morning, I placed my dad's journal next to me on the table just in case there happened to be more damn riddles hidden. I hoped not. I was tired and needed straightforward answers. Taking a deep breath, I slid my pocketknife along the sealed edge of the envelope.

Son, if you're reading this, then either one of two things has happened: you found my journal and have figured out the code, or sadly, your uncle has seen something inside of you that I'm to blame for. If the latter is the case, then I'm truly sorry and my journal is hidden on my bookshelf. You'll find it easily enough. Just remember Sherlock. Your mother and I disagreed on whether to tell you about my sickness. She thought she was protecting you. I want you to know who I am, as painful as it may be to absorb. Every day since the voices began, they have increased. They're painful and unbearable, constantly twisting my thoughts to bend to their will. My journal helped in the beginning, reading the thoughts after I wrote them, hoping that my struggling mind would see how irrational they were and correct them. But they became too powerful, overpowering the rational part of my brain. That's when I turned to your mother for help. I never told her about the journal, thinking the horrible words that I wrote would have been too painful to ingest. Your mother and I have battled this together, without seeking outside help. That was on my insistence. I feared the ridicule and judgment from society, as well as the beady eyes and sly pen marks of a staring psychiatrist. I also feared the inside of a psych ward. But I would gladly endure all of those to not have my worst fear come to life — to pass this horror onto you. I knew about my pancreatic cancer early on, though I never told you or your mother until it reached Stage Four. I am exhausted, worn to my bones. I can't take the sadness, the constant fight any longer. I'm sorry for leaving you so soon, but now you at least know the reason. I made a mistake. I want you to know it's okay to seek help. There were treatments available that could have made my life easier. By the time my mind allowed me to accept them, it was too late. The cancer had spread. There are much worse things in the world than the inside of a psychiatrist's office. Each time I heard a voice, I sent out a prayer that you be spared the hell I have had to endure. If you are hearing voices, then the Gamemakers have won another round, and for that I am also sorry. You've always been strong and will find a way to win your own battles in time, but please don't make the same mistakes I did. Son, I ask only one more thing of you: keep this knowledge I have shared here away from your mother. I prefer her not being angry with me in the afterlife. I love you.

   Dad

That's it? He wanted me to know that he never sought treatment for the voices or the cancer? He wants me to seek treatment? I'm not hearing voices. My uncle hadn't tracked me down. I found the numbers. And now I can never consult with the one person he confided in. What was I supposed to do with all of this? And who were these Gamemakers?

I was just frustrated, and wanted there to be more. Deep down I wanted my dad to have his own secret lair where he served justice. I wanted there to be pages of fatherly advice on how to proceed. But the sad truth was staring me down. I was on my own.

Chapter 26

I was on the road. I took a vacation shift from work, which was something I rarely did, and that left Dave curious when I told him. I didn't elaborate on the reason for taking off, which I knew would drive him crazy.

I planned for an afternoon of surveillance. If everything panned out, I could bring Mr. Horning back with me in the morning. I didn't have a plan B, so it had to work.

Interstate 20 took me all the way into Shreveport. The trip was supposed to take two and a half hours, but the rain and overly-cautious drivers added thirty minutes.

The call volume in Shreveport is incredibly high for its size. Per capita, their city made more calls than ours, and that's saying something. One of our medics, Carl, worked there before moving to Dallas and regaled us with many dark tales about certain areas of town. Thankfully, I had my GPS.

Mr. Horning's address popped up on the screen when I powered on the GPS: 1212 E. Rankin Street. It looked to be right off the interstate. Following the GPS's instructions, I took the next exit. Bars on store windows and sporadic abandoned houses were good indicators of the type of neighborhood I was entering. It was a fitting place for this Horning guy to reside.

Just as I thought, his street wasn't far from the interstate, and that made an easy exit if things went bad. Also, I didn't have to venture too far into the depths of the inner city. His small house sat on a corner lot. Half of the puke-green siding was peeling back and the windows were dark grey, as if the house had once been filled with smoke. In the driveway was the '82 yellow Bug that he had registered to him. I passed by slowly and matched his license plate with the numbers I had written down. I was in the right spot.

I drove around the block to check everything out, mostly to make sure no cops were lingering about, though I doubted any cop would be around there, enjoying his lunch under a nice shade tree and waving to the local patrons. I unpacked my lunch and decided to settle under a large pine tree, diagonally across from his house. I didn't know what he did for a living, if he did anything, and I had to be patient. It might take all afternoon for the scumbag to show his face. I was lucky that he was even home.

While I ate my turkey and cheese sandwich on wheat, there wasn't much happening on the street, just a few punks with sagging pants who would glance my way and taunt me with their stares. It was amusing, and normally I would taunt back. But I had a clear mission, and didn't need some random juvenile delinquent messing up my plans. I kept to myself and avoided eye contact. I only had room in my truck for Mr. Horning.

An hour later, a man emerged from the front door of the house as I was sipping on the last of my Diet Coke. I lowered my sunglasses to get a better look. His mustache couldn't be duplicated, and he was still bald and short. This was my man. But what was he wearing? It looked to be some sort of uniform with… I squinted. A badge?

There was no way that scumbag was a police officer. There was something else going on. He slung the last bite of his doughnut into the yard and then yanked a few times on the stubborn rusted door handle of his yellow Bug before it squealed open. A plume of heavy smoke blew out of the exhaust when he finally got the engine started.

I followed him for a few miles as he drove into a gated neighborhood. He punched in a code on the entrance pad, opening the gate, and then pulled around the corner and parked. He was a damn security guard!

Carrying a black lunch pail, he entered the small guard shack. He appeared to be alone. He hadn't relieved anyone, which meant they likely kept security only at night. I parked a safe distance away, in an empty playground parking lot across the street.

• • •

The neighborhood traffic going in and out slowed to almost nothing after eight o'clock. It was a weekday, and most normal people were putting their kids to sleep or relaxing in front of the TV. The guard shack appeared to be rudimentary. I saw no cameras. My guess was that the whole shack and guard were merely a visual deterrence, and his only job was to operate the electric gate and maybe write down license plate numbers if he felt like it. That shouldn't be too difficult for a guy who used vehicles to slaughter innocent families.

I waited until 0100 so he could get nice and settled for the evening. While I waited, I pondered how the scenario was going to play out — not so much the initial act, but the aftermath. His vehicle was parked close by and many people saw him as they entered and left during the evening. I wasn't too concerned about the rest of the night, but tomorrow evening when he didn't show up for work, it would certainly cause suspicion, especially with his yellow VW parked on the side.

I briefly thought about performing the act locally, at his house, but I didn't have all of my equipment. Besides, that wouldn't be conducive to my whole process. He needed to be back where it all began, so he could be released in a suitable manner.

It was time. I rolled down my window to let in the quiet. Closing my eyes, I deeply inhaled the humid night air. I pulled up to the gate as if I lived there and stopped beside the open glass door to the shack. He was sound asleep with his stubby feet propped on the counter. Before I proceeded, I needed to be absolutely sure there weren't any hidden cameras. I craned my neck to peer inside the small room. There was only a small black and white TV that was set to static. There were no radios that I could see. Only a phone against the far wall.

I slammed my left hand against the side of my truck. He jumped from his slumber, knocking an empty Styrofoam cup from the counter. I stifled a laugh as he shuffled to his feet and straightened his pants and shirt. I tipped my hat down so he couldn't see my face. It was for annoyance purposes only. I didn't care if he saw me. He would see me soon enough.

His voice sounded old and forced for a man in his fifties.

"What's your business here?" It was obvious he didn't get too many people at that hour, and he didn't recognize my truck, so he knew I didn't live there.

"I'm visiting an old friend," I said in a friendly tone. I raised my hat so he could see my smiling face. He now had a clipboard in his hands and was checking some sort of guest list as if to appear professional.

"What's the address you're heading to?" he asked, staring down at the board with a pen in hand.

"Actually I'm here to visit Steve Horning." He immediately raised his eyes from the board to mine. I was grinning. "You don't remember me?"

He looked uneasy. I mean, who shows up out of nowhere at one o'clock in the morning for a reunion? He looked at me more closely, but still no recollection in his eyes. Not that there should have been. I'd never met the guy.

"No… Who are you?"

My right hand was steady and gloved in dark latex. "Have you ever visited Dallas, Texas?" I said in a soft whisper. I figured it would have spooked him, but it didn't. He was still searching for a solution to my riddle and becoming frustrated, tapping his pen repetitively on the clipboard.

I decided to cheer up the conversation a little. "I'm Tom, you old fool. It's been too long!" I laughed out loud like we were old friends. Everyone has a friend or acquaintance named Tom or Tommy. He lowered his heavy shoulders and took a step closer to my truck, trying to get a better view of me through squinted eyes.

"Tom who?" he asked, placing a hand on my window seal. Thankfully, our vision fades as we get older, or he would have noticed when I clumsily hit the steering wheel with my right hand and nearly dropped the needle. He must have thought I was reaching my hand out to shake his.

He went down quickly. I secured him in the back seat for the long drive and retrieved his car keys from his pocket. I hurriedly got into his rusted car and pulled it forward behind a large tree covered by thick brush. The car was a mess, with empty fast food wrappers and a stench of soiled socks. I wasn't surprised. The car fit perfectly in the hidden spot. It would stay out of sight for a few days.

• • •

He snored the entire trip back. As annoying as it was, I was thankful he didn't wake up. It would have brought on unnecessary suspicion, not to mention an awkward conversation, if a patrolling state trooper had been in the vicinity while I was pulled over on the side of the interstate administering another dose.

I made it back by 0430 and unloaded Mr. Horning. I needed to get him up the stairs and secured before dawn.

• • •

I woke to a shuffling sound and banging metal. I looked down at my watch, 1130. The muffled sound of the generator must have allowed me to drift off longer than I normally could have.

"Good morning, Mr. Horning," I said.

He turned his head toward me, wrinkling his brow and mumbling something through the piece of cloth that I had wrapped around his mouth. I'm sure it was some sort of morning greeting, just not as friendly as mine.

I got up and stood over him. "I trust you are well rested, but I'm not quite ready to release you just yet. We'll have our conversation soon enough." Seconds later, he was snoring again after I gave him another dose of slumber. "I'm hungry and we've got a long night ahead of us," I said. "I'll be back in a little while. You stay put."

• • •

My mom's house was the perfect distance away to get some lunch and some leftovers for dinner. I didn't want to go out again once I'd returned. It was too risky. I was already risking enough by leaving this time.

She looked pleasantly surprised when I opened the door. She rarely saw me at lunchtime unless it was one of my days off, and with my sleeping habits, it still almost never happened.

"What are you doing up so early?" she asked as I entered. She looked good. She didn't have that permanent solemn expression plastered on her face anymore. It was another step out from the depths.

"I didn't have any groceries in my apartment, and I thought we could have some lunch together."

"I'm not hungry," she said, "but I can whip you up something. How about a grilled cheese sandwich and some chips, and another to go?"

"Sounds perfect, thank you. Hey, I saw Uncle Frank the other day."

"Oh, so how's he doing?" she asked, turning the surface knob on the stove. She slid a pad of butter from a knife onto a non-stick pan.

"He looked good. He still thinks he's Wyatt Earp running around in his detective car. I wonder if he'll ever retire."

"Probably not until he's forced to. His wife was the only one who could get him to slow down. It's probably good for him to keep going. Sometimes I wish I had worked after your father died." She fell silent for a moment. Not the silence again. It was time to change the subject. "I've been thinking about taking an art class," she spouted. Whew, that was close. I thought I had lost her again.

"That's a great idea," I said. "You were always so good at it. I don't know why you ever stopped." My dad told me that mom painted a lot before I was born, but pretty much gave it up to spend time raising me. Now I was wondering if she had to quit to help my dad with his voices. Maybe taking on such a dark and disembodied foe had drained her creativity. I desperately wanted to ask her about it, but I couldn't. It was my dad's last wish.

"I don't know, lack of energy and ideas I suppose. But I want to be around other artists. I think it will help, and it will get me out of the house." She didn't know how long I'd waited to hear her say those words.

But I needed to get back to my lab. Even though I'd given Mr. Horning enough sedative for a small rhino, it still made me nervous to leave him alone; anything could happen. I kissed her on the forehead and thanked her again for lunch. Before I left I made one more comment to promote the art class.

I was having a pretty good day. I retrieved Mr. Horning, my mom seemed to be recovering, and a large batch of thick clouds was moving in from the west and offering some future relief to the scorching sun overhead.

Halfway back to the lab, my phone vibrated in my pocket. I pulled it out and was surprised to see the number. I didn't get very many calls. My mom would call on occasion, and sometimes my relief at the station would phone to say they were running behind. And lately, Lesley. I answered.

"Tryke." It was Dave.

"Yep, it's me," I said. "What can I do for you, Dave?"

"Why didn't you tell me?" he asked. He sounded frantic.

Chapter 27

Not many things are kept secret for long around the station, or hospitals, for that matter. And don't let the stereotype fool you: guys are much worse than women when it comes to spreading rumors.

"What was I supposed to tell you?" I asked Dave. I felt a nasty feeling in my stomach when the thought of Mr. Horning alone in my lab crossed my mind. Where was Dave? Had he gone there?

"Why the hell didn't you tell me about your date with Lesley, you sly dog?"

I relaxed my tense shoulders. "Oh… that. I didn't think I needed to consult with you when it came to my personal life. What little I have of one."

"Come on, I'm your partner. Besides, I told you about my failed marriage." He had a point, but I never pried. Actually, he hadn't given me a choice but to listen and intervene. He was a regular Crying Betty during the separation period with his wife.

"Yeah," I said. "I guess I should have told you. I just didn't think it was a big deal."

"Not a big deal?! Are you kidding me? Since the first time you two met, I've watched her throw herself at you every time we dropped someone off at that hospital. Everyone kept asking when you were going to either admit you were gay or ask her out."

"Wait a damn minute! There was talk about me being gay?"

He fell silent for a moment. "Yeah, but I told those morons that you just liked being alone and preferred not to be in a relationship. They bought it, but I'm not sure how much longer I could have kept that story going. Anyway, you're in the clear now."

"Thanks, I'm so relieved. I can get back to my life and the bystanders can finally take a breath. I had no idea I was that entertaining."

"You know women, and heck, guys too. They like to talk about other people, partly to draw attention away from themselves."

"I guess. But can we finish discussing my sexuality on our next shift? I have some things I need to take care of." I had reached the bottom of the stairs leading to my lab. I was eager to power up the equipment and begin a most memorable release party.

"Sure thing. You only took off the one shift, right?"

"Yeah."

"Okay, see you then. And tell Lesley I said hi."

"Whatever," I said, and hung up the phone.

I was still in a good mood, despite Dave's phone call and the intrusion into my personal life. I guess it was inevitable that people would find out. Relationships in general made me nervous, and talking to others about a brand new one didn't interest me. Dave liked to open up about his feelings and troubles, but mine are good right where they are, hidden behind an impenetrable door.

After climbing the stairs, I activated the alarm at the top. Mr. Horning was right where I had left him: still passed out and firmly secured to the metal table. I didn't like having to leave my work when it was incomplete, but I knew it was going to be a long night, and I was hungry. I couldn't enjoy a party on an empty stomach.

I had planned a little speech for my number-one customer. I needed him to know that his acts had consequences. We were going to take a journey together to serve a greater purpose. Hopefully, by the end, both of our needs would be satisfied.

As I sat in my trusty multi-use chair waiting for him to wake up, I felt my phone vibrate again. What was going on today? Why was I suddenly so popular? I didn't recognize the number, but there was something familiar about it, and that motivated me to answer. I walked to the top of the stairs, just in case Mr. Horning decided to regain consciousness and make a ruckus.

"This is Tryke," I said.

"Is this Tryke Harper, mother of Sylvia Harper?" a female's voice said.

"Yes, it is. What can I do for you?"

"My name is Melissa. I'm an RN at Mercy General. Your mother drove herself here about thirty minutes ago complaining of a headache. I'm afraid your mother has suffered a mild stroke."

I didn't hear the rest of her words. I became dizzy and confused. This couldn't be happening. My mother had a stroke and was in the hospital? I just left her an hour ago, and she was fine.

"Mr. Harper, are you there?"

"Yes… Sorry."

"She's stable at the moment. She asked me to call and tell you what was going on. We'll be moving her to room 232, and running a few more tests when our CT machine is back up. But she'll have to stay with us overnight for observation.

Maybe longer, depending on the results of the CT scan."

"Thank you, Melissa. Can you please tell her I'll be there as soon as I can?" I hung up and stared at the complication that was now shuffling around. I took a deep breath and pondered the situation. Our party would have to be postponed once again.

I checked my supply of meds. I had enough to keep him out for a while longer. On top of being worried about my mother, I now had the risk of leaving my work a second time. I grabbed my duffel bag and slipped back into my overalls.

On my way to the hospital, my phone vibrated yet again. This was getting ridiculous. I pulled my phone from my front pocket and glanced down at the number. This one I knew well.

"Hey, Tryke."

"Lesley, what's going on?"

"I just wanted to tell you that I had a really good time with you the other night, and was wondering when we were going to do it again?"

I didn't have an answer at that moment. I was juggling two complications already. "I… had a good time, too. We can do it again whenever you like."

"Am I interrupting something? You sound distracted."

"Yeah, sorry. I am a little distracted at the moment, but nothing I can't handle."

"Anything I can help you with?"

"No," I said quickly, and then immediately realized that I had spoken with too much curious conviction.

"Tryke, what's going on?"

"The hospital just called and said my mother had a stroke. I'm on my way up there now."

"That's horrible. Is she okay?"

"Yes, from what the nurse says. But their CT is down, so they really don't know the extent of what happened."

"I'm coming up there. I get off work in a few minutes."

"Lesley, you don't have to —"

"Tryke, it's no problem. I like being with you and if we're going to be dating, I want to be there for you." I knew Lesley well enough to realize that arguing would only make her more determined.

"Room 232 at Mercy," I said.

"I should be there within a half-hour."

"See you then," I said.

This was becoming a full-blown mess. Not only was my mom in the hospital and Mr. Horning patiently waiting in a sedative dream, but now Lesley was entering the picture. I had been hoping to make a quick visit to the hospital and then return to finish what I had begun.

• • •

I avoided going through the ER entrance. I didn't need anyone else knowing more of my personal business. Standing in the elevator, I tapped my foot nervously as two old ladies shuffled in. One of them lifted her shaking right index finger and moved it toward the buttons. I stared impatiently. She paused, inches from the circle that I was eager to light up for her, and looked to her friend to ask for the floor number.

"What floor?" I asked abrasively. It wasn't like me to lash out, especially to a stranger. And most especially to an elderly stranger.

The lady looked back at me as if I had just pushed her down a flight of stairs. "None of your business, young man." I would have laughed at such a response if I hadn't been so scattered and tense.

"Sorry," I said.

Her friend pressed the button quickly. The doors shut and I had to ride up with them for just one floor. As I left the elevator, I waved back at them and apologized again for my rude outburst. I didn't look, but I wondered if the first woman was now giving me a shaking middle finger. The thought made me smirk.

It's a very real and humbling experience to see the person

you love the most in the world lying helpless in a hospital bed. "Hey, mom," I said, knocking on the open door.

"Tryke, I told them to tell you not to worry. There was no need to come up here. I'm doing fine. They said I had something called a TIA, some sort of mild brain attack, and that I would be out tomorrow, probably."

"Yeah, they told me," I said. "But let's wait until after the CT results before you plan your exit strategy. I'm still worried about you. How are you feeling?"

"They said the machine would be back up in under an hour. I'm feeling good. I can move my right hand again. It scared me when it happened."

"You should have called 911. Or at least me."

"I know… I just don't like bothering anybody."

"You're not bothering —" I was interrupted by a knock on the door. A nurse entered, with Lesley following right behind.

Lesley lunged toward me and hugged me. I hugged her back, slightly embarrassed in front of my mom and the nurse. I knew I shouldn't feel that way, but the situation was still new to me. "Mom, you remember Lesley, don't you?"

"Of course I do. How are you, sweetie?" The smile on my mom's face told me she knew about us, and approved.

"I'm doing okay," said Lesley, "but it's you we're worried about."

"I'm feeling much better, thank you," my mom said.

Lesley looked me up and down and asked, "What's with the overalls, Farmer Joe?"

I had forgotten I was wearing them. "I was doing some maintenance on my truck today."

"Oh, sorry," she said. "Mr. Goodwrench then." We both let out a gentle laugh. Lesley sat in a chair next to my mom and they began conversing as if I wasn't even in the room. It was intriguing to me how women had this genetic ability to connect, a skill that seems to elude most of the opposite gender.

I kept glancing at my watch and thinking about Mr. Horning. I knew I had given him enough sedative, but for some reason I was second-guessing myself. My mom saw me checking the time. "Do you have to be somewhere?"

"I offered to help Dave with his boat tonight. He's putting a radio in it and asked if I would give him a hand. But I called him on the way over here and told him I might not be able to make it, depending on how you were doing."

"I'm doing fine. Go help your friend. That is if it's all right with Lesley." My mom smiled slyly toward her.

"It's okay with me," said Lesley, "but only if he promises to set a time for our next date." Now they were smiling at each other. Clever girl. I knew she was good at this, but she was pulling out the big guns, using my sick mom as leverage. I liked her tactics.

"Next Tuesday night," I said. "Six o'clock." They both grinned, no doubt happy that they had accomplished what they set out to do. What they didn't know was that I had already planned for next week to be our second date. That was why I blurted out the day and time so quickly. But even as clueless and inexperienced as I was at relationships, I didn't think it wise to let them in on that bit of information.

As my mom was smiling, I noticed that the right side of her face was drooping. And seconds later, her nose began to bleed. "Mom, smile for me again." She saw the alarm on my face and quickly did what I asked. "Lesley, can you please grab the nurse?" I spoke as calmly as I could manage.

Lesley glanced over at my mom and then bolted for the door. I quickly wiped the trickle of blood from my mother's nose with the tissue that she had in her hand and shoved an oxygen mask onto her face.

Chapter 28

Lesley returned to the room a few seconds later with the nurse. In the short time that she was gone, my mom had lost complete control of her right arm and her speech began to slur. While the nurse fumbled with a vial of medication, my mom attempted to ask me a question, but I was unable to understand her words. I pulled her hand close, kissed it, and whispered, "I love you." I was fighting back tears and on the verge of losing all control, myself. The feeling of helplessness was too overwhelming for me to push aside.

Another nurse entered the room, followed by two doctors. I reluctantly let go of her hand and stepped out of the way. I needed some fresh air, but I couldn't leave her alone. I'd seen too many of these scenarios go bad, and quickly.

I felt my hand being squeezed and tugged on. I looked down and saw Lesley biting on her fingernails and staring forward. I turned my attention back to my mom when I heard one of the physicians ask for the intubation equipment. All I could do was watch from the doorway as my mom slowly slipped into unconsciousness.

They lowered the bed back and began the procedure for intubation. I shut my eyes and drifted away, trying to get a grasp of the situation. I began counting each of my breaths, attempting to slow them to a relaxed pace, a method I used to manage my OCD when it got out of control. I ignored the familiar medical jargon everyone was spouting, and concentrated. A few seconds later, the noise in the room calmed to a soft humming sound.

When I opened my eyes, the scene had been transformed into a tranquil setting. The nurses and physicians were performing much more smoothly and methodically. My mom was intubated and a machine was now effortlessly inflating and deflating her lungs. The heart monitor above her head was steady and normal, flowing like a piece of music.

Lesley was right about the fast-paced movements of a hospital room, and how they were like a symphony. You only had to step back and see it for what it was. My mom was away, lost in the place between body and soul. I wanted to be with her and comfort her as she made the transition, but I wasn't ready for her to leave. I was feeling selfish.

"Tryke, she'll get through this," Lesley said, releasing my moist hand and placing her head on my shoulder.

I knew the odds were against that, but I've also heard that positive reassurance can help people get through hopeless situations. Deluded optimism wasn't something I believed in — it only seems to prolong the anguish. I've seen the look of false hope spread across too many faces while I was going through my motions on their loved ones. On so many occasions I wanted to yell out, "They're gone! Please give me permission to stop this poking and prodding. Look into their eyes and see that the soul has left."

One of the physicians yelled out toward the nurses' station. "Call Radiology and tell them to get that damn machine going. We're on our way." A young male nurse fumbled with the phone and quickly dialed the extension.

As they wheeled my mother past me, I looked down into her eyes and wanted to believe that she was still in there. Couldn't I enjoy a little taste of that false hope, like so many others? I wanted to understand what was so irresistible about it.

Out in the hallway, I spoke with the remaining physician for a few minutes. After he explained what I already knew, we discussed the paperwork that needed to be filled out. It was the same inevitable end-of-life red tape that my mom had to fill out for my dad. Now I was going to experience the same pain that she had.

It was agonizing to read the words "ceased efforts" and "life sustaining measures." I understood very clearly what they meant, but I just couldn't deal with it at the moment. I wasn't signing anything yet. Needing a few minutes to think, by myself, I handed the paperwork to Lesley and walked calmly to the elevators.

Outside, the warm evening summer wind caressed my face and hands. I was officially stressed out. I don't like not having control over myself. It's unnerving and dangerous. I had already seen what my impulsiveness was capable of. I had to get hold of this situation. Vulnerability was not a state that I wanted to linger in.

I did what any other self-obsessed person would do, given the circumstances. I went to check on my work, to finish what I had started. And at the same time, keep hope nestled safely by my side, the hope that my mom would hold on long enough for me to finish the job and get back to her. I wasn't proud of my decision to leave, but it had to be done.

• • •

I dialed Lesley's number.

She answered on the first ring. "Are you okay?"

"Yeah. I just needed some air. Son of a bitch! Sorry, some asshole almost ran me off into the median."

"Where are you? I thought you were just going to step outside. The nurse is asking me about the paperwork, and I don't know what to tell her."

"That's part of the reason I left. I needed to go by my mom's place and find the papers that she filled out after my dad passed away. Her last wishes. I didn't think much of it at the time, and now I can't remember exactly what she wanted or didn't want done."

"What should I tell them?"

"Just stall them as long as you can," I said, "and call me if anything happens. And, Lesley… Thanks for doing this."

"You're welcome, Tryke. Just please hurry."

"I will." I hung up and parked my truck right up against the back loading dock, near the stairs to my lab. The story about the papers was the only thing I could come up with to tell Lesley. I knew well what my mom's wishes were. She'd made them clear to me after having to deal with the back and forth at the hospital with my dad. Neither of them wanted to be kept alive in a vegetative state. I was afraid that if my mom's stroke was as bad as I suspected, I was going to have to make that decision.

All was dark and quiet from the outside. There was no sign of intruders or escapees. I flipped on the generator and the machines beeped and revved to life. Mr. Horning was still knocked out. If he didn't wake soon, I was going to have to do this without a reunion speech.

As I waited impatiently, I kept glancing at my phone, hoping it wouldn't light up with a call. My original plan was to drive Horning back to Shreveport after everything was finished. Every part of the operation was risky, but I didn't have much choice. I was insistent on him being back here.

I needed a solution. I sure wasn't letting him go; that was never an option. I could get it over with quickly, but that still didn't solve the problem of what to do with the body. Even if I sped to Shreveport, I wouldn't be back to the hospital for five hours.

As I pondered the dilemma, Mr. Horning began waking up, groggily moving his neck around. I made my decision in that instant. If my phone remained quiet for the next fifteen minutes, I was going to take him to Shreveport. It was really my only option. I had to get him back to the guard shack before dawn.

He was gagged, but I could sense his trapped anger burning inside. He glared at me with his cold, blank eyes and then yanked his head away. My new plan didn't allow for a lot of conversation, but he could listen. After removing my overalls, I spoke.

"Mr. Horning." He continued to stare forward, avoiding eye contact with me. "Before we begin, let me introduce myself. I haven't much time, so you'll understand if I skip to the point and make this short." I tilted the vial over in my left hand and withdrew the medication into the syringe. Pulling my chair close to him, I sat down and placed the syringe onto the table.

"I'm Tryke Harper, the little boy you left behind to fend for myself in a vehicle engulfed in fire. I survived the accident, thanks to my dad, but my aunt and uncle weren't so lucky." My hands started shaking. "They were burned alive. Their skin literally melted as the flames licked up and down their bodies, until nothing was left."

I stood up and kicked the chair back against the wall, and swiped the syringe from the table, sending it flying across the room. He didn't flinch, or close his eyes in fear. He appeared to be processing what I had just told him, filtering through the lives he had taken.

Burning mad, I stood over him and tried to regain control of my breathing. I'd never intended for this to turn into a raged-filled revenge ceremony, nor was I going to let it. We were supposed to have meaningful dialogue, an epiphany conclusion to end the release party. I had been imagining the scenario ever since my mom told me the truth. A part of me wanted Horning to pay for what he had done, to feel the pain that he had caused others to feel. But that wasn't the primary goal I had set out to accomplish. I'm not so shallow to think that my efforts would be his only justice.

When I regained my composure, I picked up the syringe from the floor and calmly returned to him. With my hands now just mildly shaking, I continued. "Of course, I don't expect you to recall the event. It's been over twenty years. I'm sure you've killed more innocent people since then. However, there won't be any more memories to suppress or faces to haunt your dreams. You will finally be free from the restricting body and the tormented mind. It's time for you to move on."

The anger had left his eyes. There was no arrogant smirk or grin on his face, like my dad had described at the trial. He turned his gaze toward the camera at his feet.

As the medication flowed through his narrow vessels, we knew one another for that brief moment. We were both stuck in this dimension, this plane of evil, only we weren't the same. We had traveled very different paths that happened to eventually cross. He knew this had to happen.

I caught a glimpse of relief in his eyes as the monitor let out a long, constant beep. I didn't see a soul exit, nor did I hear an alarm from the stairwell. The room was eerily quiet. I should have been spooked, not knowing where he had gone. But for a reason I cannot explain, I knew that he had left — departed his prison calmly, without agitation over the person he had been.

I was satisfied with how the release went. I had expected more, given the twenty-two-year suppressed memory, but some things are better with just a neutral ending. There doesn't have to be an extravaganza or a long-awaited revelation. In the end, it left us both in peace. It was as if our souls bowed to one another in understanding. And then it was over. We could now both move on to wherever that may be.

My phone was still silent. I needed to get moving, even

though I was five minutes ahead of schedule. After loading Mr. Horning's empty body into my truck, I went back upstairs to make sure I had turned everything off, and to wipe the place down one more time.

Before switching off the generator, I stood in the doorway and gazed into the empty room. What would come next, now that I had completed the release of my number one specimen? Was this all over? Was I headed back to my mundane life as a paramedic?

My world was definitely changing. Mom was hanging onto life, and Lesley was gripping me with all that she had.

• • •

As I began my drive along I-20 back to Shreveport, I continued to think about my next move now that I was done with Mr. Horning. It was keeping me awake, along with two sugar-free twenty-ounce energy drinks. I was deep in thought when my cell phone rang.

"Where are you?" Lesley asked from the other end.

"I'm still searching for those papers. I know they're somewhere in this fire hazard. Any news yet?"

"They won't give me much information because I'm not family, but I walked over to Radiology and talked to one of the techs who works with me part-time. I saw the CT."

"And?"

"Tryke, there's a mass." I suddenly felt emptiness in the pit of my stomach. A mass was never good. That tiny string of hope that I had been loosely holding onto had now flown into the air, and was lost with the night breeze.

"How big is it?" I asked.

"Just get back here. I heard the doctors discussing surgery, and they keep asking where you are. I told them that you were searching for her living will. They need you to sign things."

"I'll be there as soon as I can. What do you think about the surgery? Is the mass treatable? Do you think she'll be disabled if she lives?"

Even though I didn't know how large the mass was or even if it was malignant, I knew the statistics and that she was rapidly declining. But for some reason, I lost all of my ability to think rationally. I forgot all of my medical training and leaned, like so many before me, on others for false hope. I wanted to be charmed into a state of bliss, where I could deny life's cruel hard truths.

"You know I can't answer that, Tryke. But I want to think she'll be okay. I really do."

"I'm sorry. I know those are questions you can't answer. I'm just not thinking straight. I'll call you when I'm heading back up there."

"Don't worry. We'll take all of this step by step. Together."

"Thank you, Lesley. I mean it."

"You're welcome. I'll call you if anything else changes."

• • •

I was in Shreveport, just a few miles from the guard shack. The closer I got, the more anxious I became, as possible complications cascaded through my mind. I was mostly concerned that someone had found his car.

I checked his cell phone for missed calls. There were none. He was the only guard working that neighborhood, I believed, but I might have been wrong about that. I parked in the same spot as before, back when I was first scoping the area, and cautiously watched the gate for a few minutes. The shack looked empty, as did the small parking lot beside it. I spotted the front of his yellow Bug in the brush, and breathed a sigh of relief.

Slowly, I moved up to the gate and typed the code I'd found in his cell phone. It was listed as "work gate code," which made it easy to find. I backed his car out from the brush and returned it to the very spot where he'd left it.

Parked in the exit lane next to the shack, I scanned the

area for wonderers and witnesses. All was still, desolate, and quiet. I wedged the door open and placed him back into his rickety chair in front of the small, perpetually-fuzzy black and white TV. I tilted his hat over his eyes and positioned him to look as though he had never left.

I had dropped his phone, and as I was bending down to pick it up, I heard footsteps approaching. From my kneeling position, I poked my head just far enough outside the door to see down the road. An older man was striding swiftly in my direction, arms swaying. He appeared to be some sort of late-night walker, wearing shorts and a reflective vest. Why couldn't he stay in the malls like the other old people?

For a brief moment, I thought that he would continue on around the curve of the street, but no such luck. He undoubtedly knew Mr. Horning and wanted to say hello. I had to somehow deter him from coming any closer, and I had to do it quickly. I couldn't let this old-timer see my face, or my truck's license plate.

Chapter 29

I began flailing my arms in the air. "Call 911. I don't think this man is breathing!"

For a second I thought the old man might not have heard me. He wasn't slowing his rapid mall-walking pace. But then he stopped twenty yards away as if the information suddenly processed. I stepped back into the shadows so he couldn't see my face, but I could see his clearly — eyes bulging and mouth hung open. Without so much as a stutter, he turned on his heels and shot off in the other direction. I wasn't sure how far he would have to go to fetch someone, and I didn't stick around to find out. My only mission was to get the hell out of there.

I waited until the man passed under a dim yellow streetlight and faded into the darkness before I pushed the button to open the exit gate. I said my goodbyes to Mr. Horning's previous prison and then eased out of the neighborhood.

A few minutes down the street, I passed the ambulance

responding to the old man's call, and now screaming toward its patient. I smiled and tipped my hat as they passed, but of course they couldn't see me in the night. And that was okay with me. An undercover salute to my fellow street warriors sufficed.

• • •

I was barely an hour away from the hospital and was relieved to see that Lesley hadn't called yet. Over the last hour and a half, I hadn't stopped worrying about my mom. I contemplated what it was going to be like without her, how much sadder and bleaker my world was going to be.

For me, the most difficult part of human interaction has always revolved around trust. I've watched so many people fail in relationships, and not only because of romantic deceit, but family deceit, too. Blood relatives can be just as selfish and cruel. Single parent beats child, mom drowns children then shoots herself, child kills parents in rage. I can go on and on. The world is a dirty place.

I called Lesley when I was fifteen minutes from town.

She picked up after the third ring. "Hello…" she said. She sounded groggy.

"Did I wake you, Sunshine?"

"Yeah…" she said, yawning. "What time is it?"

"Almost midnight. Any news?"

"They still have her sedated. The last thing they told me was that they were waiting until morning to talk to you before making any decisions about the surgery. Did you find the papers?"

"Yeah, after going through about ten boxes. I should be there in a few minutes."

"Okay, see you then." She hung up.

I swung by my apartment to change, and then by my mom's house to grab her a few items — it would be part of my alibi. I even went so far as to ruffle a few of her boxes in the back room.

• • •

Lesley handed me a cup of coffee when I entered the room. "It was hot when I got it for you," she said. "I thought you were only going to be a few minutes." She was too tired to be suspicious.

"I needed to change my clothes. I didn't want to be called Mr. Goodwrench anymore." Lesley yawned again and then looked at me with a half smile. "At least she looks peaceful," I said, standing over my mom. I ran my hand through her dyed dark hair, imagining that it would start turning grey if she wasn't out of the hospital soon.

"She's been like this since you left," Lesley said.

"Do you have work in the morning?" I realized how selfish I had been and how selfless and caring Lesley had been. It wasn't fair that she had to spend so much of her free time at the hospital.

"I called in sick."

"You didn't have to do that. You've done more than enough. I can handle it from here." By the look on her face, I knew I had said something wrong again. Failure number... who the hell knew? I had lost count.

"You can't just boot me out like that," she said. "First you leave me here alone for hours, to answer questions that I don't have the answers to, and now you tell me you don't need me anymore?"

"I'm sorry. I didn't mean it like that. I was only thinking of you."

She stared at me silently for a long few seconds. She then sighed and smiled wearily, her entrancing blue eyes heavy with fatigue. "I'm not leaving you alone during this. Look, we're both tired, it's ok," she said, picking up her purse from the chair beside her. "I would like to run home and take a shower, though."

"Of course," I said.

"Do you need me to pick you up anything while I'm out? Did you bring a bag with you?"

"Crap, I forgot. But I just need a cheap toothbrush."

"It must be nice to be a guy and only need a toothbrush in the morning."

"Sorry for being low maintenance."

She hugged me tight before leaving. I hugged her back with much more confidence than I had at the restaurant. She'd be all I had left if my mom did pass. I was glad we had decided to date, even if it did go against my rules against romance.

I sat in the chair that Lesley had been sleeping in beside my mom. Even though she was unconscious, I wanted to ask her about my dad, and especially about the voices. But I couldn't. For one thing, my dad had asked me not to. For another, I didn't know what good it would do.

I began reading a book to her that she used to read to me when I was younger. I had seen its familiar worn cover on her nightstand while I was gathering a few items to bring to the hospital. Hearing a group of words she used to read over and over might help her somehow. I was feeling lost, and didn't know what else to do. We were both helpless and at the mercy of the Gamemakers. All we owned was what we had created between us, and our own little secrets that had formed along the way.

After giving my dad's letter more thought, I realized who the Gamemakers were. Before now, I hadn't given them a name.

"The Hobbit, Chapter 1..." As I read to my mom, part of my mind focused on the ventilator steadily pumping oxygen into her lungs and the whirring of the air conditioner. I thought about how peaceful the room felt. My mind was calm and clear. There were no repetitive numbers going through my head, or chaotic dilemmas to solve. I was a little boy again, back under the covers and listening to my mom's soft voice.

At the end of the chapter, I would beg her to continue a few more pages, never wanting the story to end. I didn't like what came next: the darkness, and the loneliness of sleep. Little did I know that in a few short years, the nightmares would begin, the ones that would leave me alone and scared, dragging me to a world of nothingness, as if I'd never existed.

It wasn't the accident when I was a baby that had caused the fear. It had been there the entire time, waiting to pounce on my young and vulnerable mind. That fear is implanted in each of us. It was all part of the Gamemakers' plans. They think they're clever, but I'm on to them.

I've changed, and my fears have changed along with me. I'm no longer afraid of the dark, or of being alone. The shadows in my room now give me comfort and cover. The justice gives me purpose and hope for something different. I can see through the peephole beyond the Gamemakers' board to a new place, one with different rules. Fair rules. Someday, the once grim and unjust world will no longer pursue us, like demons on our heels.

My dad will be there in his freshly-starched shirt and recently-shined shoes, seated on a park bench, his mind no longer burdened by disembodied voices. He's reading his morning paper with crossed legs, waiting patiently for my mom. I can't let you have her yet, dad. I haven't accepted the outcome. I can't process it, for some reason. I'm sure in time, I will make the transition, but for now you'll have to wait.

I woke with the book draped over my left leg. It took me a few seconds to gather my wits and comprehend my surroundings. I'd actually slept a few hours, just enough to make me groggy. I wasn't complaining, though. A little sleep was better than none at all.

When I saw my mom next to me, I snapped back to the cold reality. This was all actually happening. There was no escape. At least not for now.

Chapter 30

Lesley was waiting for me in her car as I reloaded my bag for another night at the hospital. The doctor had called a few minutes ago and said that my mom was awake. But from the tone of his voice, I could tell he wasn't promising she would stay that way. I was briefly excited, though trying not to get my hopes up just yet — not until I had seen her for myself, and heard her voice speak my name. Lesley was more optimistic.

"It's good news, her waking up," Lesley said, as I hurled my bag into the back seat.

"I hope so. But I'll wait until I see her before calling it good news." Lesley's continued optimism was beginning to scare me. We both had relatively dismal outlooks on the world. Of course, she would add an artful and humorous spin on whatever the subject happened to be, but it was far from unicorns and butterflies, or dancing fairies sprinkling happy dust. We both knew that things weren't really going to be okay, but I was fine with her supportive approach for the moment. Thankful even. Besides, she deserved to be hopeful. She'd already spent as much time with my mom in the hospital as I had.

"You're right," she said. "Let's wait and see."

The rest of the ride was quiet. I didn't have much to say. I was irritated, and my brain was exhausted. Lesley wasn't to blame. It was the yanking and tugging on my soul, a constant feeling of helplessness as my mom was slowly taken from me.

• • •

When I opened the door to her room, I saw my Uncle Frank seated in a chair across from her under the TV set. He was wearing his usual cowboy detective attire. I'd forgotten that I had called him and left a voicemail about my mom.

"Uncle Frank," I said. "I'm glad you came."

"I got your message the other day," he said, "but work wouldn't let me get away." He winced as he slowly got up from the chair. "My dang knee is acting up again. So, who's this lovely lady by your side?"

"This is my uh…"

"I'm Lesley," she said, reaching out her hand. "His girlfriend." I was caught off guard by her words. Girlfriend? I suppose it was appropriate. If she wanted to label us that way, I was surprisingly fine with it.

He lowered his hat like a gentleman cowboy and shook her hand politely. She looked over at me, grinning slyly.

"So how's she doing?" I asked. "The doctor called and said she was awake." I turned to look over at my mom.

"I haven't been here long," Frank said. "But I talked to her for a minute and she responded with facial expressions."

The vent was still pumping oxygen into her lungs, but to my surprise her eyes were open. Heavy from the sedation, but still open. She looked terrible and older somehow, and seemed to be in pain. The medication being pumped into her IV wouldn't help. This was a different pain, the kind that I'd seen shortly after my dad died. It was a hurt that drugs wouldn't relieve. It had to be let go.

Mom had always been a believer in a heaven, and was more than determined to see my dad again. She missed him so deeply that it shadowed her will to live, but she also knew she would have to wait. Death wasn't her decision to make. She would have to endure this place, this life, until she was released.

I didn't like seeing her suffer, but what could I do? I certainly wasn't about to cross the line that now vaguely brushed itself against my thoughts. My lab was reserved for the wicked and cruel, and that was final.

I didn't know what to say to her now that her eyes were open. I wanted to apologize for being so helpless. I wanted to tell her how much I had missed her since my dad had passed on. But I didn't say any of those things. All I could manage was a half-smile and a soft squeeze of her hand.

She pointed to a pad of paper sitting next to the bed. I handed it to her, along with a pen. She slowly wrote a few short sentences and handed the pad back to me. Lesley and my uncle walked across the room to give us some privacy.

When I read the words, I felt a sudden rush of relief. She knew I had found my dad's journal and was fine with it. But there was more she wanted to tell me. "When you're better, mom," I said. "Soon, okay?" She nodded and a tear rolled down her cheek. She closed her eyes and drifted back to sleep, releasing her firm grip from my hand. I could be wrong, but I didn't think it was coincidence that she happened to wake up for that brief moment.

One of mom's physicians came in a few minutes later and broke the silence of the room. He wanted to check on her before his shift ended. Dr. Snead was a young guy, in his mid-thirties, with a pleasant demeanor. Also, he was articulate and down to earth. I liked him. He wasn't the surgeon, but he had been taking care of my mother since she was admitted. I met with him briefly in the hallway with Lesley.

As we talked, I watched through the crack of the door. Uncle Frank was standing over my mom and talking to her through broken sentences. He was holding his hat over his chest. I couldn't hear what he was saying, but I imagined he was expressing gratitude about her and his brother, how he missed my dad, and that he was sorry for not visiting more after his death.

Meanwhile, Dr. Snead and I discussed the surgery they were contemplating. It was risky, but the choices were limited. If she was going to have any chance of survival, she needed the operation. I told him I would sign the paperwork in the morning when he returned.

Frank asked if he could have a few words with me before leaving. We walked around the corner to an empty waiting area. Lesley stayed in the room with my mom.

He sat down across from me and placed his cowboy hat on his knee. "After you were born, your father came to me with some disturbing news that I hadn't had a clue about up until then. He told me about the voices, and the pain he was trying to hide from the world. I didn't know how to take it at first, mainly because I didn't know much about the sickness. Heck, I don't think he did himself at the time, but he said he was dealing with it. He was communicating with your mother and their attempts seemed to be working, keeping the voices somewhat quiet. But I knew him better than that. His drinking was his real source of medicine. And when your sister died, he doubled up on it." Frank sighed deeply and stretched his eyes as if trying to hold back the tears. He wiped his nose and continued.

"I'm going to tell you something that he never wanted you to know, something about your sister." He shuffled around a bit, and placed his hat onto the chair beside him. "One night, a few months before she died, she came to your parents and told them she was seeing things in her room. Images, like ghosts. Your father said she didn't appear scared of them, so he didn't think much about it, and marked it off as her imagination. But a week later, she came to him again. This time she saw something outside, in the neighbors' front yard. Multiple dark objects. And she was frightened, to the point of hysteria. He couldn't ignore it this time. The cold, hard truth was that she had the sickness. It ripped him from the inside out. Did more damage than any cancer could have."

By now I was in shock, and didn't know what to say. Not only was my dad sick, but my sister, too. Everything had been hidden away from me, in an attempt to preserve my innocence.

Frank continued. "Before your father died, he gave me that letter, along with instructions. The numbers were just another way to tell you that even though he had died, he could still show you the world through a different perspective. He was always one for teaching you things, in unconventional ways. He would sway you in one direction, with subtle hints, but ultimately he let you guide yourself. His past teachings were always included in his future ones."

I smiled and shook my head. "Well, this one was a pain in the butt."

"Mission accomplished, then," Frank said. "Anyway, he wanted me to keep an eye on you, watch for symptoms of the sickness. And if I ever saw them in you, I was to give you the letter and get you some help. I trust you're old enough to make the decision for yourself. I have no idea what he wrote to you in that letter, but I want you to know I'll always be here for you if you need anything."

I stood up to stretch my legs. He seemed to be waiting for me to give him an answer. "Uncle Frank, I'm fine. Seriously. I know the consequences of not getting help. My dad made it clear in the letter."

He stared at me for a few seconds and then nodded, placing his hat back on his head. "Okay, then." We walked back around the corner and he poked his head in the door to say good-bye to my mom and Lesley.

When I thanked Frank for coming, he reached out his

hand and then pulled me in for a hug. It was an unexpected gesture, but something he needed to do. Raw emotion seeped out from his pores as he squeezed tighter and tighter. He had obviously been holding it all in for years, through so many difficult times with his wife, niece, and brother. And now my mom.

I saw Lesley out of the corner of my eye. She was watching us, looking like she had just witnessed a puppy being rescued from the jaws of a coyote. I suppose it was one of those spontaneous, candid family moments that people love so much to see.

• • •

Lesley fell asleep shortly after one of those late-night talk shows ended. I thumbed through a few magazines, listening to them both softly snore, along with the low hum of the hospital air conditioner. I must have nodded off myself for an hour. I woke in the chair with a stiff neck. Lesley was still sound asleep next to me. Luckily, her chair was a recliner. My mom was still lost in narcotic land. The way I felt, I wouldn't have minded a boat ride along with her.

I peered through the thick hospital curtains. It was still dark outside. The hallway was quiet, except for a male nurse sitting at the nurses' station, lightly tapping the desk with his thumbs, one earphone hanging loosely in his right ear. I could faintly hear George Michael singing "Careless Whisper."

I decided to go for a stroll along the empty corridors. The quiet was nice. It didn't hold anguish or tough decisions, or ask questions that could end with horrible consequences. I took the long way around, past the morgue to the ER ambulance entrance. I didn't feel like conversing with anyone, and just wanted to observe. Sometimes it was entertaining to watch from the outside looking in. Dave was working that shift, and I wondered if I'd get to see his permanent night frown from the perspective of a hospital visitor.

The ER looked to be fairly quiet for Mercy General — no ambulances parked in the driveway and no nurses or techs smoking outside. I sat down on the curb and watched the sporadic clouds hug the full moon. The humid air felt oddly pleasant. Normally, I would be cursing the way it caused my shirt to cling to me, but now I was grateful for any feeling that might distract my thoughts.

The driveway wasn't empty for long. Fifteen minutes later, I heard sirens approaching from a few blocks away. Medic 3 pulled in a minute later. I listened to the familiar hissing from the air brake, and the lowering of the back as the double doors were opened.

The two medics didn't recognize me as I sat in the shadows ten yards away. I was glad. They were a fitting pair of certified douche bags, and would likely embellish their call, as usual, for recognition. I wasn't in the mood to hear their tales.

They pulled the stretcher from the back. The patient was a female child who looked to be around five or six years old. An oxygen mask was fitted to her face and her hands and chest were partially wrapped with bandages. She had soot smeared across her face and legs. A house fire, I presumed, when I didn't see any parents in the back with them. Unless it was something worse and the police had the parents in custody. As much as I was longing for a distraction, I didn't need to see that.

I heard another ambulance approaching. They pulled into the driveway and turned off the lights. I saw the familiar "Medic 15" outlined in reflective paint on the side of the rig. Dave exited the driver's door, moving more quickly than I'd ever seen him move at night. I stood up to get a better look. I was curious to know what was behind this rare event. I stepped from the shadows and watched as Dave pulled open the double doors. That's when I knew.

Rick Darvon exited the back, slinging his stethoscope over

his shoulder and yelling for Dave to move faster. Rick was a far more dramatic medic than Dave, and had a few more years under his belt, so Dave always gave him a little extra respect. I, on the other hand, didn't feel that length of service did anything to make up for douche bag status.

Behind Rick, I saw a fireman doing compressions on a tall adult male.

"Hey, buddy," Rick yelled at me. "Can you give us a hand here?" I was caught off guard and didn't acknowledge him. "Hey, over here, pal," he said again, this time snapping his fingers.

Now, normally I would handle this situation much differently. I would ignore a dick like him until he pushed past the point that I couldn't. Even though they were more than capable of handling this without me, and Rick was being a lazy prick, I quietly avoided direct conflict. I had a feeling that the man in the back was the father of the little girl Medic 3 had just brought in.

When I approached the back of the rig, Rick still didn't recognize me. He was way too caught up in his own voice and movements. "Grab the stretcher and assist him with it," Rick told me, pointing toward Dave, who hadn't recognized me yet either.

"That son of a bitch is lucky I'm a nice guy," I said to Dave, grabbing the stretcher handles beside him.

He briefly paused his grunting noise and looked over at me with a look of bewilderment. He smiled when he recognized me. "Hey, man, what are you doing here?" I could tell he was past aggravation by the way he cursed the slow battery-operated wheels of the stretcher.

"My mom, remember?"

"Yeah, sorry. Give me a minute, and let me drop this guy off." He pantomimed a gun to his head and pointed at Rick as they wheeled the dead man through the ER doors.

Rick never acknowledged me. I wasn't surprised. Guys like him expect everyone to bow to their every word and command. But I have a little something for him. If there's one thing that medics, firemen, and police officers know, it's how to exact revenge. I racked my brain for a suitable retaliation. Lube on the door handle, or saline in his seat wasn't nearly good enough for an ass-hat like him.

I struck quick, before Dave saw what I was doing. It was going too far, and he wouldn't have let me do it — even the new *I don't give a shit* Dave. I injected a dose of Lasix into the bottle of water he had on the dash. He would be up and pissing every five minutes the rest of the night.

Just as I tossed the residue of evidence into the trash, Dave came out pushing the stretcher. "I'm sorry," I said. "I didn't know they were going to stick you with him."

"He sure is an ass, isn't he?" said Dave. "I'm sorry about how he talked to you. If I'd have known it was you, I'd —"

"It's okay. I have more pressing matters going on at the moment."

"Of course. How's she doing?"

"She opened her eyes a little while ago, but I'm not sure for how long. They're going to operate on her in a few days. I'm really not too optimistic. I just don't want her to suffer. She looked like she was in a lot of pain."

"All you can do is pray, I guess."

What, pray to the Gamemakers for mercy? I'd been down that path, and was feeling forsaken. "Sure," I said. "I guess I can give that a try."

He looked stunned, as if I'd said something in an unfamiliar language. I must have given him the impression that I prayed everyday, like a good boy. I felt a lecture coming on.

"Don't lose hope. I'll pray for her, too." It was a valiant gesture on his part, but I doubt they would listen to him either.

• • •

Before I left to go back upstairs, I asked Dave about the little girl and the man they brought in. As I'd assumed, it was a house fire. The little girl had attempted to wake her dad, but he was already dead. He must have died in his sleep sometime before the fire. She ran next door to wake the neighbors and they called 911. Life strikes again and a little girl loses her dad. Gamemakers 1, little girl 0.

The door to the morgue was cracked open when I passed by on my way back to the room. I peeked my head in just to glance around. I had always been curious about morgues, having never actually ventured inside one.

The room was smaller than I had expected, especially for a hospital the size of Mercy. If I were frightened of the dead, I would definitely have found the scene more than creepy. A flickering light in the far corner dimly lit the space, giving it the appearance of a deserted motel that dared anyone to approach. Three metal examining tables were arranged in the center, with a large sink behind them against the wall. I pictured the sink opening its wide jaws to accept mouthfuls of blood. Each of the tables had its own stack of metal bowls and a scale. Directly across from the middle table was a set of three metal doors that I suspected was the freezer, where the waiting bodies were stored.

I was about to be on my way when I saw that the middle freezer door was hanging open, exposing a black body bag. It appeared to be unzipped. I was intrigued by so much sloppiness, and wanted to take a peek. The freezer was only about fifteen feet away. Thirty seconds and I would be out. No one would ever know.

I looked around one last time and then swiftly walked toward the bag. I felt the chill of the freezer as I approached. The light was now flickering continuously, strobe-like. The body was on the second shelf, just below my waist. I peered down at the half-unzipped bag, but I could see only a glimpse of the mottled pale skin. I inched my hand toward the bag to unzip it farther. The lights in the room suddenly flipped on.

"Boo!" said a voice from behind me.

I let go of the zipper and jumped. I turned around to see a short, pudgy guy in his late twenties, wearing loose, bright green scrubs and a ridiculous smile. He had evidently amused himself.

"You scared the living shit out of me," I said, exhaling loudly.

"Better than the dead shit. Am I right?" he said, laughing and motioning toward the body. "What brings you to the morgue this time of night, Mr.…"

"Rick," I said. "I couldn't sleep as usual and saw that the door was open, so I took a quick peek. I didn't mean to interrupt —"

"A fellow insomniac. Nonsense, stick around if you want." He stepped closer to me, staring at me with his right eyebrow arched. "Unless you're going to rat me out to my superiors."

"My lips are sealed."

"Good," he said, patting me on the back. "I was about to prep the body for Dr. Peters."

He was nice enough, though a little kooky. I'm all right with kooky; it's much better than an asshole. "He's doing an autopsy this time of morning?"

"In a few hours, yeah. He gets up at three a.m. everyday. I don't mind, really. I'm up at night anyway. Though, it does get kind of lonely in here." He turned his gaze toward the far wall and stared silently. After a few awkward seconds he turned back toward me and said, "I'm Marvin by the way."

"Nice to meet you. So, how'd she die?" I helped him lift the stiff body of the middle-aged lady onto the table.

"Cancer, supposedly. But the husband wanted an autopsy performed. He's pissed off at the hospital for something. Not sure what."

Marvin started drawing lines on the body with a purple skin marker and began complaining about how the nurses in ICU on the third floor wouldn't give him the time of day. While he ranted, I pictured my own mother on the table. Even though her body was merely an organic suit, I didn't want it to be violated. I suddenly felt nauseous and dizzy, with sweat beading on my forehead and neck. I didn't want to see any more, not with my mom in her brittle state. I couldn't deal with the realness of it all, and needed to get out of there.

Marvin was still talking, but I cut him off mid-sentence, just as he was beginning to elaborate about a particular redheaded RN named Rhonda.

"Sorry, man, but I need to go. The smell in here is giving me a headache. Thanks for letting me watch." I made my way toward the door, which now seemed much farther away than it had when I entered.

"Anytime, Rick. You know where I am." I leaned against the wall outside the door and took a few deep breaths.

Down the hall, I laughed quietly to myself. I had almost forgotten that in my desperate moment of being caught, I'd used the bastard's name. I wondered if the Lasix was working yet.

• • •

My mom and Lesley were both still sound asleep. I sipped on a cup of coffee that the male nurse had given me. He was still jamming to George Michael, though I didn't recognize the song.

Chapter 31

The last three weeks had been both odd and revealing to me. I spent a great deal of it in my lab going over all of the events that had taken place there, but didn't know if I had the stamina to continue. My mom being in the hospital had drained me; when her energy left, it took mine with it.

She'd made it through surgery, but had yet to regain consciousness. And even though she never wanted to live that way, I didn't have the strength to do what I'd promised her: pull the plug. I was still holding on, wanting, wishing, dreaming that she would wake up and yank us both out of the nightmare.

Lesley relentlessly tried to pull me out from the dark well I had fallen into. Even Dave had taken a break from his own needy emotions to offer advice and support. But they both knew I had to do this alone; the path I was on didn't allow for companions.

We had a ride-along at work the next day. Dave had valiantly volunteered to be a backup preceptor, and his duties were needed. The moment I heard about it, I advised him that I wouldn't be available to assist in his training endeavor. My head was still aching from the previous night's binge of solo drinking at my apartment. The only thing that made the morning bearable was a heavy shield of clouds that blocked the bright rays of the cheery morning sun.

His name was Jared. Skinny and twenty-one years old, with neatly-parted blonde hair. He was fresh, right out of paramedic school, and this was his first shift. I noticed the panic and uncertainty in his voice as I went through my morning routine of checking the rig. Dave and Jared were methodically going over the drug box. As Dave quizzed him, Jared's mind stumbled for the answers.

I was fortunate enough to grasp this job with little effort. Not that it was easy. I sometimes wonder if I missed the most important part: the fear that comes with discipline and understanding. I had never suffered enough to appreciate that.

The caffeine from the coffee hadn't yet kicked in when the dispatcher's harsh and piercing voice amplified over the radio, causing me to flinch and nearly spill the hot liquid all over my shirt. Someone had turned the volume of the radio up to full blast. Probably Jared.

"Sorry, that's my fault," Dave said, seeing me wince in pain. "I showed him how we did the morning radio test a few minutes ago."

"I'll live," I said. I looked over at Jared. "You might want to take notes on what not to do." He kept his head pointed to the floor.

"Yeah, don't drink yourself into a coma the night before your shift," Dave said, patting me on the back.

"Up yours," I said. I quickly downed an aspirin before we took off down the road. It was barely eight o'clock in the morning and we were already on our way to an apparent suicide attempt. This one was a seventy-five-year-old male. Green Jared was most likely going to get a taste of death on his first run. It should at least be easy for him, the paramedic aspect anyhow.

We arrived before the police. We usually waited a few houses down from the address of the call, out of sight, until they arrived. But Dave messed up on the address. We were now in front of the house with a distraught wife staring at us.

"Jared," Dave said. "Now, normally we would wait for police to secure the scene on these calls, but since the wife is staring us down and I messed up on the address, we might as well go in."

"Watch your ass, though," I said to Jared, lowering my sunglasses to the ridge of my nose for effect. "You never know what people are capable of, and they just might try to take you with them." I smirked as we dragged the stretcher up to the front door behind the panicky wife. Jared was frantically looking around like a skittish dog, and treading closely behind Dave.

The two-story house was eerily quiet and pristine. We entered through the living room, passing shelf after shelf of what I assumed were family photos. If the end result was what I suspected, it was going to devastate a lot of people. I wanted to stop and examine a collection of bonelike pieces displayed in a large wooden case against the wall. But Dave persistently pulled on the head of the stretcher, forcing me forward. Still, I managed to catch a glimpse as we passed by. They were dinosaur bone fragments. One of them — husband or wife, or maybe both — had been a paleontologist. Oddly cool, I thought. You don't come across many of them. The house was most likely their retirement home, built with years of savings.

The wife hadn't spoken to us yet. Shock is good at keeping humans quiet. We followed her through a kitchen that smelled of recently-cooked bacon. I spotted the cast iron skillet on the stove; the grease had congealed on the bottom.

We exited the kitchen through an open sliding glass door that led outside. The porch was saturated with hanging plants and had two yellow and white lawn chairs set neatly beside one another. It was a peaceful space, with two rotating fans blowing overhead. I looked back at the wife for further directions, but she was turned away from us, with her face implanted into her cupped hands. Apparently, she expected us to find her husband on our own.

Dave was in front of me, with Jared between us. The lawn chairs were facing in the opposite direction. One was occupied. When Dave and Jared walked around to the front of the chairs, our young student's face instantly turned pallid. He staggered a few feet to the grass and hunched over, spilling his breakfast in chunks.

"Tryke, we're going to have to work him," Dave said.

The husband still had a forty-five-caliber revolver in his left hand. He had a single bullet hole in his left temple with blood seeping from it. It was pulsing with his slowing heart rate. Brain matter was sprayed along the chair's arm. He would certainly have met the DRT criteria if it weren't for the pulse.

This was going to be messy and I wasn't in the mood. The man was going to die anyway, but we couldn't let him expire in front of his wife without at least making some futile attempt at resuscitation. He didn't need our drugs, the bullet had reduced his brain to mush.

"Jared, a little help would be nice," I said. "That is, if you don't mind putting a halt to your vomiting for a minute." He looked up at me apologetically and wiped the residue from his mouth. "Open the yellow blanket on the stretcher so we can move him," I instructed. He would learn soon enough how to push aside unneeded emotions. Either that, or he wouldn't make it. But he suddenly focused and pulled himself together, unwrapping the blanket and spreading it out across the stretcher. He may have a future on the streets after all, I thought. Dave moved the gun to a nearby table. As we hoisted the man onto the stretcher, I managed to avoid getting a single drop of blood on me.

We left the backyard through the side fence. The wife didn't need to clean blood from inside the house, too. I tilted his head and covered the wound as best I could, as we made our way to the truck through the rocky gravel terrain. The cops arrived just as we were loading him into the back of the rig. I was more than sure that Dave and Jared could handle the quickly deteriorating man, and went over to the patrol car to inform the officers where the gun was located, and what the scene had looked like when we got there. It wouldn't hurt Jared to have some one-on-one with the patient before he departed.

I poked my head into the back of the rig a few seconds later. Jared was holding the man's head, the wound now gushing blood like a recently primed beer keg. He had the sheet wrapped behind his head, using it as a catchall. Dave had given Jared the responsibility of the head while he started the IV. He knew that the catchall would soon give way, and when it did blood would fly. Jared would have plenty more opportunities to insert IVs in the future. For now, why not immerse him into the profession right?

"Y'all ready?" I said. "This should be a good learning experience for Jared." I smiled at Dave before shutting the double doors. It was going to be a fun trip.

I watched from the rearview mirror as Jared clumsily squeezed the BVM, introducing oxygen with one hand while his other held onto the quickly filling sheet. It was only a matter of time before it toppled over. Sure enough, a mile down the road, I heard, "Crapola! It's all over me!"

"Don't worry about the blood," Dave said. "Just keep bagging him. You can clean off at the hospital." I couldn't see Dave's face, but he was probably biting his lip to keep from laughing.

We arrived at Mercy General five minutes later. I glanced in the back as we pulled up to the entrance and saw that Jared was now doing compressions and Dave was bagging.

"He needed the practice," Dave said, when I opened the

double back doors. He was referring to Jared doing compressions on an obviously dead man, someone we weren't going to bring back. I had to move back a few steps as the overwhelming amount of blood funneled out when the air ride lowered. "Sorry, it was filling too fast. Jared decided to just let the rest pour out."

I frowned at Jared and shook my head disapprovingly, while holding back a laugh. "Who says crapola anyway?" I asked. "I bet you say gee-whiz too, don't you?" His face turned the same color as the crimson life now covering the floor of the rig. The apologetic and stunned look on his face made my day. My headache was finally gone, and I smiled for the first time in weeks.

Before we entered through the double doors to introduce our suicide victim to Mercy's ED, I gave Jared quick instructions on proper compressions from the side of the stretcher. He thought it was the coolest thing he'd ever seen. He propped himself on the side and began copying my technique as we wheeled into the trauma bay, and didn't stop until the physician made him quit. I let him have his false hero moment. He would learn the truth about this profession — and the world — soon enough.

The physician called it as soon as we transferred the man to their stretcher. There was nothing they could do for him. The staff knows our hands are tied in the field when the patient still has a pulse. We have to work them, even though they aren't viable. We're not allowed common sense, mostly because lawyers are too expensive. And then there's morality to consider. That's where it really gets complicated.

Jared unraveled the water hose in the bay and began washing the blood from the back of the rig while Dave sat inside the ER, writing the report. I knew better than to hang around Jared by myself. It was only a matter of minutes before the questions would begin. And as I doused the back with an entire bottle of disinfectant, cabinets and ceiling included, Jared didn't disappoint.

"Hey, Tryke," he said timidly.

"Yes?"

"I know I should be talking with Dave about the call, since he's my preceptor, but for some reason I think you'll answer me more honestly. Not that I think he's dishonest. It's just... I don't know. You're more forward."

"I get it," I said. "So what is it that you want to know?"

"It doesn't make sense to me why we didn't try harder to save him. Aren't we out here to save lives? We didn't even intubate the guy."

"I'm going to tell you something that you will eventually figure out for yourself. And if you decide it's too hard to grasp and you erase this conversation from your memory, you won't be alone. There are many individuals stuck in wonderland." I had his full and eager attention now. In fact, he was unaware that water was flowing onto his boots from the hose in his right hand. He was ready to absorb the shocking conclusion.

"It isn't easy to buck the system of the Gamemakers," I said. "You have to find a loophole and then pounce as hard as you can. It may not always seem clear at the time of your rebellion, but in the end you'll find your way."

He silently processed the words. "Maybe you're not as straightforward as I thought," he said.

I laughed. "It'll click one day. You'll find your own answers eventually, even if it has to be at the moment of your own death."

"I just wanted to know why we didn't do more for the guy." Obviously, this kid wasn't grasping what I was chunking his way. The mind can live in such denial that it will slow to a near stop in order to avoid a collision.

"That's all I have for you," I said. "There's a reason Dave's your preceptor, and not me." He didn't respond, and returned to his task of cleaning the stretcher.

When I stepped out from the side door of the rig, I noticed that blood had seeped down and out onto the wheels.

Whatever poor sap was behind us on the interstate got his windshield sprayed. Huh, that's a first.

"Jared, if you wouldn't mind, can you rinse off the wheels, too?"

"Sure," he said.

"Tryke, I need to tell you something." I flinched. It was Dave, from behind me.

"You scared the crap out of me," I said. "You done already?" He didn't have the clipboard in his hands. He pulled me away from where Jared was working. "What is it?"

"It's your mom," he said, softly.

Chapter 32

Dave asked if I wanted him to join me, but he was just being polite. He knew my answer would be no, and that I preferred to suffer alone. Though he may not have agreed with my ways, he has always respected them. If Lesley had been there, she wouldn't have allowed me such freedom. She would insist on taking the walk with me, holding hands. More and more, I liked holding her hand. I would definitely not have brushed it away at that moment.

The walk through the ER to the elevators was the most grueling I had ever taken. Paired eyes in scrubs followed me, pitied me, no doubt relieved that they weren't the ones having to take that walk.

I could hear my mom's soft, encouraging words whispering in my ears. "Don't worry about me, I'll be fine. You're strong and handsome like your father. Hold your head up high, don't slouch." I was struggling to hold back the tears that had eluded me since my dad's death.

• • •

Her voice continued to comfort me as I rode the elevator up to the second floor. The hallway that I had traveled so many times recently looked narrower and somehow longer, as if it had been stretched. "We'll all be together again soon enough. Take care of Lesley, as she cares for you." My father's boisterous, happy laugh echoed through my ears, followed by his voice: "I love you, son."

One of my mom's physicians, not Dr. Snead, met me at the closed door, accompanied by a nurse. When the doctor uttered the words that I have had to say myself so many times, they stung my face like a brutally cold wind. My stomach knotted and I instantly became enraged, overcome with irrational anger. I grabbed the physician by his lab coat collar with both my hands. He was bigger than me, but I didn't care.

"Not yet. She wasn't supposed to go! Not yet!" His face didn't show surprise. He was blank, emotionless. This wasn't his first time delivering that message. I wondered if my own face was just as cold and emotionless all of those times I had to relay those same words. I loosened my grip and quickly apologized, realizing what I was doing. "I'm… I'm sorry." A few of the nurses had stopped and stared at the commotion. I had forgotten my own advice to Jared.

I took a few deep breaths and entered the room.

It was quiet. The vent and monitor were turned off. Her body was eerily still, with the ET tube protruding from her mouth. Her hair was greyer, her eyes were shut, and her skin was pale and cool. She was gone, leaving behind the lifeless prison as a reminder of her stay. The flesh was dead without her.

There was no reason to linger in the room. I had seen enough. I didn't need time or silence with my mom's body. But I stayed to calm my fury before I faced anyone else.

• • •

I gathered the few items she had in the room, including the book, *The Hobbit*. I wanted to cry, to lose control and destroy the room's contents. "I can't do this here," I told myself, trying to remain calm. Before leaving the room, I began to count my breaths until I was sure there wouldn't be another outburst. I made my way to the elevators, avoiding eye contact with anyone. Still, I could feel their gazes touching and patting me, some hugging me, as I trudged back through the ER to the rig.

Dave was waiting for me, seated in the passenger seat with the door slung open. Jared stood beside him, talking, but stopped midsentence and moved to the side when he saw me. Dave immediately informed me that he had spoken to our supervisor and arranged for a replacement, so I could go home. He had taken it upon himself to know what I needed. I thought my anger had subsided, but I was wrong. I snapped.

"I don't need your pity, Dave, or anyone else's. I'm here to work and save lives! Right, Jared?" I looked over at Jared, who was now ducking his head. "Run up there to the second floor and ask those bastards why they didn't work harder! Why they didn't save her life! Why she had to die!"

"Tryke, I didn't mean —" Dave said.

"Don't, Dave. Not right now. We're all fucking clueless, and they like it that way. Fuck it all!" I trudged down the ER driveway and sat down on the concrete. I deserved a few minutes of self-pity and destruction, and didn't care who saw me. Everyone else in the world seemed to get more than their share of it. There wasn't a shift that went by that didn't involve some attention-seeker.

This wasn't me though. I didn't want attention. I was trusty Tryke, the one who was steady as a dead man's hand, the guy who could always be relied upon to keep a cool head. Maybe I wasn't any of those things, and I'm just like everyone else in this game. The tears were on the verge of falling, but they held on stubbornly behind the anger.

After a few minutes of deep repetitive breathing, I managed to regain my composure. I felt like an idiot for losing my cool for the second time. I now had to face Dave and Jared.

I apologized to them both on the way back to the station. I'd never shown a vulnerable side to Dave, or anyone for that matter. Dave understood and apologized to me once again. He probably felt better, now that he knew I was human after all.

Jerry, our supervisor, called the station when we arrived and insisted that I take off a few shifts. Actually, it was mandatory. I didn't like the policy, but I did have to finalize some things. And then there was the funeral to arrange.

Lesley called me on my way home. Dave must have contacted her and told her the news. She was going to find out anyway, and at that moment, it was better that someone else told her. I was still on edge and didn't want to snap at her. She didn't deserve that.

Halfway to my apartment, and after hanging up with Lesley, the overwhelming flow of emotion that had stayed hidden finally revealed itself. I sat at a red light, quivering. I wanted to punch the steering wheel to stop the shaking, but it was too powerful. I lowered my fists in submission and let go. The tears fell like a welcomed afternoon summer rainstorm, bringing relief to a cracked and thirsty desert floor. I wasn't sure how to react to it, so I didn't. For the first time in my life I unclenched everything. The heavy rusted chains unlocked and slid off, retracting under the door of the prison cell. I began to laugh through my tears.

A horn blowing from behind brought me back to reality. I wasn't mad. I was exhilarated with sadness. It was a curious feeling, and one not easily explained. I drove the rest of the short distance to my apartment wielding a wide grin, and draining my tear ducts at the same time.

Lesley was there waiting for me when I pulled in. How the heck did she get there so fast? I didn't feel much like talking, but I was glad to see her. My emotions were still on a rollercoaster, riding up and down, and circling. The truth was, I didn't know what I wanted, but discussing my feelings and coming to terms with my mom's death wasn't it. I'd just experienced a curious breakthrough with my emotions, and there was much to sort out.

After Lesley pulled the tailgate of my truck down, I sat beside her and she grabbed my hand, holding on tightly. We stayed in that spot for two hours, silently, just holding hands. It was exactly what I needed.

Chapter 33

I sat quietly in my dark apartment, wondering how the hell everything had gotten so out of hand: my mother dying, my dad's letter, my sister's condition. It felt like someone had jammed a faucet into my veins and left it on, slowly draining my blood away. I was exhausted, physically and mentally. The only thing driving me was a tiny sliver of anger that stubbornly hung on.

I was officially lost, just as my mother had been for so long, deep in the mind's underworld. I didn't have any more answers to soothe my worries, choosing my dad's approach instead. I began sipping my worries aside. But no matter how much I drank, I couldn't quite shake the experience that had started it all — my sister's death.

After her drowning, and seeing the image surrounding her body, I started noticing other things. None was as pronounced as her soul had been, but other blurs and shadows. Back then, I thought perhaps she was signaling to me beyond the grave, but now I'm not sure.

What if none of it was real? What if I had the same sickness as my father and sister? I was likely carrying the gene; there was no disputing the possibility. How could I avoid the surrounding facts? The idea was terrifying. Why didn't I see it when my uncle talked to me in the hospital? Where the heck was I?

But I still wasn't entirely convinced. I saw those images clearly, just as I see my hands now. I sensed the presence of an escaping soul. And more than that, I had proof on the video of Mr. Crow. Memory chips don't lie, do they?

I was overcome with trepidation as I powered up the camera and slowly flipped open the display. My hands were shaking so badly I had to brace the equipment against my leg. I fast-forwarded until I reached his release, and then slowed down to half speed.

The image was gone.

I squeezed my eyes shut and wiped them repeatedly, then rewound and played the video back several times, hoping there was a glitch. But nothing changed.

I had made it all up in my mind.

Without another thought, I hurled the camera across the room, shattering it to pieces.

I sat down against the wall, squeezing my head for answers, but I knew the truth. The undeniable reality was that I was indeed sick. Now I had to face the consequences, whatever they might be. I certainly wasn't sure anymore. It seemed that everything I thought I knew wasn't real, and my entire life had been a lie. What else wasn't really there? I began questioning my whole existence, trying to distinguish what had been tangible from what I had simply imagined.

I broke out in a cold sweat and started tapping on the floor with my index finger, repeatedly counting to ten. I couldn't control my breathing, and was reaching the point of hyperventilation. My upper body tightened as my heart continued rapping at my chest wall. I was on the brink of losing all reality. I clenched my fists and tried to slow down the counting, repeating each number twice. But I couldn't stop the influx of thoughts.

The room began to spin. I felt tingling in my hands and feet. I was falling prey to an invisible foe that I had always thought of as a weakness. Many times I had rolled my eyes at it, impatiently dismissed the very thought of it, and ridiculed my patients for it.

I was experiencing a full-blown panic attack.

I knew that if I didn't regain control, I would pass out, and then my body would take over and steady my breathing for me. Fighting it was futile. I had to let go, allow the thoughts to flow, and unleash them. It was the only way.

And finally, I did.

• • •

It was time to say goodbye.

The Gamemakers had won. In the process, they had also taken what they came for: my will. They struck hard with false visions, death, and even a panic attack to seal the deal. They fought dirty, but ended by revealing the truth. My ambition to trump them was gone. I would now spend the rest of my life in anguish and regret, battling to stay on the plane of reality. I had been reduced to a sniveling boy awaiting trial.

I flipped on the generator and started stacking all of my equipment in one corner. I covered it with a large white sheet and began a final wipe down. I would come back for the equipment later. My journal, along with my dad's, would soon be destroyed by fire.

Before turning off the generator for the last time, I pulled the keys from my front pocket and prepared to leave. Along with the keys came a tiny object that landed on the floor next to my right foot. I stared down at it, unsure if I should pick it up or crush it with my boot. The memory card was the only piece left from the camera I had destroyed. I must have placed it in my pocket while cleaning up.

What the hell, why not have one more look for shits and giggles?

I pulled the sheet back, found the one camera that was still intact, and placed the memory card into the slot. When you're down, why not kick yourself one last time, just to feel the cool wind in your face as you plunge to the depths? Sure enough, the camera revealed the truth one more time. There was no soul or blurred dark image. There was only the alarm from the stairs.

I plopped down in my chair and ran my hand through my hair. A few minutes later, it hit me. Wait a damn minute! What about the alarm? What had triggered it? I hadn't found anything lurking around that night. Only the wind and rain, neither of which could have reached that far up the stairs to the alarm trigger. What did it mean?

The answer was simple. It meant they hadn't won yet!

How could I have been so blind, so weak, as to give up without a fight? I was done cowering in the corner. The game was far from over.

Everything became instantly clear, and that last sudden glint of hope was now forming itself into a full, bright fireball of rage.

Those who have seen this room deserved their fate. They made their choices and now it was my turn. We all win in the end. They get to leave their prison here and make more choices somewhere else. Hopefully they learn, but somehow I fear they won't. Not if the Gamemakers have anything to do with it. This world is fucked up and always will be; there's no getting around that. We don't make the rules, but no one says we have to follow the ones set out for us. Free will is the only weapon we possess to battle the evil that's all around us, the evil placed here by the Gamemakers. And I wasn't about to give that up without a fight.

My family was taken from me, and revenge will be had. Seeing the visions was a distraction to the truth and to life itself, the true mask of deception, a pain-ridden ride to the suffering of mankind.

This venture had always been meant for retaliation. It was my only move in the Gamemakers' tournament of torment.

Wielding my newfound energy, I slung the sheet back from over the equipment. I would continue releasing souls from the world until I was released myself. There would always be plenty of evil to go around, and I wouldn't have to hunt for it. In fact, it would continue to arrogantly walk up to me and ask for help.

I was no longer a distraught bystander. I was a player in the game.

Ready, player one.

Chapter 34

When I sat up in my bed the next morning and stretched both of my arms out over my head, I felt reborn. I was back. For the first time in months, I had actually achieved absent consciousness. I passed N1, N2, and N3, reaching the elusive REM stage of sleep. The foggy feeling was gone. I told my old enemy goodbye, at least for now.

I had finally come to terms with my mom's death, realizing that she and my dad, along with my sister, were all back together. I also had a purpose, until it was time for me to join them.

As Dave would have put it, I was pumped. My mind was clearer than it had been in years. I called my partner that afternoon and told him I was ready for the trip to the gulf. He couldn't believe my demeanor at first, twice asking me to repeat what I had just said. After realizing that I hadn't lost my mind, he became ecstatic, letting out a boisterous "Yee-Haw" in my ear. I called Lesley next.

"How are you feeling?" she asked.

"Strangely well. I'm okay with everything now."

"That was fast. Are you sure you're not back in the denial phase?"

I laughed. "I'm sure. I just skipped over a couple of the grieving stages. My mom is with my dad and sister now. That's where she wanted to be. I'm good. Seriously."

"If you say so." I could tell by her voice that she still wasn't entirely convinced.

"I talked to Dave earlier, and we were wondering if you'd like to join us on a trip to the gulf. I know it's not a normal date, but I think it'll be a good time."

"Are you kidding me? I would love to go," she said.

"Oh, and I kind of told Dave you would get your friend Angie to go with us."

"You did, did you? Then you've lucked out, because she's been bugging me about him ever since they met."

"I knew this was going to work out," I said.

• • •

The end of the vacation season was the perfect time for a visit to the gulf. The crowds had thinned and the water was still warm. Dave finally named his boat. It wasn't something that I would have picked, but it fit him for the moment — though I made him aware that the next girl he became serious with would make him change it. He'd decided to call the boat "On The Prowl". I laughed when I saw it plastered on the back, while Lesley frowned at me and shook her head. She did it playfully, of course. I doubt she would have cared even if I'd had it written on my own boat. They were just words, and our relationship was far greater than anything verbal. In fact, that's what she told me the night before we left. I still twitched at the word *relationship*, but I was working it out.

On our trip down to the gulf, we witnessed a wreck on I-49 near Lafayette, Louisiana. It happened a hundred yards in front of us. A midsized truck traveling on the other side of the interstate flew across the grassy median and slammed head-on into a small compact car. Of course, we stopped, and Dave pulled a full jump bag from under his back seat. We were never off duty.

Lesley quickly dialed 911. I grabbed a few items from the jump bag and checked on the occupants of the car, while Dave headed for the truck. I saw only one person in the vehicle, a woman who appeared to be in her thirties. The child seat in the back was empty, but that was the only good news about the accident. The vehicle was ancient and didn't have airbags. The woman had been wearing her seatbelt, but it didn't matter. The impact from the truck had sent the dash into her, instantly draining her life. There was nothing I could do.

After covering the lady with a blanket Lesley had brought along for the trip, I went to assist Dave. The driver of the truck looked to be relatively unharmed. He was out of his vehicle and pushing the blood pressure cuff away, but Dave wasn't going to let the man rest until he'd obtained a set of vitals.

Just out of curiosity, I went to check the inside of the truck, and the smell of alcohol was overwhelming. I found the broken culprit on the floor.

Dave had finally convinced the guy to let him take his blood pressure. I smirked at my partner's valiant effort to keep a wobbling drunk still long enough to get the cuff around his arm. The smell of alcohol emanating from his pores was just as strong as it had been in the truck. Dave was clearly annoyed, sighing repeatedly and slamming his equipment back into his bag. He was more than grateful when I offered to wait with the man until the ambulance arrived.

The man clumsily sat down on the pavement, leaning against his wrecked truck for stability. I sat across from him so I could see his face. I had only one question. And it wasn't about his level of intoxication, because that would not have been answered truthfully. He was clearly plastered, and would either say he hadn't had a drink or tell me the infamous two-beer story, while never revealing the size of the containers.

"So, what's your favorite drink?" I asked.

He didn't hesitate. He spouted off, "Whiskey, straight, with three ice cubes." He hiccupped and slapped his arm on my leg like we were old pals. I quickly grabbed his arm and flung it away. I didn't want that piece of shit touching me. As I watched his total disregard for the destruction he had just caused, I felt the anger building inside me. I stood and took a step toward him, and then glanced around to make sure no one was looking. I grabbed a fist full of his stringy hair and rammed my right knee into the side of his head, knocking him unconscious.

I regained control of my emotions and sat him upright against the mangled door of his truck. I leaned over and whispered to him, "You're lucky I'm on vacation." When our fellow paramedics arrived on scene, I requested that they let the man know he had killed an innocent woman. It was the least I could do for the guy.

I walked back toward Dave's truck and stopped a few feet away. I glanced up at the vast sky, then down at the black pavement between my boots, and whispered.

"Nice move. I can't get them all. I'll give y'all that. My turn now."

• • •

The humidity was low, which left the constant easterly breeze a perfect temperature to cool our sun-drenched faces. The water was a beautiful mixture of blue and green that pleasantly contrasted with the pure white sand on the shore. It was a nice change to have the aroma of coconut suntan oil and salty air saturating my senses, rather than potent disinfectant and the metallic scent of blood. Michael Buble' was amplified over the boat speakers, singing *Come Fly With Me*.

As Dave steered his new boat, he finally looked to be at peace with himself. He was wearing a permanent grin, and he periodically glanced over at his date and then at me, raising his eyebrows toward her in his typical cheesy manner.

Lesley and I sat in the rear of the boat. She had her head tilted back, letting the sun bathe her face. She looked beautiful with her eyes loosely shut beneath her sunglasses and her dark hair slow dancing with the wind. I lightly brushed my fingertips along her toned legs that were slung over mine, and placed my hand in hers. A broad smile unfolded underneath her shades. I lay my head back next to hers and closed my eyes. The warm sun felt good, though I do enjoy a dark and rainy day.

Journal Entries

*Number mystery solved. (The lone number above each new entry is a number system devised to determine the possibility of a visual release. Each entry receives a number from 1 to 10, with 10 being the highest possible chance of visualization.)

7

Entry No. 12, 42 y/o male, name: Travis Fritz. His overwhelming desire to abuse his mother and her nursing home roommate is obvious. We have made several calls on her and he's been there each time, watching our every move and giving the impression he was a caring son. But I could see him for what he was. His avoiding eye contact and swift movements when we neared an injury site while examining her were amusing to watch. Though his mother was unable to talk, she showed enough skittish behavior around him to reveal his secret.

3

Entry No. 18, 34 y/o male, name: Jeff Roberts. Intoxicated driver killed family of four, all dead on scene from major trauma and burns. While transporting to emergency room, he grinned and hummed happily while I radioed the report. Afterwards he inquired about the occupants of the vehicle he hit. When I told him that all of the occupants were dead, including two children, he showed no emotion. He continued his ominous humming all the way to the ER. This obviously wasn't his first time.

4

Entry No. 23, 45 y/o male, name: Tate Burns. Injured when burglarizing a home while family was asleep. Tied father to chair and beat him in the garage; then robbed home. Transported father for neurological damage below waist from the beating. He will most likely be paralyzed for the rest of his life. Transported Tate a few hours later after police tracked him down and shot him in the leg; lucky for me the bullet narrowly missed the right femoral artery.

6

Entry No. 27, 29 y/o female, name: Carla Krupp. Coded her four- and six-year-old daughters at their home. She claimed that she was asleep during the incident. When she woke she found both of her daughters dead in the backyard, face-down in the above ground pool. She didn't attempt resuscitative measures. She claimed that she was too distraught to do anything other than dial 911, despite her five-year experience as an ER nurse. The two girls both had mild bruising on their arms and missing patches of hair that looked to have been pulled out. Her demeanor didn't coincide with a mother who had just lost both of her daughters in an accident. I have seen many faces of parents after losing their children and hers was much different. There was definitely pain behind her eyes, but not a grieving pain. She wanted release.

5

Entry No. 32, 30 y/o male, name: Todd Wilkes. He's an ED physician at Corvine Hospital, deliberately killing elderly patients. These are not mercy killings. I have overheard his loud opinion on several occasions about his disdain for the elderly and their drain on the health care system. He carries a full syringe in his lab coat at all times. I'm not sure what the substance is, but will further investigate when time comes. I have caught him on three separate occasions leaving an elderly patient's room, and a few minutes later the patient codes. On one of those occasions, he was unaware that I was watching through the curtained door while he introduced the substance into the patient's IV line.

5

Entry No. 53, 60 y/o female, name: Ms. Dundee. She is a regular patient of ours, a stubborn diabetic who insists on avoiding her medications. She has a mentally-impaired son who lives with her. He has saved her life on many occasions, though I believe she is less than thankful to him. We found him beaten with a phone in her house. Dave and I both suspect she is the culprit.

Addendum: Karl, her son, is currently in a vegetative state in a local nursing home after the beating. She will be my first experiment, my first attempt to visualize the soul. I feel she will be a good start.

Results: The soul didn't reveal itself to either my eyes or the camera's. For now it continues to be elusive. An afterthought I have is to change the camera to thermal imaging. Why shouldn't the soul carry some residual heat from its warm cage? The premise was there.

Miscellaneous: Her glucose levels were low, but due to her body's unrelenting compensation, I had to intervene. I used insulin to complete the task. I set a time limit of five minutes before attempting resuscitation. Failed, after three cycles of medication.

4

Entry No. 57, 34 y/o male, name: Mr. Crow. I didn't bother to learn his real name. His drug habits led him to rob and beat my neighbor, Mr. Thompson. He has also neglected his own child resulting in the child's death; upon coding the child, the wounds were consistent with a fall.

Addendum: Mr. Crow was my third attempt to reveal the soul. I used his own mixture in his pocket to release him. I don't know the exact contents of the mixture, but it was most likely heroin.

Results: My first success. No resuscitation attempted; a door slamming — that turned out to be the weather — interrupted the process. The stair alarm was also triggered, but not from the weather. The camera revealed a dark blurred image from behind his body seconds before the alarm. I believe it was Mr. Crow's soul that triggered it when released. Due to the unforeseen weather complications, I wasn't able to visualize it with my own eyes.

Miscellaneous: What happens next?

5

Entry No. 65, 53 y/o male, name: Mr. Laurence. He likes to beat children and burn them with his cigarettes. I decided quickly that he was going to be my second experiment. I was angry and the choice was made on **impulse**. It was a **dangerous** move, but for some reason I felt I had to get it done.

Results: I used epinephrine. The substance worked quickly, ending his reign of terror. No resuscitation attempted. No soul visualized, but it didn't matter. It felt good to rid the world of a dirty lurker.

Miscellaneous: If I am to survive, I must control my anger. Hastiness increases the possibility of mistakes.

3

Entry No. 72, 51 y/o male, name: Mr. Horning. This one is very personal for me. This man is responsible for killing my aunt and uncle, and nearly me, when I was very young. He has murdered many others, using his vehicle as the murder weapon. He currently resides in Shreveport, Louisiana. It is imperative to have him back where this all began.

Results: No resuscitation attempted. No soul visualized. I managed to get him back to my lab. It was another risky effort, and with much stress and some close calls, it was accomplished. I didn't have time for my prepared speech due to unforeseen circumstances. I expected more of a show or at least an epiphany due to the subconscious feelings that had been building over the years. But I realized in the end that it wasn't necessary. I didn't need to see him leave; a calm bow out and silence was a suiting ending to it all. I accomplished what had to be done and am more than satisfied with the results. My aunt and uncle's souls can now rest in peace. And mine also, for the moment.

A note from C.S. McMillian

Thank you for reading Dark of the Mind. I am currently in the process of writing the sequel. Please, don't hesitate to connect with me on Facebook: www.facebook.com/darkofthemind